Praise for

The Blumkin Project

The Blumkin Project

ALSO BY CHRISTIAN SALMON

Storytelling: Bewitching the Modern Mind

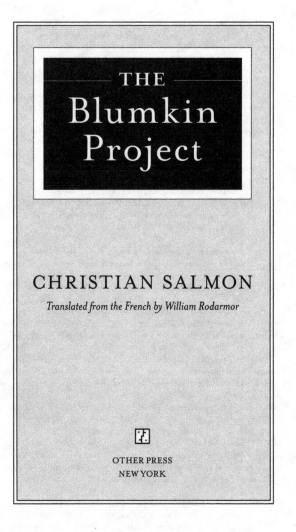

THE
Blumkin
Project

CHRISTIAN SALMON

Translated from the French by William Rodarmor

OTHER PRESS
NEW YORK

Production editor: Yvonne E. Cárdenas
Text designer: Jennifer Daddio / Bookmark Design & Media Inc.
This book was set in Mrs. Eaves
by Alpha Design & Composition of Pittsfield, NH.

1 3 5 7 9 10 8 6 4 2

Library of Congress Cataloging-in-Publication Data
Names: Salmon, Christian, 1951- author. |
Rodarmor, William, translator.
Title: The Blumkin project : a biographic novel / Christian Salmon ;
translated from the French by William Rodarmor.
Other titles: Projet Blumkine. English
Description: New York : Other Press, [2022] | "Originally published
in 2017 as Le projet Blumkine by Éditions La Découverte, Paris"
Identifiers: LCCN 2022012622 (print) | LCCN 2022012623 (ebook) |
ISBN 9781590511541 (paperback) | ISBN 9781635429978 (ebook)
Subjects: LCSH: Bliumkin, Iakov Grigorʹevich, 1900-1929—Fiction. |
Partiia levykh sotsialistov-revoliutsionerov (Russia)—Fiction. | Russian
S.F.S.R. Chrezvychainaia komissiia po borʹbe s kontr-revoliutsiei i
sabotazhem—Fiction. | Spies—Soviet Union—Fiction. | Soviet Union—
History—1917-1936—Fiction. | LCGFT: Biographical fiction. |
Historical fiction. | Novels.
Classification: LCC PQ2679.A523858 P7613 2022 (print) |
LCC PQ2679.A523858 (ebook) | DDC 843/.914—dc23/eng/20220318
LC record available at https://lccn.loc.gov/2022012622
LC ebook record available at https://lccn.loc.gov/2022012623

*Romance had singled Jim for its own—and
that was the true part of the story,
which otherwise was all wrong.*

—JOSEPH CONRAD, *LORD JIM*

Once upon a time, I was a Bolshevik.

A fictional Bolshevik, but a flesh-and-blood Bolshevik just the same, with a leather jacket, a red bandanna around my neck, and a glint in my eye. In those days, the walls of my apartment were covered with posters from the October Revolution. You could see entwined rifles and hammers, circles penetrated by triangles, raised fists, and slogans shaped like allegories: "Beat the Whites with a Red Wedge!" Locomotives roared skyward, and workers in red tunics pointed at the class enemy or the deserter. Astride a globe with a broom in hand, Lenin swept the last exploiters from the surface of the Earth. My dreams echoed with onomatopoeia written in gigantic repeated letters, as in Eisenstein's films:

HO, HO, HO.

Streaming in from everywhere, the masses became a physical force on encountering the Marxist theory of surplus value. From the moment I awoke, the picture on the wall of a man with a bloody bandage around his forehead charged me with his implacable energy. The genie of electricity lit up the world. The Soviets did the rest.

The masses rushed into the great theater of history. In the wings, the actors waited for the curtain to go up to run onstage and deliver the words that the crowd had been anticipating for so long. Slogans burst from fiery mouths. It was no longer the orators speaking to the people, but History itself dictating their words, as if the aim of those Bolsheviks with nerves of steel was to melt and merge with it.

During revolutions, women's charms fade in the eyes of men, they say. History takes their place. It haunts men's dreams. In one such dream, Lenin is forever haranguing the Petrograd crowd from his balcony, cap in hand. Trotsky's train is thundering after Kolchak's and Denikin's armies, spanning vast spaces and desolate distances.

A youngster of seventeen shoots an ambassador at point-blank range. "The revolution chooses its lovers young," Trotsky told the German generals, who were astonished at having to negotiate peace with adolescents. The reason is simple: they kill more easily.

———

Back then, I could recite whole passages of Isaac Babel's *Red Cavalry* and had embraced Dziga Vertov's manifesto "I Am an Eye!" ("Flee the sweet embraces of the romance, the poison of the psychological novel, the clutches of the theater of adultery"). This was probably the source of my later rejection of psychological narrative and the so-called bourgeois novel.

But my breviary, my bible, was *The Iron Heel*, by Jack London, though I have forgotten its plot and major episodes. I only remember the scene in which the hero Ernest Everhard proved capitalism's inevitable breakdown. "You say I'm dreaming?" said the young labor leader. "Very well, I'll demonstrate the mathematics of my dream!" Ernest Everhard was my politico-literary superego: he had an answer for everything.

Those were the richest, craziest, most passionate years of my life. I was in love with Alexandra Kollontai, history's first female ambassador. Isadora Duncan and Sergei Esenin were the most extravagant couple in Moscow. She had abandoned the stages of Europe for an unheated palace in Moscow, where "she made proletarian children dance." From Bolshevism, I especially retained its period of genius, history's first proletarian revolution, and maybe also its last. My historical clock stopped in 1923, when the New Economic Policy (NEP) followed the heroic years of War Communism. What happened afterward, the trials and Stalinism, didn't concern me. That was another period, Thermidor or Restoration. My subject was the transition.

I was a Bolshevik of the 1980s, further to the left on questions of society and culture than on the role of the vanguard party or the collectivization of farmland, for example. I was very free concerning morals and the institution of marriage, but inflexible on principles of communal life and the sharing of domestic chores. With Bolsheviks like me, the tsar could rest easy.

Once a week, all of us Paris Bolsheviks would gather in a big auditorium at the École des hautes études en sciences sociales on rue de Varenne. In a dense fug of cigarette smoke, our professor of Bolshevism would explain—with statistics at hand—how the failure of grain harvests at one particular moment led to the fatal rupture of the peasant-worker alliance, and everything that followed. We wanted to understand the specific conditions of the processes of transformation, its dead ends and historic errors, so as not to repeat them in the revolutionary period that was sure to begin for us. Sometimes the seminar would go on late into the evening in a back room of a bistro near the Arts-et-Métiers metro. When I was feeling melancholy, I would sometimes repeat the famous testament by Nikolai Bukharin—condemned to death by Stalin—that his young wife, Anna Larina, learned by heart during his years in exile: "Comrades, know that on the banner you will be carrying in the victorious march to communism there is also a drop of my blood." Confronted with Stalin's crimes, we wanted to rebuild Marxism on the bedrock of lived experience. And to do that, we focused on field study: the "Bolshevik years" were ending, and we were turning into sociologists.

It was in the course of moving that my Bolshevik past resurfaced. Thirty years had passed. I had just moved into a house on the banks of the Marne. The electricity hadn't been turned on yet, and the house lay in semidarkness. Using my smartphone flashlight, I picked my way among the piled chairs, box springs, trestle desks, and boxes of books stacked to the ceiling.

For the first time ever, I had enough room to unpack my library. Up to then, it had been scattered among various storage units. Years passed between one box and the next, and moving among them gave me the impression of crossing decades, disturbing slumbering periods. Breathless from my comings and goings, I sat down on an old trunk that the movers had left in the middle of the living room. It was a greenish tin trunk with dented corners, covered with freight stickers. Taped to the lid was a half-erased label I could just decipher in the dim light: BL KIN JECT 79—probably a shipping label.

Intrigued, I released the hook holding the two metal tabs of the latch and lifted the lid, which opened with a creak. The trunk was full of books, lying side by side in a single patchwork layer. They had spent years in the dark, huddled together like stowaways, migrating from one basement to another without ever seeing the light of day.

I picked one up and shone my phone light on its cover. *The Start of an Unknown Era*, by Konstantin Paustovsky, published by Gallimard in its Soviet Literature collection. On the back cover, this sentence appeared, after a date: "1917: The story of a man is written in the story of a country." I gently laid the book at my feet and reached for another one, whose title in red capital letters filled the entire page: *People and Life*, by Ilya Ehrenburg. On its back cover: "A patriot says he comes from the biggest country in the world, the country that is pursuing the most fascinating social experiment."

The cover of an old paperback showed a drawing of a mustached man staring fiercely through the bars of his cell at prisoners exercising in a snow-covered prison yard. This was Arthur Koestler's famous novel *Darkness at Noon*. Opening it to the frontispiece, I saw the first and last names of a sixteen-year-old girl, written in an adolescent's rounded letters. At some distant time the book had belonged to the person who became my daughter's mother. As I leafed through a volume of V. I. Lenin's *Complete Works* published by Éditions sociales, a few grains of sand fell from between the pages. So I'd been reading Lenin at the beach! *My Life*, Leon Trotsky's autobiography, lay next to *The Noise of Time*, a collection of prose pieces by Osip Mandelstam. Trotsky and Mandelstam. War and Poetry.

Sweeping my phone light across the trunk's contents, I paused at Platonov's *The Foundation Pit* from L'Age d'Homme, which had republished whole swaths of Russian literature in its Slavic Classics collection. In the same ocher binding, beneath a logo formed by the letters *C* and *K*—whose meaning I forget—was Andrei Biely's *Petersburg*, Vasily Grossman's *Life and Fate*, Yuri Olesha's *Envy*, Leonid Leonov's *The Thief*, Nikolai Leskov's *No Way Out*, Mandelstam's *The Egyptian Stamp*, Zamiatin's *A Story About the Most Important Thing*, and Sergei Esenin's *Confessions of a Hooligan*. Each of those titles had been familiar to me in a previous life, and I had forgotten their contents. Some of the books were dog-eared, tagged with multicolored Post-it notes, their covers cracked, stained with damp. Glossy surfaces had worn away, letting the paper's grain show through, like the translucent skin of an old man.

I could make out blurry pencil marks in the margins, notes from old lectures, unreadable in places, like commentaries that time hadn't retained. Passages, underlined or crossed out, revealed tastes, states of mind, opinions that seemed to belong to some other person. A drawing by my daughter at age three was slipped between the pages of an essay on the GPU, revealing the real date in my memory of that distant era with the precision of carbon-14 dating.

Under the first layer of books lay crushed archive boxes, notebooks in various formats, cardboard slips covered in blue writing that was fading to purple here and there, even an old red-and-black typewriter ribbon. There was a jumble of newspaper clippings, tracing paper covered with city maps, spiral-bound notebooks, and cassettes with unspooled magnetic tape, their plastic cases cracked, boxes of photos, ring binder sheets, handwritten manuscripts, historians' articles, accounts by GPU agents who had defected to the West, photocopies of police reports, a floor plan of the Lubyanka prison, a scene-by-scene breakdown of Eisenstein's film *Battleship Potemkin* . . . A postcard fell out of Isaac Babel's *Odessa Stories*; it had probably served as bookmark. On the right-hand side of the card was an address: "Quinta La Rivera Prolongation av. principal de Santa Ines Caracas, Venezuela." That must have once been my address, but I didn't remember it.

On the other side I read these words written in red ink:

"Salutations, oh vanished one! I got your February letter yesterday, because I have vanished as well. The beauty of clandestine life! Good luck with the writing. Best wishes, Milan."

With pins and needles in my legs, I stood up and closed the trunk. The half-erased inscription on the lid, BL KIN JECT 79, which I'd thought was a shipping label, suddenly came back to me: BLUMKIN PROJECT 1979. The Blumkin Project.

This trunk held the archives I had assembled years earlier about a legendary character in the October Revolution, Yakov Blumkin. It was he who, on the orders of his Left Socialist Revolutionary Party, had assassinated the German ambassador to Moscow in 1918. The act was a protest against the "infamous" peace treaty Lenin and Trotsky signed with Germany at Brest-Litovsk. To appease the Germans, it was announced that Blumkin had been executed. Meanwhile Trotsky, who had taken him under his wing, sent him to Ukraine to carry out sabotage missions behind White enemy lines. A year later Blumkin resurfaced in Moscow, where everyone had thought him dead. Far from hiding, he showed up at soirées and hung out in fashionable literary cafés. One evening he ran into the poet Vladimir Mayakovsky, who took him in his arms and shouted, "*Zhivoi!*"—"He's alive"—a nickname that stuck.

I sat down on the trunk and used my phone to search for Blumkin. A series of photographs appeared. I clicked on the first one: a bearded man with dark eyes surrounded by a group of Jewish merchants. The caption read, "Blumkin in Jaffa, 1928." In another he is dressed like Lawrence of Arabia and posed atop a camel in front of the Egyptian pyramids. In a third, he is walking on the Tibetan plateau. The caption relates to the Roerich expedition: "Searching for Shambhala, 1925." In yet another photo, I recognized the poet Sergei Esenin's baby face and somewhat feminine blond curls. Nearby, a leather-jacketed Blumkin seems to be watching over him. And there is Trotsky's train: on the platform, the Old Man is raising his cap and saluting the crowd in front of a huge red flag that fills the left third of the photograph. Dressed in a Red Army uniform, Blumkin stands on the train steps, scrutinizing the faces around him. The last photograph had been taken in 1923 in the Gilan Mountains in Persia, according to the caption: a group of fighters surrounding a man, apparently their leader, his head wrapped in a bloody bandage.

Was it the same man in all these photos? It was hard to say, as his appearance changed from one shot to the other. Sometimes his face looked angular; sometimes puffy. In some pictures he looked about twenty; in others, forty. Yet the dates of the photos left no doubt, as only about a decade separated the oldest photographs from the most recent: 1918–1929. This was indeed the same Yakov Blumkin, alias "Zhivoi," alias "the Lama," alias "Sultan-Zade." A Google search yielded 3,300 hits, which rose to 16,700 if the search was done in Russian, some of which I could understand thanks to translation software. This was a far richer database than the one at my disposal when I started my research at Nanterre's Bibliothèque de documentation internationale contemporaine. In the early 1980s I had spent entire days there, finding only a few lines, and sometimes just a footnote, that as often as not referred to the same episode, the most famous one in Blumkin's life: the assassination of the German ambassador in 1918.

The search results began with his Wikipedia entry in Russian—Яков Григорьевуч Блюмкин (Ukrainian: 1898–November 3, 1929). The French version gave only a summary. I cut and pasted the text into a translation program. A warning appeared on-screen: "This article violates the Russian language." Reading the translation, it was apparent that the translation software was no kinder to the French. Ignoring the warning, I continued reading. To some, Blumkin was "thin," "virile," his face framed by a heavy black beard; he looked "Assyrian," with dark eyes, a "hard" gaze. To others he was "stocky," clean-shaven, with black hair and "moist lips." "His eyes gleamed like black olives." Sometimes the automatic translator produced incomprehensible gibberish: "He looked like the female General Dima—big, complete, with thick lips, autonomous." Or again: "He accidentally dozhivshemu in peacetime."

Those words curled up like shavings from a carpenter's plane. Catching them on the fly, I assembled them like the scattered pieces of a puzzle. According to a former Cheka member who knew him well, Blumkin used makeup as skillfully as an actor, and could change his appearance in the blink of an eye. All those who encountered him agreed that he had a certain "stature." To the secret agents who went over to the West peddling their more or less reliable accounts, he had all the qualities you would expect in a spy, an array of often contradictory aptitudes: curiosity and discretion, gregariousness and a taste for solitude, rigor and adaptability, caution and daring. He was said to have exceptional gifts rarely gathered in a single person: a stuntman's physical prowess, a wild animal's instinct, a poet's sensibility, and the erudition of an old rabbi. He spoke several languages, including German, French, and Hebrew, not to mention Arabic, Chinese, and ancient Persian. The editor of his Wikipedia page thought he was a model for the character of Max Otto von Stierlitz, "the Soviet James Bond," the hero of a 1960s TV series called *Seventeen Moments of Spring*. According to Google, a map of his constant movements covered a third of the planet, and his travels, laid end to end, would circle the globe several times. On the other hand, there is no doubt about his tragic end, to which Google's clumsy translation lent a touch of unintended pathos: "Prisoner Jakob Blumkin prints on a white page of the autobiography, his last confession prison."

So many stories have circulated about "Zhivoi" that it's hard to tell true from false; some people have gone so far as to doubt his very existence. They claim that "ghost writers" in the Lubyanka invented him out of whole cloth in order to cover all sorts of shady affairs, obscure circumstances, and as-yet-unexplained murders.

The notion of creating ex nihilo a fictional character who could be charged with all of the world's sins and then killed off when his work was done isn't completely absurd. After Blumkin's execution by Stalin, the Vienna communist newspaper *Die Rote Fahne* declared that "Blumkin never existed and therefore could not have been executed." The Cheka had "disappeared" so many people that making others "appear" would be easy. A sheaf of fake passports and a dozen doubles who would emerge from the shadows at the right moment, and the trick would be done.

This secret program would have been code-named "Project Blumkin." A writer recruited by the Soviet secret services would be given the assignment of creating a fictional character along very specific lines: establish a chronology, gather a bunch of clues and evidence, and then imagine a set of circumstances that would support the character's birth, growth, and development. He would need to stress the crucial moments in the hero's life, encounters preceded by premonition. Once sworn to secrecy, the writer would be given access to the Cheka's archives: a mass of autobiographies, address books, doctored photographs, letters, mission orders, forged signatures, lists of fake names. He could turn to psychologists to decipher the existential equation of a Jew from the Pale of Settlement, draw on costume and makeup artists, cartographers, and of course historians, but also fingerprint experts, graphologists, and teams of linguists who could create a verbal style for our hero the way others custom-tailor shirts: familiar expressions, slang from the Odessa alleys that he can't shed, language tics, and made-up neologisms drawn from foreign languages.

Once this mission was accomplished, the plan would be to shoot the fictional character into the world the way Laika the dog was shot into space on *Sputnik 2*. Leaks to foreign embassies and their agents swarming over Russia would be arranged. Fake dissidents would be dispatched to European capitals with revelations about an elusive character who threatened British interests in Persia, Palestine, Egypt, and India. Secondhand information from reliable sources would be passed to them, sending them off in his pursuit. They would be given safehouse addresses, fake mission orders, and secret rendezvous places—the Anzali bazaar, a laundry in Jaffa, a brothel in Odessa, the Hotel des Grands Hommes in Paris.

I'll admit I was tempted by this version of history, which showcases the police and the secret services' imagination. It's the most romantic one, and it saves its big revelation for the end. In the book's final pages, the reader learns that the hero with whom they have shared so many adventures was a creation of the secret services. A decoy. A complete fiction.

And yet, there is no doubt that Yakov Blumkin really existed.

As my empty house gradually sank into darkness, Blumkin's ghost reappeared. Locked away in a trunk that had followed me for years, he now stood before me like those shades in *The Odyssey* who beg Ulysses for blood, to bring them back to life. As darkness filled the room, I lit a candle that a previous tenant had set above the electric meter. By its trembling light, I made my way between the piled boxes to a less cluttered corner of the room and collapsed into an armchair, exhausted.

How many times had I picked up the burden of Blumkin's sad existence to tell his story, only to stumble on some unseen obstacle, struggle for a few months, and then give it up, to deal with more urgent tasks? How often had I dusted off books and notebooks, refiled papers and maps, and protected disintegrating documents, only to quit after a few months and again rebury the living ghost they called "Zhivoi," in this very trunk? I had so often tried to revive this awkward phantom, who would neither come to life nor die for good, before giving up and putting him back in the trunk that served as his coffin along with the dusty relics of my pointless erudition.

As the years went by, the Blumkin archives accumulated in this trunk along with my personal memories. The trunk was a camera obscura where his life mixed with mine in a series of fortuitous superpositions and superimpressions. History great and small merged on photographic paper. Snapshots of my daughter at different ages in her childhood were slipped into secret Cheka reports; her earliest drawings lay next to charts and maps of Russian cities; the postcards she sent me, full of hearts and spelling mistakes, were mixed with transcripts of Blumkin interrogations.

Now that the trunk was open, those memories threatened to fade in contact with the air. They had to be fixed before they disappeared completely. His life and mine. They had been "developed" together, in a telescoping of times and places. His story had leached onto mine. The Blumkin Project that had accompanied me in my travels and my moves bore witness to a self that had disappeared, one I had strained to escape among the highlights of a legendary story. My Blumkin life! I had wound up knowing Moscow, Leningrad, Kyiv, Odessa, and Istanbul better than the cities where I had lived. The map tracing Blumkin's travels overlaid the one of my own movements. And now, with autumn drawing to an end, Yakov Blumkin was ringing my doorbell, like an intrusive friend you haven't seen in years. There he was, right in front of me, both fiction and reality, he and his many doubles, Zhivoi and zombie.

Six months later, I was on a plane for Odessa.

CHAPTER

2

Yakov Grigorievich Blumkin was born in
Odessa on October 8, 1900.

Perhaps. He himself gave that date during a deposition before a Cheka commission in 1919, but in his
autobiography—members of the Bolshevik Party had
to write their autobiographies several times during
their lives—Blumkin put down March (without further precision) and not October 8. Just a few extra
months in an existence lived at a dead run. After his
arrest in 1929, Blumkin gave yet another version,
saying he was born in Sosnytsia, near Chernigov,
in 1898. This version is cited on a website devoted
to the history of Jewish communities in Ukraine,
which mentions "Yakov Blumkin" among "Famous
Jews from Sosnitsya." Other sources give his birthplace as Lemberg (Lvov), where he supposedly studied at the German *gymnasium*. This might explain a

precocious anti-German prejudice to which he gave full rein at seventeen when he killed Germany's ambassador to Moscow, Count von Mirbach.

After Russian troops seized Lvov in September 1914, his father, Grigory Isayevich, was said to have enlisted in the Russian Army and accompanied the soldiers as they retreated to Odessa, where his family settled. But that's hard to believe. His father, a former lumber worker in Polesia, died when Blumkin was six (in 1904 or 1906, depending on the two versions of his birth), leaving his family and brothers and sister destitute. So he couldn't have joined the Russian Army in 1914.

Of the three versions recorded by historians— two of them from Blumkin himself, as I was able to verify in GPU archives—I prefer the first date, 1900, for three reasons that will have consequences for the rest of this book. One: Blumkin was born with his century, and this perfect synchronicity is the only harmony to be heard in a biography loud with the dissonances of troubled times. Two: Blumkin's birth on the "magical date of the century's change" shines an augural, almost Christlike light on our hero's humble birth to a poor family in Odessa's Moldavanka ghetto. Three: in a biography complicated by pseudonyms and a breathless succession of locales, the date 1900 gives readers an easily remembered benchmark that lets them calculate the hero's age at every stage of a life full of false trails and blind alleys.

You could give a thousand details of young Blumkin's life: the spicy scent of acacia trees, the courthouse's white domes, street peddlers' cries, the sirens of ships sailing for Port Said and Newcastle, Marseille and Cardiff, the whirling of dead leaves on the muddy roads driven by the first automobiles... The Moldavanka neighborhood, its "wind men," big-hearted bandits who robbed the rich to feed the dockworkers, the Combat Organization terrorists, whose names blistered the tongues of white-stockinged bourgeois lounging on flowered sofas, the merchants, the brokers. You would have to describe the first strikes, the garbage cans heaped in the street, the burning of the synagogue, the muzhiks sweeping through Odessa, the ransacked shops, the air choking with feathers from ripped mattresses. You would have to talk about revolts, ticking bombs, the shredded bodies of the tsar's ministers. But if we're going to say just one thing, let's quote Blumkin's grandmother, who told him, "Study, study, and you'll get everything, riches and glory. You must know everything. People will fall at your feet and bow down. The whole world must envy you. Don't trust anyone, don't have friends. Don't give them money; don't give them your heart."

I reread those lines in February 2011, on the plane taking me to Odessa. It was an excerpt from a synopsis I had written twenty years earlier for a publisher, a dozen pages that contained what little information I had collected about Blumkin. I found it in the bottom of my Blumkin Project trunk a few days before I left, and I took it along, thinking it might guide me during this trip to Odessa. I was startled by the specificity of the images: the acacias, leaves, and feathers, etc. Had I actually gone there, to question the witnesses or their descendants? Of course not, and the Internet didn't exist back then. Those images were lifted from history books, memoirs, and novels. I consulted accounts of the 1905 pogroms, the memoirs of writers contemporary to Blumkin like Isaac Babel and Yuri Olesha, images from Dziga Vertov's *Man with a Movie Camera* and Eisenstein's *Battleship Potemkin*, both of which were shot in Odessa.

That's how every biographer proceeds, borrowing memories, stories, and images from witnesses, historians, and writers to bring a tableau to life. Mixed in with these literary and cinematographic quotations were memories of my own childhood in Marseille. Wasn't Odessa called the "Marseille of the Black Sea"? For decades, cargo ships shuttled between those cities like buses serving the same line, tying up to the same docks, trading Ukrainian wheat for Marseille tiles. In my mind, Babel's Moldavanka neighborhood looked like Marseille's Le Panier, and I conflated the famous steps in *Potemkin* with those of the Saint-Charles train station. I felt I knew Odessa even before visiting it, a paper Odessa composed of quotations and personal memories. A montage of mental images.

I closed the synopsis. Its cover sheet bore a date, my name, and a Paris address near the Bastille. In taking it, I thought it might guide me during this trip, but I was wrong. Maybe I would at least find in it an explanation for the reasons that got me interested in this "elusive hero," as Emmanuelle called him when she accompanied me on this return to my Bolshevik Ithaca. As the plane flew over the snow-covered peaks of the Alps, I thought back to that distant period she once dubbed "Blumkinian." She hadn't known about him, because she was still a child at a time when I'd already gotten interested in a character who gradually took over my life, to the point that I devoted all my free time to him. Were my motives that of a historian, a militant, a writer? Did I want to write a biography or a novel? I couldn't answer those questions. The person I was then had become distant, and was as remote from me as I was from Blumkin. Far from helping me track him down, it blocked him. The two stories were mirroring each other, exchanging their own enigmas. I had to separate them, untangle them.

The plane began its descent into Odessa. Looking out the window, I watched as its white wing ripped the surrounding fog. Then the Gulf of Odessa appeared with its long arms stretching inland, the hips of its estuaries, and the jumble of basins glittering in the setting sun. Rail lines ran to the foot of warehouses where containers were stacked like Rubik's cubes and orange-clad longshoremen busied themselves around the cranes. Freed of its barge, a tugboat zigzagged back into the harbor, trailing a snake of foam. The plane banked gently, momentarily revealing the city with its grid of streets, a checkerboard on a cliff. Then it skirted the Black Sea beaches, following an invisible path toward the ground. A vacant lot with scraggly bushes appeared in the windows on either side, and the plane bumped along the runway until it came to a stop.

The Londonskaya Hotel stands a few hundred yards from the famous steps in Eisenstein's movie *Battleship Potemkin*. It overlooks the harbor and in fair weather provides a wide panorama of Odessa Bay, "like a balcony on the Black Sea," says the hotel's website. This morning, however, we could barely make out the tall rust-colored cranes dipping their long arms into ships' holds. Snow was coming down hard, and the acacias on Prymorsky Boulevard, which ran along the hotel, bowed under its weight.

It was in this hotel that the writer Yuri Olesha learned of Sergei Kirov's assassination, the event that launched the great 1936–38 Moscow trials. The guest register displayed the signatures of a constellation of writers and film people: Robert Louis Stevenson, Anton Chekhov, Henri Barbusse, Sergei Eisenstein, Louis Aragon and Elsa Triolet, Sergei

Esenin and Isadora Duncan, Marcello Mastroianni, Nikita Mikhalkov, and many others. The opera and the archaeological and literary museums were very near at hand. To my right, I could glimpse the white colonnaded facade of what had been the stock market before the Revolution and became the regional Soviet headquarters in 1917. The building housed the Odessa city museum. The monument to the *Potemkin* sailors had been removed, replaced by a statue of Catherine the Great.

On the flat-screen TVs lining the hotel walls, Euronews was replaying muted scenes of a violent demonstration. Hundreds of thousands of people had gathered on Tahrir Square in Cairo to demand the ouster of President Hosni Mubarak. The police were charging the demonstrators. Bodies were being carried away on stretchers as image followed image of streets filled with tear gas, a forest of green flags, bloodied faces. From time to time, a shot of a journalist reporting on the event would appear, only to be relegated to a corner of the screen to make room for images of the angry crowd. TV screens in gilded frames hung on every wall, with dozens lining the hallways to the ballrooms, each repeating the same images, as in an electronics store. I had come to Odessa to investigate the 1905 and 1907 revolutions, and here the news was giving me a revolution unfolding in Egypt at that very moment.

I had made an appointment with a historian who was studying police archives, and whom I'd agreed to keep anonymous. He claimed that the legend of Odessa as the mother of crime was constructed by literature and cinema. He had gotten interested in the famous bandit Moisei Vinnitsky, who inspired Babel to create the character of Benya Krik, the "King" of *Odessa Stories*. Blumkin became close to Vinnitsky after the February Revolution of 1917. The historian was late, probably because of the weather. In fact, no cars were driving on the boulevard. Outside, bundled-up crews were clearing the streets with shovels.

Very early this morning we had decided to go see the famous Odessa Steps. The streetlights were still on, their pale light filtered by the thick veil of snowflakes. Emmanuelle walked ahead of me, holding a city map and pointing to some invisible spot in the distance. With difficulty we trudged through fresh powder snow up to our calves. We retraced our path several times, searching for the start of steps that loomed so large in my imagination that we couldn't possibly have missed them. No sign indicated the spot. I had screened the scene of the steps in Eisenstein's movie so often, I was positive I would recognize them at first glance. But there was nothing in the layout of the area that matched my mental picture, neither the modest statue of Governor Richelieu, nor the huge lions from the movie, now no more than tabby cats half buried in snow.

Emmanuelle was a veteran mountain hiker and expert map reader, but it took all her powers of persuasion to convince me to try the modest stairway we eventually found. The steps looked much narrower than those in the movie, squeezed on either side by fences covered with inscriptions hiding abandoned gardens with graffiti-covered concrete borders that poked up here and there under the snow.

We took the icy steps one at a time, with my memory protesting at how narrow they were. It was only when I got to the foot of the stairway and turned around that I recognized the steps of the film. The optical illusion created by the architects gave the flight of steps a monumental dimension that Eisenstein further emphasized with low-angle shots. But how had the filmmaker managed to assemble so many extras in such a small area? There were hundreds of them, maybe a thousand. I was tempted to calculate the area's surface by pacing off the width of the steps. How often had I watched this scene precisely because of the great number of extras Eisenstein used, all of them contemporaries of my hero with a thousand faces!

Eisenstein made the movie for the twentieth anniversary of the 1905 revolution. It tells the story of the *Potemkin* sailors' mutiny. Blumkin was twenty-five years old then. I would have liked to add him to the crowd, put his face on one of those extras. I had studied each of them, looking for clues. As I climbed the steps, I could see them, one after another. The elegant woman in the feathered hat who observes the distant battleship through a lorgnette. The woman twirling an umbrella on her shoulder. The amputee who leaps from step to step, swinging his arms. The little boy with the basket who runs down the steps with his mother, and falls under the Cossacks' bullets. The foot that crushes his hand, its fingers spread. The bloody face of the woman with shattered glasses. The girl in the white blouse and knotted scarf. The little boy plugging his ears, next to his fallen father. The young woman who is shot and loses hold of the buggy that starts bumping down the steps, carrying her baby.

Whatever became of that baby, that movie extra? He was probably about six months old at the time of filming, which ran from August to November 1925. So in 2011 he would be about eighty-five. Could he still be alive? What had his life been like? Back in my hotel room, I watched the film's credits, but the names of the extras weren't listed. I tried a search on my computer. Many hits referred to the scene, to references to the scene in other movies, like *The Untouchables* and *Brazil*, and to the architects who designed the steps, but there was nothing on the identity of the diminutive extra. I gave up my search. A few days later I put the question to a film historian who confirmed that no one ever learned the baby's identity. "You have the Unknown Soldier under the Arc de Triomphe," he said. "We have the Unknown Baby of the Steps."

———

"Childhood is wonderful," wrote Victor Shklovsky, the father of Russian formalism, "it wants to dig to the depths of the world." That's probably true of any childhood, but digging takes on special meaning in Odessa. Shklovsky wrote that line in "Plumbing the Depths," his preface to the Odessa writer Yuri Olesha's book *No Day Without a Line*. After the huge success of *Envy*, his first novel, in 1927, Olesha wrote only for theater and film, but he devoted his last years to an unfinished book of memories. After Olesha's death, Shklovsky and his wife used those unfinished manuscripts to create a collection of fragments that glowed with "the brilliance of spent uranium." The first two parts, titled "Childhood" and "Odessa," offer irreplaceable testimony about the century's first two decades in Odessa. If I wanted to get a picture of Blumkin's childhood, I would have to visit the city's catacombs.

Odessa is perched on a cliff overlooking the Black Sea, but its buildings and monuments are built of stone blocks quarried underground. The yellow chalk of its downtown buildings was cut, loaded, and hauled along narrow tunnels by oxen and mules gone blind from spending their lives in darkness. The farther the city spread, the deeper its roots sank underground, excavating a maze of galleries that would extend two hundred feet below sea level and cover more than 1,500 miles. Odessa has the biggest network of tunnels in the world, more extensive and more complex than the famous catacombs of Rome (185 miles) and Paris (300 miles). Laid end to end, they would stretch from Odessa to Paris.

The city is a colossus with feet of clay. Whenever a roadway slumps, the town's underground tunnels are blamed. If a facade cracks, it's because the catacombs under the building are collapsing. After the Revolution, the Bolsheviks forbade any more excavation in the catacombs, so as not to further weaken the city's foundations. The abandoned mines became the haunts of vagabonds, bandits, and smugglers. From the very beginning, the catacombs served as storage areas for contraband, a veritable Ali Baba's cavern piled high with all sorts of merchandise offloaded from ships. Smuggling was especially easy because some tunnels led down to the sea, which made transshipping illicit merchandise simple.

After the Second World War, a museum honoring the partisans was built at the catacombs' entrance. When fascist troops occupied Odessa, the partisans went underground with their weapons and ammunition. For the next thirteen months, some six thousand fighters harassed the occupying troops. They would emerge to the surface through air ducts, launch attacks in the heart of the city, then disappear back underground. In response to this invisible terror, fascist troops tried to block access to the catacombs and pumped smoke into the tunnels to force the partisans out. They went deeper instead. Valentin Kataev describes those fierce battles in *The Waves of the Black Sea*. The tunnels still bear their marks: defensive firing slits cut into galleries, walls pockmarked with bullets and grenade shrapnel. A hot water bottle. Nazi uniform buttons. The partisans set up an underground military base with dormitories, canteens, a laundry, and working hospitals. Countless caves served as ammunition dumps. In a break room, people played chess, checkers, and dominoes by candlelight. Rooms cut into the rock on either side of the main tunnel housed men and women; hay-lined niches in the walls served as bunks. The medical wing had real beds and an operating room. The women cooked on wooden ovens built of yellow chalk, venting the smoke up to a higher tunnel. On the surface, villagers would pretend to be drawing water from wells, while actually lowering baskets of food down air shafts to the partisans.

Stories and legends of all sorts have always risen from Odessa's catacombs: unexplained disappearances, rumors of ritual crimes. It's hard to tell truth from fiction in all these stories from the lower depths, a dubious grab bag of false memories and adventures partly shaped by rumors, imagination, and mystic vibrations. Gangs kept women imprisoned down there, to be sold into slavery. A survivor of the *Titanic*, rescued by a brigantine bound for

Odessa, supposedly made a model of the liner in solid gold and hid it in the catacombs. He was afraid it would be confiscated by the Bolsheviks, who had seized control of Ukraine six years after the sinking. A century later, people are still looking for the treasure. Other stories speak of a spirit—or even a god—that watches over the catacombs. Sometimes called "Bout," this avenging divinity protects the riches hidden there. If someone tries to steal treasure buried in the catacombs, Bout will lock them in frozen darkness. According to these beliefs, it's forbidden to bring what you find underground to the surface. And if you break this law, you have to at least leave something in exchange.

Odessa is built on three levels. The city proper with its neo-Baroque monuments, flowered gardens, and wide avenues; below that is the port, with its half-moon bay and its long docks bristling with cranes; and finally the underground city of the catacombs. The psychoanalyst Mosche Wolff, a disciple of Freud who settled in Odessa during the first decade of the twentieth century, thought this three-level architecture echoed the three-part construct of the self that Freud was then developing in Vienna: superego, ego, and id. Could that be why psychoanalysis first took root in Odessa before spreading to Moscow? In 1912 Freud wrote to Jung: "There seems to be a local epidemic of psychoanalysis in Russia (Odessa)."

Odessa's id consists of that maze of tunnels, the refuge of bandits and children searching for an adventure playground in its depths. To keep them from going down there, kids were warned about children who had gotten lost, dying of thirst or crushed by rockfalls. A *Wall Street Journal* reporter found smashed VHS cassettes littering the ground: the unspooled tapes were used as guidelines to keep people from getting lost in the labyrinth. The story of Theseus and the Minotaur, reinvented.

To our psychoanalyst, the port city above the catacombs, a place of exchanges and transactions where the reality principle reigned, represented Odessa's ego. It was linked to the superego—the upper city—by the steps made famous by Eisenstein's film. The upper city rose above the Black Sea like a utopia and a strategic vision. A geometric dream, its checkerboard grid of streets laid out by French architects in the image of urban Renaissance utopias. At the start of the century, Odessa's superego, perched on its cliff above the Black Sea, suddenly blazed with a thousand lights. The city had discovered electricity.

Years later, Blumkin still remembered the day his father took him to a neighbor's house to see electricity. Above their heads hung a clear glass bulb connected to a twisted wire that ran along the ceiling and down a panel to a black switch mounted on the doorjamb. The neighbor flipped the switch, and light bathed the objects in the room, even the most distant. He flipped the switch again, and the room plunged back into darkness. The bulb didn't light up all at once but gradually, like a bowl slowly being filled with water, and it reached its greatest luminosity when it was full to the brim and the light spilled out, as it were.

Today it's hard to imagine the fascination exercised by the arrival of electricity in homes. Until then, you obeyed the cycle of days and nights. Now you could fire up a captive, domesticated sun in a simple glass bulb with the flip of a switch. Wrote Yuri Olesha in his memoir: "I remember the big crowd of people who gathered in our apartment to see the electric bulb, their faces lifted and mouths agape. It was a miracle."

Above the bulb, a white reflector hung from a braided cord that ran through a pulley. By raising or lowering it, you could adjust the width of the bulb's light. Olesha's neighbor repeated the operation several times. He climbed onto a chair to raise the reflector, and young Olesha could see faces emerge from the shadows and brighten. Then he lowered it, and the faces got dark again.

As soon as he was alone, and despite his parents' prohibition, Olesha played with the light switch, turning it on and off several times, each time varying the interval, as if to figure how it was rigged or to learn a magic trick. "*E-lek-tri-ches-tvo*," he would whisper as he turned the switch, and light flooded the room. *"E-lek-tri-ches—tvo,"* he said, separating the syllables, as the room went dark. When evening came, he leaned out the window repeating his *"E-lek-tri-ches—tvo"* mantra as the streetlights along the boulevards all came on at the same time. Electricity lit up windows, avenues, and theaters, as if a long-blind city had suddenly regained its sight. People dreamed of a city "as transparent as crystal." The heroes of those days weren't yet Lenin or Trotsky; they were named Edison, Siemens, and Marconi.

Downtown Odessa bristled with electric poles, and cables ran over rooftops, weaving a huge spiderweb between neighborhoods, their shadows crisscrossing the streets. The streetlights glowed with a steady, strong light, as if ordered to restore the right angle's prerogatives to the world. Objects' shapes no longer wavered under pale and trembling gas light. The city lamplighters, their long rods on their shoulders, disappeared one by one, departing the world like shadows chased away by electricity. "You like lightning in the sky," Mayakovsky wrote to Pasternak a few years later. "I like it in the electric iron." A veritable "electromania" hit the population as industrial and domestic uses appeared, announcing the electrification of society. Electric motors took their place next to steam engines, gasoline motors, and hydraulic turbines. Using electromagnetic waves, the wireless telegraph made it possible to imagine "a planet as transparent as crystal."

But the arrival of electricity in Odessa in 1905–06 wasn't just a technological innovation; it was a revolution of perception. "We will move from the lyricism of the machine to the undeniable electrical man," wrote Dziga Vertov, who would shoot *Man with a Movie Camera* in Odessa. This new man "celebrates the proper running of the machine, is passionate about mechanisms, marches straight toward the marvels of chemical processes, and writes poems and screenplays with electric and incandescent tools."

During my stay in Odessa, I got my hands on a real treasure: a few lines written by Blumkin in November 1929. Those few lines contained no revelations, but to my eyes they constituted a piece of evidence, and in Blumkin's own hand. I found them almost by accident, because they hadn't been filed correctly. They weren't in Blumkin's official file, but in that of Yakov Agranov, the man who interrogated him before leading him to the basement to be executed.

In his Lubyanka cell, Blumkin was said to have written a kind of memorandum summing up his periods of service. Victor Serge, who heard it from a witness to Blumkin's last days, believed he requested and obtained a fifteen-day reprieve to write his memoirs, and a long letter to his son, Martin, who had been born two years earlier and never knew his father. But this was never found, even after the opening of the archives in the 1990s. At one point I had imagined re-creating this autobiography, an insider's history of the Revolution's first ten years, as told by one of its actors. That was the original idea behind the Blumkin Project. The exercise soon struck me as gratuitous and artificial, however, and I abandoned it.

But now for the first time I was able to read something, barely a paragraph long, written by Blumkin himself. Amid the range of possibilities I faced since restarting my research on Blumkin, I finally had an established fact, a proof of his existence. I examined each of his words like a paleontologist who must reconstitute a dinosaur from a single fossilized bone. I know these lines by heart, having read them so often I can almost hear Blumkin's voice:

"I was born in Odessa to a poor Jewish family in March 1900. At the time of my birth, my father, who had been a lumber worker in Polesia, became a small merchant. He died when I was six, and my mother and my brothers and sister sank into poverty. Caught between national exclusion and social misfortune, I grew up according to my destiny as a child."

That last sentence is as concise as an equation. "Social misfortune" was the condition of children from poor families, forced to quit school and eke out a living as messengers, apprentices, hawkers, or street thieves. "National exclusion" referred to the situation of Jews who were confined to the Pale of

Settlement (*cherta osedlosti*) between 1791 and 1917. This covered the western part of the Russian Empire, which today is occupied by Lithuania, Belorussia, Poland, Moldova, Ukraine, and western Russia. "Caught between national exclusion and social misfortune, I grew up according to my destiny as a child."

In the fog of legends swirling around Blumkin's life, those few lines give a system of coordinates we can use to orient ourselves, with "social misfortune" on the x-axis and "national exclusion" on the y-axis. Using those, you could draw a curve, a mathematical function on which to arrange all the known and sometimes contradictory facts of Blumkin's life and trajectory. This is what I once called the "Blumkin function," the biography of a child of the century born in 1900.

At five, Yakov Blumkin was on the famous steps of Eisenstein's film when the sailors of the *Potemkin* sailed into port and threatened the government buildings with their guns. The whole family went out to see the battleship in the harbor. The chestnut trees were in bloom. In a family photograph, his sister Rosetta is wearing a light, flowered dress, a kerchief on her head. His two brothers are in short-sleeved shirts. Suddenly two cannon shots thundered above their heads. The *Potemkin* was aiming for the municipal theater where the military council met, but missed. The two shells landed somewhere in town. His father died the next year, plunging the whole family into poverty.

Blumkin entered Talmud Torah school at age eight and left four years later. At twelve, he was reading Jack London's *Martin Eden* and dreaming of foreign horizons: Moscow, St. Petersburg, Berlin, Jerusalem—the litany he recited to himself each evening as he went to sleep. His first theft was a map. He stole it from the cloakroom of the Odessa Maritime Company and pinned it on a wall facing his bed. He was fascinated by the dotted lines of transatlantic routes. In the evening he trained himself to memorize frontiers, the outlines of oceans and deserts, the relief of mountains. In his mind, he climbed the highest peaks in Tibet, descending on the other side to disappear into Persia and China. The Black Sea? A passageway to the Mediterranean, which opened to him the doors to the Orient, Africa, Constantinople, Marseille, Tangier, the Strait of Gibraltar.

But in the meantime, he had to earn a living. In 1913, he was a trainee in Karl Franck's electrotechnical office, then in one Inger's workshop, where he earned twenty or thirty kopeks a day. By day, he wired businesses and private homes. At night he repaired tramway lights at the Richelievski depot for a Belgian company. He occasionally worked as an assistant electrician at Odessa's Russian theater. In 1916 we find him at the Avitch and Izraïlson cannery. He hopped from one job to another without any apparent logic to this instability.

Blumkin was fourteen when war was declared, seventeen in the year of the Revolution. A year earlier he had joined the Left Socialist Revolutionaries, who enjoyed the prestige of Azef and Savinkov's SR Combat Organization, which had been spreading terror in tsarist Russia since the beginning of the century. Blumkin read a lot. He wrote poems—pretty bad ones, apparently. Still, his verse appeared in various publications: *Kolossia*, *Gudok*, and once even in *The Odessa Paper*. Brochures with red covers lined his shelves, their titles outlining an intellectual itinerary and a path to action. At night he painfully deciphered Marx's *Das Kapital* and recited aloud entire passages of Sergei Nechayev's *Catechism of a Revolutionary*.

Tossed onto the street very young, Blumkin discovered class struggle, the world of Moldavanka bandits, Odessa's Jewish elite, and street fighting. His brothers Isaiah and Leo, the youngest, worked as journalists for Odessa newspapers. Nathan, another brother, would become a well-known playwright under the pen name Basilevski. Leo was an anarchist, their sister Rosetta, a Social Democrat; you can imagine the arguments around the dinner table. From 1905 on, they never stopped. Peasantry and proletariat. Strikes. Occupations. Demonstrations. Bolshevik party brochures. Lenin's complicated articles. The theory of imperialism.

Discussions raged over billiards in the harbor's Greek bistros, between Mensheviks, Bolsheviks, People's Will populists, and Socialist Revolutionaries. Blumkin was still finding his way.

Two tutelary figures emerge from the mists of Yakov Blumkin's childhood, a writer and a bandit. One ruled the y-axis (the condition of Jews in the Pale of Settlement); the other ruled the x-axis (the condition of the poor). The writer was celebrated, the bandit legendary. While the first owed his fame to his works, the second became a literary character, the famous Benya Krik, the great-hearted bandit in orange pants that Isaac Babel immortalized in his *Odessa Stories*. But you have to be careful not to confuse the "King" of Moldavanka with his model, a certain Mishka Vinnitsky—dubbed Mishka Yaponchik ("Mike the Jap") supposedly because of his slanted eyes—who had his hour of glory in Odessa in 1917–19. As Babel writes in "Justice in Parentheses," "There is no other like Benya the King! He stamps out lies in his quest for justice—justice in parentheses as well as justice without parentheses."

Mendele Mocher Sforim (his pseudonym means "Mendele the book peddler") was Mike the Jap's total opposite. Where Mendele's knowledge and experience gave him sway over people's minds, Vinnitsky ruled Odessa by stealth and strength, committing burglaries, robberies, and expropriations. He stole from the rich and gave to the poor. But both men were driven by a desire for justice, and shared the same love of their people. They differed only in how to put it into practice. Mendele believed in cultivating minds through education; Mike the Jap couldn't stand to wait. Mendele gave Moldavanka's people the dignity of their language; Mike the Jap fed and armed them. In his autobiography, Blumkin pays homage to both his masters: "One opened my mind, the other taught me the most basic of skills, how to kill a man."

In 1908, when Yakov Blumkin entered Odessa's Talmud Torah, Mendele Mocher Sforim was seventy-three and had been running the school for a quarter century. He is considered the founder of modern Jewish literature, one of the greatest scholars of the Bible, Talmud, and Hebrew authors. The publication of his complete works is under way.

On the first day of school, Mendele received young Blumkin in his book-lined office, which reeked of tobacco. He was an old man with a neat white beard, rimmed glasses, and surprisingly liberal ideas. As the principal, he felt that Jewish children should pursue more than just religious studies. He encouraged them to learn foreign languages and to free themselves from the yoke of the religious community. He severely criticized his so-called benefactors for their bigotry, cruelty, and cynicism. He admired the Renaissance.

Called "the grandfather of Yiddish literature," Mendele during his lifetime was celebrated all over Europe and as far as the United States. He would be a national treasure, except that the Jews in the Russian Empire had no nation, merely a "zone of residence." That's where nearly five million Russian Jews, mostly peasants in shtetls, lived at the start of the twentieth century.

Mendele's great merit was to capture shtetl life just as it was disappearing, and give written form to its humor, anecdotes, and language. From his travels through the Pale of Settlement, he brought back the lives of men and women accustomed to making the best of their bad luck. He wrote: "My fate was to go down to the lowest level, to the basement of Jewish life. My merchandise is rags and tatters. The people I deal with are the poor, beggars, tricksters, charlatans, the dregs of life, the lowest of humanity. Mendele took Yiddish—despised as "a language of stutterers" "for women and the ignorant," "bastardized German," "a cursed jargon"—and turned it into a literary language. In 1909, during a lecture tour from Vilnius to Bialystok and from Lodz to Warsaw, thousands awaited him in train stations, jostling each other to get close, to catch his eye or shake his hand. But in Odessa, Mendele passed unnoticed. Visitors were surprised to see him strolling the streets incognito, eavesdropping on conversations in search of popular expressions and bursts of spoken language. A modest hero who cared nothing for glory, he wanted only to be useful to his people.

In 1923 in Berlin, Dora Diamant, Franz Kafka's last love, read to her ailing lover stories from *Fishke the Lame* and *The Travels of Benjamin III*. The latter is a picaresque tale often compared to *Don Quixote*, and it earned Mendele the title of "the Jewish Cervantes."

The centenary of Mendele's birth was celebrated on February 10, 1936, also in Berlin. A Jewish restaurant was booked, supposedly for a wedding reception. The would-be bride was none other than Dora Diamant. A Warsaw Yiddish newspaper gave a moving account of the event: "Around us were a few dozen members of our now defunct cultural club who were still in Berlin, along with some other lovers of Yiddish. Standing at the head of the table, Dora read a chapter from Mendele's favorite novel, *The Wishing Ring*. We all sang Yiddish songs, thrilled that a group of persecuted Jews in Nazi Germany had managed to join in celebrating the centenary of our great classical writer." It was Diamant's last evening in Berlin. Next day, she took the train to Moscow to join her husband, a German communist who had left Nazi Germany and moved to the Soviet Union.

We don't know much about Blumkin's second mentor, Mishka Vinnitsky, alias "Mike the Jap." Very few documents survive that would help reconstruct his life. It should be noted that in 1918 Vinnitsky himself attacked the state police archives and destroyed the registration files of some sixteen thousand criminals. All the hard data about Mike the Jap having disappeared, Isaac Babel and his imagination stepped in.

This reshaping of reputation is a fairly common phenomenon, whereby a person is turned into a hero by entirely literary means. These people often come across as hybrid beings, men of flesh and paper who rise above the human condition to reach the kind of universality only attained in books. Once a flesh-and-blood man has been transformed into a hero, it's very hard to start with the romantic hero Benya Krik and work backward to find the real Mike the Jap. But we can try.

He was born Moisei Vinnitsky on October 30, 1891, to a lower-middle-class Jewish family in the Moldavanka neighborhood. He had high cheekbones, olive skin, and the slanted eyes that gave him his nickname. His life story preceded Blumkin's by a decade. Like Blumkin, Vinnitsky was born and raised in Moldavanka, lost his father at six, and very early experienced poverty. He also was a student at Talmud Torah, but had to drop out. He even became an apprentice electrician, too. There's nothing miraculous about this repetition, however. Those were the material conditions of Moldavanka's impoverished Jews, and they turned the children of wig-wearing Jewish mothers into bandits and revolutionaries. In 1905, at age fourteen, Mike the Jap joined a Jewish self-defense detachment formed to protect the community against pogroms. The triggering event was the murder of a gentile boy in Dubossary, a little town near Kishinev, in April 1903. Following Easter celebrations a few days later, a mob attacked Jewish neighborhoods. In three days, they sacked hundreds of stores, burned hundreds of homes, and killed dozens of Jews. The forces of law and order didn't lift a finger. Starting in 1904, the pogroms spread, to peak in late 1905 and early 1906 amid a general climate of revolutionary agitation. The last two months of 1905 saw no fewer than 657 pogroms, with more than three thousand killed and fifteen thousand wounded, mainly in Bessarabia and Odessa (eight hundred killed, five thousand injured in late October 1905).

A year later, Mike the Jap joined an anarchist splinter group, attacking stores, munitions depots, even private homes. This politics of expropriation led him to participate in terrorist acts. While still an adolescent, he was sentenced (apparently unjustly) to twelve years in prison for killing a policeman. Only the fact that he was a minor saved him from hanging. In February 1917 he was amnestied, along with other criminals convicted of political crimes.

Vinnitsky returned to Odessa in the summer of 1917, on the eve of the Revolution. He formed a gang of robbers that quickly became known throughout the city. Merchants, restaurant owners, and brothel keepers paid him protection money. He also paid off the police (for their passivity). And he remembered the poor when spreading money around, which earned him a reputation as Odessa's Robin Hood. He fed this reputation by publishing a letter in the Odessa Soviet deputies' *Pravda*, in which he rejected the accusations of banditry in the name of a very personal concept of class struggle. "Personally I would be very happy if someone asked a worker or a peasant if I had ever harmed them. I know in advance that no one could answer in the affirmative. Concerning the bourgeoisie, if I have undertaken offensive actions against it, no worker or peasant can condemn me. The bourgeoisie rob the poor, so I began robbing it in turn. I am proud to be called a robber, and I will be a threat to capitalists and the enemies of the people wherever they are for as long as I live."

At seventeen, Yakov Blumkin encountered Mike the Jap in the Jewish self-defense groups he later called his "school of life." There he discovered a whole fauna of adventurers, activists, Zionist militants, bandits, and terrorists, and it wasn't always easy to tell them apart. From self-defense committees to expropriations, from terrorism to state violence, the ranks of the Revolution's clandestine movements were full of Jews frustrated at the slowness of Russian society to accept them.

Future Zionists first took up arms in Russian revolutionary terrorism. In Odessa, Jews like Blumkin turned to political violence. Self-defense groups organized in response to the pogroms, determined to break with the victims' legendary passivity. Vladimir Jabotinsky, who would later found Revisionist Zionism, tells this story: "We traveled to Moldavanka and met a few young men in a big room that looked like an office. They gave us about twenty pistols as a gift, and sold us the rest at cut-rate prices, mostly on credit and without hope of repayment. We stored our weapons—pistols, iron bars, kitchen and butcher knives—in that office, which two people guarded day and night. The other part of the office held the mimeo machine on which we printed flyers in Russian and Yiddish. Their content was very simple: two penal code articles that clearly stated that someone who kills in self-defense is not punished, and a few words of encouragement to young Jews, that they not let themselves be led to the slaughter."

In his obituary of Theodor Herzl, who was also a cosmopolitan Jew, Jabotinsky contrasted the ghetto Jew, whom he called "ugly and sickly, without external charm," with the real Hebrew, "the ideal image of male Hebrew beauty, tall, broad-shouldered, and graceful." To the "fearful and oppressed Jew who prefers to hide and avoid meeting strangers' eyes" he set a bold Jew unafraid to "look anyone in the eyes" and raise a banner before him, declaring "I am a Hebrew."

Mike the Jap's reign as king of Moldavanka was tumultuous but short, less than two years in all, from 1917 to 1919. But what years those were! Blumkin was with him during that period, before leaving Odessa, which was occupied by French and Greek forces, to settle in Moscow in the spring of 1918.

When the Soviet Republic of Odessa was proclaimed, Mike the Jap understood the need to collaborate with the new authorities. He went to the Cheka and offered to form a detachment that would be part of Odessa's Soviet Army. His troops displayed great style, as described by a witness who saw them marching through the streets of Odessa: "Musicians that Mike the Jap had gathered from all over the city led the parade. Trumpet players and flutists from the Opera, wandering street fiddlers, and accordion players from outlying taverns all walked in step together, playing appropriate marches and well-known Moldavanka tunes. Following the orchestra came the Jap himself, riding a white stallion and wearing a leather cap, white tunic, and baggy, dark red pants." According to another account, Mike's horse was black and not white, and the commander led the parade and was followed, not preceded, by two Jewish Moldavanka bands. Then came the parade of infantry, two thousand men armed with rifles and Mauser pistols, dressed in long white pants and smocks, but with a wide assortment of head coverings, from top hats and boaters to felt bonnets and kepis.

In May 1919 Mike the Jap's 54th Revolutionary Detachment was battling troops under Symon

Petlyura. In letting Mike the Jap organize a revolutionary battalion, however, the Soviets had laid a trap. By sending him to the front, they got him out of the city. Vinnitsky never saw Odessa again. He was shot in the back in a little train station. His funeral became a key moment in the construction of his legend. All the Jews of the region, including many from Odessa, were said to have gathered for the funeral. The funeral service was sung by the Great Synagogue's cantor, joined by the soloists of the Odessa Opera.

Two years later, Mike was resurrected on the page and on-screen under the pseudonym "Benya Krik." Everything suggests that Isaac Babel knew the details of Mike's death. He describes it with what in Odessa is called "scrupulous inexactness," except for the critical event, the bullet in the back.

In the years that followed, Mike the Jap's life ceased to belong to the real world and entered legend. A clear sign of this switch was the proliferation of different versions of every event in his life. Stories about him multiplied and contradicted each other. They spread by word of mouth and were enriched with extravagant details. They came from a number of sources: from Vinnitsky and his lieutenants, who ruled the city, from Soviet authorities who understood the danger of the popular Jap's two thousand bandits, from the press, and from the street. All of them passed on stories of the struggle, the ultimate goal of which was control of the city.

———

That's how "Mike the Jap" became "King" Benya Krik in Isaac Babel's *Odessa Stories*. And what Babel knew, he could only have learned from the Jap himself. As he wrote in "Justice in Parentheses": "The King speaks little and speaks politely. Who can fathom the meaning of the King's few words? Between yes and no, a five-thousand-ruble commission hangs in the air... The words of the King lay like a stone block across the road where hunger roamed."

You could also say that they lay like a stumbling block across the path leading to the facts. Who could have told Babel about Mike the Jap's activities? Who described the funeral of Josif the shop assistant, shot by one of Krik's drunken men? Who drove the red car in which the gangsters showed up at Josif's funeral, where they were certainly not welcome? Whose guns kept the crowd in check while Krik gave his speech?

In 1925 Babel began writing the screenplay of *Benya Krik* for Goskino, the state's first movie studio, drawing on two of his stories: "The King" and "How Things Were Done in Odessa."

It was obviously impossible to bring Babel's prose to the screen without losing something, especially since the film was silent. The script was offered to Eisenstein, who was getting ready to shoot *Battleship Potemkin*. If he had accepted, it would have changed the history of film. Instead of *Potemkin*, we might have a Soviet *Godfather*, born of the Moldavanka Jewish ghetto.

To the censorship board, the film's director, Vladimir Vilner, declared: "I had to be constantly vigilant not to let myself be influenced by the rumors from Odessa, which repeated a thousand romantic legends about Mishka the Japanese, 'the big-hearted robber,' and take care to avoid anything that would make crime seem heroic...We tried not only to avoid romanticism, but also not to focus too much on the main character."

It wasn't enough. The "Benya Krik" myth resisted demystification. Wondered film historians Yuri Morozov and Tatiana Derevianko: "Why was the real Jap so popular in Odessa? Why couldn't the film's opponents forgive him for it?" Mike the Jap became famous in many Odessans' eyes for reasons other than his skills as a burglar and bandit: in caricature, he personified the Jewish street's defiance of authority.

The censorship board's verdict was final. According to its members, the film tried to romanticize the criminal underworld by lending it a certain "Odessan charm...The scandalous treatment of the Bolshevik character who tries to use Benya Krik's gang to lead a revolutionary activity is a defamatory distortion of historical truth."

Benya Krik wasn't distributed in Ukraine. (In English, its title is *Bennie the Howl*.) It is said that the premiere was held in January 1927 in Kyiv, and that

the film was immediately banned on the order of
local Party organs. Another source says that Lazar
Kaganovich, the general secretary of the Ukraine
Communist Party's Central Committee, attended
the film's premiere in Kharkov, which was then the
republic's capital. He emerged very unhappy about
its "romantic treatment of crime."

So was Odessa the capital of organized crime, as
it was described? If you believe the police department's data, no organized Jewish criminal gang
existed in Odessa before 1917. Mike the Jap spent
the ten years before the Revolution in jail, convicted
of participating in anarchist expropriations in his
youth. So he couldn't have been the author of the
exploits attributed to him. The only acts reliably
linked to Mishka Vinnitsky when he belonged to the
anarchist group Molodaya Volya (Young Will) were
a break-in at the Lansberg flour store and the bur-
glary of a certain Lander's home.

Isaac Babel's Benya Krik is as far from its model
as his Odessa is from the city I had before my eyes.
Babel hadn't only told the stories of the city; he had
created a myth. He built Odessa the way Catherine
the Great's minister Potemkin built villages. Anyone who writes about the city today runs the risk of
writing about Babel's Odessa, Babel's bandits, and
Babel's Moldavanka. Odessa is a city that now only
exists in the imagination of its inhabitants and their
descendants scattered throughout the world. Its Jews
have been driven out or exterminated, but Odessa

can't rid itself of their presence. Moldavanka has become a Ukrainian neighborhood, but its back alleys still ring with the sound of Babel's parties. As Benya Krik says at the funeral of Josif the shop assistant: "There are men who are already doomed to die, and there are men who still have not begun to live."

CHAPTER

3

The Czech Airlines Airbus A320 had been sitting on the tarmac at the Odessa airport for half an hour. Snow was coming down in heavy flakes. By pressing my face against the window, I could make out the headlights of the backhoe in front of the plane clearing snowdrifts away. The machine's jaws scraped the ground, then its arm jerked upward, made a quarter turn, and dropped blocks of snow and dirt along the edges of the runway.

To pass the time, I thumbed through the photos of Odessa I had taken with my smartphone: yellow facades, marble elevator shafts, balconies with caryatids, Moldavanka courtyards jammed with cars, the building where Gogol lived (if you stand on the balcony and lean to the right, you can see the sea), the Richelieu statue at the top of the *Potemkin* steps, arms outspread and head whitened by snow, the rust-colored cranes on the docks, the downtown business section's glass block, lit up like a satellite ready to be launched, the big abandoned park facing the sea, a picture of Vladimir Jabotinsky.

I had also taken pictures of the little Jewish museum, the smallest museum in the world, so tiny it probably doesn't even deserve the name *museum*, much less *memorial*. It took us hours to find the place, located in a three- or four-room apartment with electric radiators, on the ground floor of a shabby building. Its walls were covered with yellowed photocopies; a few farm tools stacked in the corners, as if at the end of a day's work, bore witness to shtetl life. In glass-topped cases, ritual objects and photographs of the founders of Zionism stood next to newspaper clippings announcing the opening of Odessa's Maccabee Sports Club with its young people in tank tops.

Odessa has been invaded, occupied, and liberated several times, and has been the scene of violent battles and mass executions. Its Jewish population has been exterminated or scattered to the four corners of the Earth. All that remained was gathered in this minuscule museum, its rags and spoken language becoming inaudible within its four walls. It was staffed by a history teacher bundled up in a worn overcoat. For a few euros he will tell for the hundredth time the legend of the Odessa of Babel and Mike the Jap, the pogroms of 1905, and Mendel Beilis's 1913 ritual murder trial in Kyiv, which Kafka followed in the Prague newspapers and which inspired him to write *The Trial*. The Jewish presence in the city was now nothing but a ghost. Wherever you looked around this little apartment, all you saw was Mendele's tattered travel bag, "that old and familiar Jewish travel bag, as discreet and elegant as a piece of calf liver dangling from your nose." It didn't add up to a story, much less a biography, just bits of debris that can't be assembled in a world in pieces.

We last left Yakov Blumkin in Odessa in 1917. Since dropping out of Talmud Torah at age twelve, he continued to grow up "between social misfortune and national exclusion." He was poor and Jewish, intelligent but half educated, hungry for bread and poetry. How can you reconcile war and poetry, intellectual life and material survival, collective action and adventure? An adolescent limbo where frustrations grew more acute.

He quit school to work, took all sorts of odd jobs, buying here and reselling there, unloading crates in the market, stacking melons and watermelons into pyramids in market stalls, aligning the plucked heads of chickens with the little signs stuck in their flesh, rabbits with veined skin and bound paws, and fish curved around on themselves, its eye looking like a marble that had rolled into a corner. He went down to the harbor to watch ships and shoot marbles with the stevedores. He sometimes went to the library to read novels by Jules Verne and Jack London. Reading sparked his imagination. He saw himself as an explorer of unknown lands, but also an inventor of new languages. He filled notebooks with quotations and made lists of words in Hebrew, Yiddish, and Russian, with a preference for complicated ones, like *palimpsest*, *jasper*, and *onyx*. The uncertain definition of things. The obscure nomenclature of objects. He admired Mendele for supposedly having invented words that didn't exist in Yiddish: *iceberg*, *shipment*, *shirt*, *crane*, *rhinoceros*. To Blumkin, a man who could create a word was the equal of a god.

To this picture we can add a trait that people regularly mention about Blumkin: his behavior lacked simplicity, as is often the case with people from the South. His affectation was spun out in words. Loquacious wherever he went, he walked the streets accompanied by a flight of words. To write his biography, it wasn't enough to simply re-create the thread of historical events he'd been involved with; you also had to round up all those scattered words. List them, establish the web of their exchanges, chart their affinities, measure their spread over the years, and bury those that hadn't found employment. Words can move or frighten, seduce and convince, but in certain situations could be strangely impotent. Then other weapons were called for.

Blumkin very early encountered violent anti-Semitism, and gravitated naturally to the Jewish self-defense committees. These comprised a counter-society of battle-tested young people, radicalized intellectuals, and the ex- or future terrorists who would blast a bomb-strewn path from Odessa to Moscow and Jerusalem. And let's not forget the brotherhood of Moldavanka bandits over which Mike the Jap ruled like sunshine on a puddle. Mendele taught Blumkin the power of words, but Mike the Jap taught him how to use weapons, precisely so as not to be only "paid in words"—his favorite expression. With the Jap, Blumkin began pillaging Odessa's department stores and shaking down the local rich for "the needs of the Revolution."

The heroes of Blumkin's youth didn't step out of those French novels that revolve around a few individuals standing apart from the world. They came from the ranks of the Combat Organization, people like Boris Savinkov and Yevno Azev who coolly shot the tsar's ministers at point-blank range, or threw themselves under horses' hooves to be sure, in dying, that they hit their target hidden behind the carriage's curtains. They spent months noting itineraries, observing habits, and watching the target, and put their lives in the balance. How many of these heroes had he passed in the streets of Odessa, men and women with burning eyes who had abandoned their class origins without being able to connect with the proletariat or the peasantry, deracinated people who were fading away along with tsardom's final hours?

These were players of an endgame, diggers of the old world's grave. They belonged to the same vanishing tsardom they thought they were fighting. The oldest certainties on which life in society was built were falling into disuse. Everything had to be made new, laws both written and unwritten. Moral precepts, laws, the political system, the principles of education, all eddied around in a whirlwind that people called "The Century," for lack of a better word. For them, the magical date of the change of century meant much more than the change of a date on the calendar. "You were lucky to be born on the cusp between two centuries," Blumkin's father once told him, "because you'll live a second childhood, the childhood of a new world." A "beautiful, pitiful age," whose "spine is cracked," wrote Mandelstam in his famous poem "The Age." This fracture in time would force each person to choose sides. The Blumkins in the Pale of Settlement would hear the call of the century expressed in Eduard Bagritski's then-celebrated verses:

> Our age is awaiting you out in the yard,
> Alarmed and alert as a well-armed guard.
> Go, stand by its side, don't hesitate.
> Its solitude is at least as great.
> Your enemy's everyone you meet,
> You stand alone and the age stands still,
> And if it tells you to cheat—then cheat.
> And if it tells you to kill—then kill.

Blumkin would not tell stories, as his mentor Mendele did. Instead, he would write history in letters of blood. Living history that resembled nothing you could read in books, history whose legend hadn't yet been written. A metamorphosis that was hard to discern with the naked eye would turn those little Odessa Jews, who grew up worshipping books and fearing pogroms, into Bolshevik commissars and leather-coated Chekists. Blumkin now had people call him "James" or "Jack," in honor of Jack London, his favorite writer. Instead of fighting fictional wolves in the Far North, he would battle real wolves with a brand-new Browning automatic, a gift from Mike the Jap.

February 1917: strikes and demonstrations were spreading in the main industrial centers. On March 8, International Women's Day, several parades of women (students, employees, and textile workers from the Vyborg suburbs) demonstrated in downtown Petrograd, demanding bread. On March 10 the strike became general. Next day, police and troops opened fire on a column of demonstrators, killing more than a hundred fifty. Overnight, the two elite regiments that had been ordered to fire on their "brother workers" mutinied. On the morning of March 12 soldiers and workers fraternized, seized the arsenal, distributed rifles to the crowd, and occupied the capital's strategic points. During the day, the entire Petrograd garrison (some 150,000 men) went over to the insurgents' side. The tsar abdicated the next day.

The regime that had ruled the Russian Empire for three hundred years collapsed in five days. In the countryside, vast tracts belonging to big land-owners—left fallow for lack of manpower—raised the question of land ownership in the peasants' eyes. The tsar had abdicated, leaving a power vacuum. On one hand was the Soviets' direct democracy; on the other, the Duma's parliamentarianism and its provisional government. The country stood between two revolutions. One was ending; the other had not yet begun. Between the two, history hesitated, the calendar lurched forward.

March 1917: in St. Petersburg the poet Osip Mandelstam was walking through "gardens heavy with greenery and cardboard streets" along which "provisional government cars raced." Thanks to two of his works, we know what he was thinking about: a 1922 essay called "The End of the Novel," and a prose piece five years later, *The Egyptian Stamp.*

In "The End of the Novel," Mandelstam reports a strange phenomenon: his European contemporaries were being "thrown out of their own biographies, like balls out of the pockets of billiard tables." How can someone be expulsed from their own biography? The idea shocks us, we who identify with our history from the cradle, and whose life can be summed up in a curriculum vitae. For a life to become a biography, says Mandelstam, a man acting through time must become the thematic pivot of significant facts. "The sense of time that man possesses in order to act, to conquer, to perish, to love," he writes, is what gives a biography its framework. "The same principle that governs the collision of billiard balls governs the laws of their actions: the angle of incidence is equal to the angle of reflection... It is clear that the moment we enter the era of powerful social movements and organized mass operations, the acts of isolated individuals lose their importance."

Mandelstam's family moved seventeen times during his childhood. Seventeen beds. Seventeen bedrooms. Seventeen childhoods. In "The Egyptian Stamp," he calls the kingdom of childhood a broken mirror, with dreams, images, and memories scattered, the "dear Egypt of objects," whose pieces Mandelstam strained to gather. "The clear eternity of dining room, bedroom, study... Dawn breaks her colored pencils, which gape like the beaks of nestlings... My shoe came untied and because of that I was seized with the feeling of great guilt and disorder... It was impossible to recoup anything or repair anything: everything went backwards, as always happens in a dream... It is terrifying to think that our life is a tale without plot or a hero, made up of desolation and glass, out of the feverish babble of constant digressions, out of the delirium of the Petersburg influenza."

Making a virtue of necessity, the 1917 revolutionaries gave this pulverizing of individual biographies an ideological meaning. As the anarchist writer Victor Serge says: "Individual existences—beginning with my own—are only of interest to me in relation to the vast collective life of which we are only parcels, more or less endowed with consciousness. Thus the form of the classic novel seemed impoverished and dated. The banal French novel in particular, with its dramas of love and ambition, centered at most around a family, seemed to me a model not to follow in any case."

"In principle, we Bolsheviks don't write a comrade's biography until after they're dead," said Mikhail Olminski, the president of the Society of Old Bolsheviks from 1922 to 1931. But Olminski's "principle" is less ideological than you might think. The lives of individuals had tumbled into a kind of weightless narrative. In relegating individual biographies to a storehouse of accessories, the revolutionaries were recognizing an upheaval of perception, a revolution less political than anthropological, an upheaval of the relationship between time and space. The Russian Revolution broke with romantic individualism. Its art was cinema. Its hero, the crowd in movement. Anyone who hopes to describe the life of one of those revolutionaries, ripped from chronology and whiplashed by the acceleration of history, is confronted by this fragmentation of places and times. For want of personal memoirs, we try to weigh the impact for those shocks on individuals, and tell the collective history of a rattled generation, the biography of a generation without biography.

After World War II, German philosopher Theodor Adorno gave almost clinical expression to this smashing of biography that is common to great changes: "Life is transformed into an atemporal series of shocks, between which yawn great gaps, empty, paralyzed intervals."

Blumkin's life certainly had no shortage of dramatic events. What is disconcerting is their chaotic chronology, the dizzying succession of locales, his unexplained disappearances, the legend that follows in his wake. The ground shakes under the hero's footsteps. Chronology ceases to be of any help. The struggling biographer must become an archaeologist, or rather a seismologist.

"I was in Odessa at the time of the February Revolution," writes Blumkin in one of the three autobiographies he drafted during his ten years in public life. "I was seventeen when I participated in the Revolution as a propagandist during a campaign for the election of the first soviet of worker deputies. I called on people to support the Revolution and to elect their deputies to the soviets." At night he worked as an electrician at the Richelevski Tramway depot. He found the time to write feverish, peremptory poems for an audience less impressed by the

quality of his verse than by the vigor of this young firebrand with the Assyrian-style beard.

In the spring of 1917, Blumkin's grandfather died, leaving him an inheritance of three hundred rubles. He took the train to attend the funeral in Sosnytsia, in northern Ukraine, a thousand-mile journey. Looking out the window, Blumkin saw assemblies of peasants gathered in wheat fields. In the stations, strangers were kissing each other. Manifestos slipped under windows showed the sun breaking through clouds. The walls were covered with posters showing a broken chain or an overturned throne or crown. The imperial eagle was being stripped from public buildings everywhere. Statues were torn down. Images of the tsar were trampled underfoot or burned in joyous bonfires.

At the cemetery, where many victims of the 1905 pogroms were buried, Blumkin said Kaddish for his grandfather.

A week later he found himself in Kharkov, where he contacted the leaders of the Left Socialist Revolutionary Party. They put him to work doing propaganda ahead of the elections to the Constituent Assembly. He worked for a few weeks in a business, Goldmann & Chapko. In mid-August he was sent to Simbirsk in the Volga region, the birthplace of Kerensky and Lenin, where he spoke at a number of meetings. He was elected to the town soviet, but promptly left for Alatyr, a little town a hundred miles to the west. There he learned the news about the Bolshevik insurrection in Petrograd, and immediately returned to Odessa.

Two weeks later, with a mask on his face and a Browning in each hand, he and Mike the Jap robbed the State Bank of four million rubles for the Left SR Party. That night Blumkin recited his poems in an Odessa café and collapsed under a table, dead drunk.

In early 1918 Blumkin was fighting on the Romanian front, where his comrades elected him commander of the detachment. In March his detachment joined the 3rd Soviet Army of Ukraine as it was leaving Odessa and retreating to Theodosia, in Crimea. Blumkin joined the army's military council and was named first deputy chief of staff. A month later, he had become the chief of staff of the 3rd Soviet Army of Ukraine, the "Odessa." At seventeen he commanded an army of four thousand bayonets resisting the advance of the Romanian and Hungarian armies. Shortly after he turned eighteen, the 3rd Army was dissolved.

Between March 1917 and April 1918, when he settled in Moscow, Blumkin moved seven times, led a constituent assembly election campaign, and within the space of three weeks was elected a deputy for three different soviets hundreds of miles apart. By turns, he had been a courier, apprentice electrician, electoral propagandist, bank robber, deputy, army commander, and chief of staff. By the time he reached his majority, he had held a list of positions worthy of a general on the verge of retirement.

But let's return to the terrible winter of 1917. Blumkin was in Odessa. The poet Sergei Esenin, who had not yet become his closest friend, was at the front, serving as a nurse on a medical train. Lenin was still in Zürich. A month earlier he told a group of young socialists: "We older people may not see the decisive struggles of the imminent revolution." In March, after the violent repression of demonstrations by the police in St. Petersburg, the tsar abdicated. A provisional government was formed. Ending his lengthy deportation to Siberia, Stalin hurried back to Petrograd. Trotsky had sailed to Manhattan, "its streets a triumph of cubism, its moral philosophy that of the dollar." Informed of events in Petrograd, he turned around and returned to Russia.

Driven only by the centripetal force of events, all those personalities wound up in Moscow a year and a half later, in a proximity no one could have predicted a few months earlier. The Kremlin, the Metropol and National hotels, the Bolshoi Theater, and the Poets' Café on Tverskaya Street were all one stage, whose boards were trod by commissars, deputies to soviets, speculators, activists, adventurers, and poets. Nobody quite knew who anyone was, or what they did. Usurpers were legion. Decrees flew out of the Kremlin, their ink barely dry, and hovered above the city, unsure of where to land. All night long, Commissar for Foreign Affairs Georgy

Chicherin received journalists and foreign delegates in a Metropol room that served as his chancellery. The Bolshoi Theater welcomed thousands of delegates to the worker and peasant soviets. Kremlin porters bowed to ill-dressed, ill-shaven Bolsheviks. The Lubyanka's cells held a little of everything: speculators, ancien régime dignitaries, conspirators, foreign spies, and political opponents, who were the largest group. Offices, bedrooms, cells, theater boxes, and balconies all traded roles. Hastily outfitted with a leather coat and a brand-new Browning, adolescents made arrests with and without warrants. No one individual was leading the dance. Instead, it was a blind force that for lack of a better word we can call History, which has little regard for individuals.

In the spring of 1918, Blumkin settled in Moscow, to which the Soviet government had retreated in the face of Denikin's advancing White Armies in the south. The treaty of Brest-Litovsk had reduced the empire's surface to the dimensions of the former Moscow duchy. The Soviets were encircled and deprived of the former empire's resources. Moscow was a ghost city, haunted by famine. Yet the theaters were full, and polemics between various avantgardes raged in the literary cafés.

Blumkin had no sooner arrived than he was assigned to the All-Russian Extraordinary Commission for Combating Counter-Revolution and Sabotage, created in 1917. Like many of the new revolutionary institutions, it would become known by the acronym formed by its initials in Russian: Cheka. In the beginning, there was nothing especially sinister about the Cheka, or the Lubyanka building, for that matter. Once the headquarters of an insurance company, it stood a stone's throw from the Hotel Metropol, the Bolshoi, and the Duma, and a few hundred yards from the Kremlin.

The Cheka seemed so inoffensive when it was created that Blumkin even suggested to Mandelstam that he collaborate with the new institution, for which he predicted a great future. "In Blumkin's view, this organization was bound to give shape to the new era and become the focus of power," writes the poet's widow in her memoir, *Hope Against Hope.* "Mandelstam took fright and refused to work for it—this at a moment when nobody yet knew exactly what the nature of the new institution would be. He only had to learn that it was powerful to keep right away from it." Others were less cautious. Isaac Babel did some translations for the Cheka, and not a few intellectuals lent it their talents.

At seventeen, Blumkin was in charge of German counterespionage within the new organization. His functions and power shouldn't be overestimated, but he did have a budget and some autonomy of action, reinforced by improvisation amid the reigning disorder. Still, the irresistible rise of this young provincial to the heights of power raised questions. The Left SR Party enjoyed a lot of influence in its coalition with the Bolsheviks, and was suspected of having placed its young recruit in order to prepare attacks against German officials in protest against the "shameful peace" that Lenin and Trotsky had signed with Germany at Brest-Litovsk.

What role in his nomination did Blumkin's links with the British poet-spy Erdman, whom he knew in Odessa, play? Were the English trying to revive war on the Russian front? Whatever the case, Erdman was in Moscow in April 1918, where he took control of a number of armed anarchist groups while collecting information on German influence in Russia for the Entente. Who was passing him information? None other than Blumkin. After all, the British could manipulate the opponents to the famous Brest-Litovsk treaty that ended the war with Germany in the spring of 1918. Did the English secret services inspire the creation of a Foreign Department within the Cheka (later the NKVD and GPU) under the control of the Left SRs? Blumkin had helped create it along the lines of Britain's famed MI6, and spent his whole career there. Given the confusion that reigned in Moscow at the time, it's not impossible. And it would explain his blazing ascent in 1918.

The Cheka's move from Petrograd to the heart of Moscow fed every fantasy, especially since the new organization's functions were still somewhat vague: an intelligence service, but with an office designed to fight sabotage. In its early days, the Cheka was hardly the political police it would later become during the Civil War. The men in their leather coats—about a hundred of them at first—embodied the armed fist of the Revolution in a period of confusion where it was sometimes hard to tell where political action ended and banditry began.

Shortly before its move to Moscow, the Cheka had shot a criminal, the self-styled Prince Eboli, who had been extorting funds by claiming to be a Chekist. Anarchists calling themselves the Black Guard had taken over twenty-five Moscow villas abandoned by their owners, from which they launched attacks and expropriations. Their misdeeds accomplished, "they indulged in incredible orgies," according to the historian Orlando Figes.

In cafés, confrontations broke out between Chekists and customers—labeled "hooligans" in the police reports—that sent people to the hospital without the real reason for the disputes being apparent. This comedy of errors lasted for several months, and Blumkin contributed a few jokes of his own, contributing to his legend.

The most remarkable story from this tragicomic period was the arrest of the clown Bim Bom for his circus act, in which he mocked the Soviet government. Thinking it was a farce, the audience laughed when a detachment of heavily armed Chekists burst into the big top, until their favorite clown fled under the real bullets of his pursuers. I used to imagine a black-caped Blumkin riding a white horse at the head of this anti-clown detachment: the theatrical

Chekist in hot pursuit of a facetious clown. You can almost hear the laughter in the front row. The burlesque flight of the clown, caught at his own game. The cavalcade of men in black. Shots fired, followed by panic in the bleachers. A novelist could make a memorable scene of it.

Georgy Ivanov, a friend of Mandelstam and a member of the Acmeist poetry circle in 1910–22, tells the following story in his memoir, *Petersburg Winters,* which he wrote after going into exile in Paris. On a spring night, he says, Mandelstam was at a drunken party of Bolsheviks and Left SRs at the Poets' Café, at a time when the two parties were sharing power. Blumkin was sitting at a table, working at a macabre task. "He was dead drunk," writes Ivanov, "and filling out blank execution orders [previously signed by Felix Dzerzhinsky, the head of the Cheka] with the names of 'counter-revolutionaries' picked at random from other lists." The horrified poet observed the Chekist in his leather coat. "After anguished deliberation, as one could imagine," he jumped from his seat, yanked the papers from Blumkin's hand, and tore them to pieces "under the other's stupefied gaze." He then "rushed headlong out of the room."

Ivanov claims that Mandelstam "wandered in the snow that evening, reciting poems, his and those of others, smoked, and eventually sat on a bench near the river at dawn and wept." Finally at daybreak, he went directly to the Kremlin, to the apartment of Trotsky's sister, who was married to Lev Borisovich Kamenev, one of the most powerful Bolsheviks. When she awoke, she found the poet in a state of shock after his night spent out in the snow. She helped him clean himself up, served him tea, wrapped him in her husband's coat, and took him to see Dzerzhinsky, "the signer of the fatal execution orders."

Upon hearing the account by Kamenev's wife, Dzerzhinsky—who was as rigid as the tall statue of him that for years would dominate Lubyanka Square—thanked the poet and ordered Blumkin's immediate arrest, so he could be judged "at this very hour by a summary tribunal." Again according to Ivanov, Mandelstam haltingly tried to plead Blumkin's cause, suggesting exile instead, as he was hostile to the death penalty, but Kamenev's wife dragged him out before he could formulate his request. She accompanied him back to his house, gave him some money, and advised him to stay hidden for at least two days. Blumkin was arrested at noon. At two o'clock, some good soul telephoned to warn Mandelstam that Blumkin had been freed and was searching the city for him.

Ivanov's story is so extravagant that it wouldn't be worth a second glance if it hadn't played a central role in building Blumkin's legend. Most of the accounts about his personality in those years cite Ivanov's apocryphal account. Early in my research, whenever Blumkin's name was mentioned in works on the Revolution, I kept encountering this story, which was cited so often, it had become mythic. Yet Ivanov's account is full of unlikely and even absurd details: the presence of snow in Moscow at the end of June, the execution orders filled out by Blumkin during a "drunken party," Mandelstam's hysterical attitude in the night following the incident, his bursting into the Kamenevs' apartment in the Kremlin at dawn. All of these should have been warning flags for anyone tempted to repeat Ivanov's account. As for the poet's presence at a drinking party of Chekists and commissars, it is so improbable that one of his biographies tried to argue that "Mandelstam was present because you could get candies there (his almost pathological taste for sweets was well known)."

We would have to wait for the publication of Nadezhda Mandelstam's memoirs in 1970 for Ivanov's incorrect and embellished account to be definitively discredited. In *Hope Against Hope*, she writes: "Georgy Ivanov, pandering to the tastes of his least discriminating readers, has given such a highly colored account of the whole story that it becomes meaningless—yet respectable people continue to quote his version, ignoring its logical flaws." Ivanov claimed that Mandelstam took a sheaf of arrest warrants from Blumkin's hand and tore them up. But that would be meaningless. "A piece of paper can always be replaced," Nadezhda points out. "What kind of warrant could it have been?"

Following Nadezhda, Mandelstam's biographers have tried to scotch the legend, but that hasn't stopped it from spreading. Even Isaiah Berlin repeats Ivanov's account almost word for word in his celebrated 2004 book *The Soviet Mind*. From an intellectual as rigorous as Berlin, this is incomprehensible. Drawing on the Nadezhda memoir and Clarence Brown's authoritative 1973 biography *Mandelstam*, Berlin trots out the opposition between the Chekist, drunkenly copying the names of men and women to be executed, and the poet: "timid, frail, affectionate, always in love, infinitely vulnerable, compared by his friends to an elegant but slightly ludicrous small bird."

Going by what Mandelstam told his wife, Blumkin boasted of having life and death power over people, and that he planned to have "a dirty little intellectual" shot, who had been arrested by the "new organization." "Mandelstam said that he would not stand for it," she writes. "To this, Blumkin said he would not tolerate any interference in his business and he would shoot him too if he dared to 'meddle.'"

Nadezhda continues: "It was fashionable in those years to speak with contempt of the 'spineless intelligentsia' and to talk blithely about shooting people." With great honesty, she admits that she briefly caught the virus, too. "I even had a slight bout of it myself, but was cured in time by a wise doctor. This happened in Eckster's studio in Kyiv where a visitor read out some couplets by Mayakovsky about how officers were thrown into the Moika Canal in Petrograd to drown. This brash verse had its effect and I burst out laughing. Ehrenburg, who was also there, at once fiercely attacked me. He gave me such a talking-to that I still respect him for it, and I am proud that, silly as I was at the time, I had the sense to listen to him and remember his words forever afterward."

Writes Nadezhda: "Brandishing a revolver, shouting and raving like one possessed, Blumkin was simply indulging his temperament and his love of external effects—he was by nature a terrorist of the flamboyant type which had existed in Russia before the revolution."

After that, whenever Blumkin ran into Mandelstam, he would pull out his pistol and threaten him, and the poet would back away. But he told his wife he didn't think Blumkin had any intention of killing him. He had threatened him several times before, but had always let witnesses disarm him, and in Kyiv Blumkin himself had once put away the pistol. Writes Nadezhda: "Mandelstam thought it was all an empty threat and put it down to Blumkin's love of melodramatic effects: 'What's to stop him from shooting me? He could have done it a long time ago if he wanted.'"

This little game ended in 1926, when Mandelstam happened to get into the same train compartment as Blumkin. "Seeing his 'enemy,' Blumkin demonstratively unhitched his holster, put his revolver in his suitcase, and held out his hand. They then talked amicably for the rest of the journey." Not long after this, they learned of Blumkin's execution by firing squad. Mandelstam was stunned by the news, she says. "Blumkin, terrible as he was, was by no means an utter savage."

A half century later, the linguist Roman Jakobson, who knew Blumkin in the early 1920s, remembered him more as a scholar able to read the Avesta, the holy book of pre-Islamic Iran, or some old Hebrew book, than as a killer of diplomats. But "he tried to risk his life any way he could," he said. It is rare, writes Nadezhda Mandelstam, to find a true lover of poetry and a born killer in one person. "Only the historians may be able to make sense of this when they come to study this strange time and this outlandish man."

The question remains: Why did Ivanov so distort this story as to make it incomprehensible? He was friends with Mandelstam from 1910 to 1922 and had no apparent reason to so misrepresent his biography, writes Clarence Brown in his authoritative biography, *Mandelstam:* "That is the problem and the tragedy. Ivanov's testimony to the period that he lived through, one of the most interesting and inaccessible periods of Russian literary history, simply cannot be believed. He made no distinction between what was and what merely might or even ought to have been the truth. But the literary artist's perfectly commendable desire not to bore his reader led to the vicious practice of attaching real names of living people to his fictitious personages ... Ivanov was a poet first of all, and a publicist *faute de mieux*."

The problem is that he was a poet in exile. In moments of loneliness, Ivanov must have felt that the Russia he had known was nothing but a dream. Had people like Akhmatova and Mandelstam really existed? Was it possible to resuscitate those lost years and the desperate gaiety that reigned then, even at the height of the Revolution, when every poem had an audience waiting for it at every street corner? When one of Ivanov's friends questioned him about some episode or other in his memoirs, he laughed and said that he had given free rein to his imagination. As quoted by Brown, he said: "There are memories like dreams. There are dreams like memories. And when you think about what happened 'so recently and so endlessly long ago' you sometimes don't know what is memory and what is dream."

The explanation may help us understand Ivanov's tendency to embellish his recollections, even to invent them. But how could such an exaggerated, highly improbable story be so successful? I have a lot of experience from my work studying storytelling, and I know that stories are viruses; they are contagious. If the story is a good one, we hurry to repeat it, without bothering to tell whether it's true or false. But what makes a story "good," that is, worthy of being told, believed, and repeated? What are the conditions under which an anecdote becomes a legend, to the point of influencing a historian? Two conditions must be met. First, the story must fulfill an expectation, fit into a familiar horizon, a collection of presuppositions already accepted by the reader. Second, it must be freighted with possibilities. It must carry one or several stories. A good story fulfills an expectation and exceeds it, by announcing what comes next.

I think the tale told by Ivanov made its way into the history of this period of the Revolution so readily because it fulfills that expectation, the opposition of the poet and the terrorist. Variations of these would soon be seen in history, to which Arthur Koestler gave the form of the dilemma in *The Yogi and the Commissar*, reflecting the conflict between end and means. Ivanov's anecdote had all the elements of a vignette: on one hand, the drunken Chekist with a gun; on the other the frail, unarmed poet. One signs death sentences under the influence of liquor and probably drugs; the other tears them out of his hands. One boasts of being able to cause people's death; the other rises up to stop him. A fatal duel between the bullet and the ballad, clearly echoing the legendary duel between Pushkin and the French officer who shot the great Russian poet in the stomach and killed him.

But another reason can explain the success of a story: its augural, premonitory character. Ivanov's unbelievable story was credited by History writ large. A few days after the argument between Blumkin and Mandelstam, an event occurred that shook the chancelleries: the German ambassador was assassinated in Moscow, and the killing threatened to revive war between Germany and Russia. In the hours afterward, it was learned that the author of the attack was none other than Yakov Blumkin. The insignificant argument at the Poets' Café retrospectively appeared in a new light, rising to the level of an event with worldwide impact. The argument between two drunks soared on its own wings toward a future full of omens, where it found its meaning, impact, and moral. If Blumkin's threats against Mandelstam had been taken more seriously, the assassination might have been avoided.

News of the October Revolution reached the West in the middle of the Great War, and the names of the new people's commissars didn't mean much to the journalists or diplomats. To a public eager for news, the press served up the most fanciful biographies. This is always the case when a revolution takes place. It thrusts unknown faces, unpronounceable names, and characters without biographies to center stage. The names of Lenin and some of his companions, like Trotsky and Lunacharsky, were vaguely familiar to a very small circle of socialist leaders who had attended the international congresses. But the lives of those émigré Russian revolutionaries, whose differences and internal struggles caused the Internationals so much concern before 1914, were no longer of much interest now.

They would have to wait for the Revolution's tenth anniversary to see 246 biographies and authorized autobiographies of the great men and actors of the Revolution collected in the famous *Granat Encyclopedic Dictionary*. Georges Haupt and Jean-Jacques Marie were the first in France to present and translate this rogues' gallery in their *Les Bolcheviks par eux-mêmes* (*Makers of the Russian Revolution*). "The names and faces were personalized by multiple collective biographical dictionaries," they write. "Listed were not only the leaders, but every professional revolutionary of any importance."

From the simple militant to the highest Party leader, each had to prove their devotion to socialism and their loyalty to the Party by agreeing to describe their life in the minutest detail. This was often repeated several times in the course of a lifetime, and could prove perilous later. The different versions might contradict each other, and certain facts might disappear as others emerged from the shadows. All this autobiographical material, with its variants, contradictions, even its lacunae, could serve as evidence held against their author, feeding the authorities' suspicions,

This biography fever only lasted for a while, however. When the era of the great Moscow trials of the 1930s arrived, biographical notices disappeared along with their authors, and memoirs were locked away in secret sections of libraries, or burned. Stalin set about imposing his own version of history. He made actors and authors disappear, and wrote out of history his adversaries' names and stories, even their faces.

In that way, the "glorious October Revolution" became the object of three successive accounts: first as a collective, anonymous epic of peasants and workers; then as a novelistic work of Bolshevik theoreticians and strategists; and finally as proof of one man's genius. Soviet historiography successively followed three literary genres: epic, novel, and hagiography. But the transition from one to another wasn't easy. To accomplish it, faces and voices had to be erased. Entire lives were made to disappear—a colossal and difficult undertaking, because it's easier to get rid of bodies than living memory. After Stalin's death, "ghosts" began coming out of the closets. They had to be given names, and their biographies reconstituted. Names reappeared on the occasion of a birthday or a rehabilitation. Faces erased from official photographs resurfaced. In cemeteries, flowers appeared on graves decades after the deaths of their tenants. A game of hide-and-seek with memory, subject to the political necessities of the moment, futile games played by the living with the dead.

Nikolai Bukharin, whom Lenin once called "the Party's darling child," both the most brilliant and the most sensitive, was executed in 1938 after the Moscow trials. But he got posthumous revenge thanks to his widow, Anna Larina: during her years in the gulag, she had memorized his "Letter to the Future Generation of Party Leaders." The Italian communists made Bukharin their spiritual leader and the inspiration of Eurocommunism, a reformist current that broke with Moscow. I devoted several years of research to Bukharin and made him the subject of my thesis. But no sooner was the thesis finished than the impulse that led me to those revolutionaries took a different turn. In the 1970s the biographies of many revolutionaries became accessible in French. First, thanks to Georges Haupt and Jean-Jacques Marie, then to the memoirs of Nadezhda Mandelstam and Anna Larina Bukharin. Published in Paris in 1973, Alexander Solzhenitsyn's *Gulag Archipelago* emerged like a sunken continent peopled with phantoms and specters. We were the first to discover them, the first to welcome them into the world of the living. Those men and women, whose stories had remained buried during the entire Stalin era, fascinated us, not as historic characters but as revenants. Solzhenitsyn, who gathered their stories, wasn't a novelist. He was an archivist, an archaeologist.

Displaced people who have lost their nationality are called stateless. But what do you call those who have been excluded from their own history? Memoryless? Placed by history on an ejection seat, they were all projected into "the present, that invisible point, that nothingness moving toward death," as Milan Kundera writes in *The Book of Laughter and Forgetting*, his first novel written in exile and published in France in 1979.

The book begins with a description of a photograph familiar to every schoolchild in communist Czechoslovakia. It shows a communist leader waving to a crowd in 1948. He is wearing a fur hat. Another leader named Clementis, who was standing next to him, had loaned him the hat. Four years later, Clementis was accused of treason and hanged. So he was made to disappear from the legendary photo, leaving just a blank section of wall. All that remains of Clementis, notes Kundera, is the fur hat on the leader's head.

CHAPTER

4

They say that Kolyma's frozen soil preserves corpses so well that when dead people are dug up, their faces still wear the expression they had at the moment they died. I read this story in the memoirs of former gulag prisoners, maybe in Varlam Shalamov's *Kolyma Tales* or Yevgenia Ginzburg's *Le Vertige* (Vertigo), unless it was Ryszard Kapuściński's *Imperium*. The image of those faces with features perfectly preserved by ice came to mind as I was walking the streets of Moscow in November 2015.

I came out of the metro at Smolenskaya Square, at the foot of the building that houses the Russian Ministry of Foreign Affairs. It's one of the seven skyscrapers that sprang out of the earth in the 1950s, and which Muscovites call the "Seven Sisters." Exemplars of Stalinist neo-Gothic, they are the fruits of an unlikely cross between the styles of the Kremlin towers and 1930s American skyscrapers. This unnatural union produced concrete mastodons that, when sprinkled with snow in winter, look like giant waffles.

It was unusually warm for the season, and I wondered if it might be due to global warming. I don't know which of the two thoughts preceded the other—the warming trend that was melting ice floes or the frozen Kolyma soil that preserved bodies so well—but the image of those faces with their eyes closed followed me as I turned into Denezhny Lane and headed toward Villa Berg, the site of the German embassy after the Revolution.

The metaphor of freeze and thaw has been used pretty regularly in Soviet historiography. But the division into two historic periods—the freeze under Stalin and the thaw after the revelations of the Twentieth Congress in 1956—doesn't account for Soviet history's upheavals, entanglements, and reversals. The thaw image is opposed to the freeze the way memory is opposed to forgetfulness, and good versus evil. But Soviet history doesn't obey such a neat division. It strings periods of forgetting together like episodes in a serial. It is riddled with cracks that have continued to extend and deepen long after the collapse of the Soviet Union. Russian society isn't done with forgetting. It is continually recycling the dead and rewriting the past.

The ideological and political reasons that got me interested in the actors of the October Revolution suddenly appeared almost pointless when confronted with the image of those faces emerging from the frozen earth, their questions still unanswered, like clues at a crime scene that police investigators carefully collect in hopes of making them speak.

The crime scene metaphor isn't fortuitous. It came to mind as I approached Villa Berg at 5 Denezhny Lane, where Yakov Blumkin and his accomplice Nikolai Andreyev assassinated German ambassador Count von Mirbach on July 6, 1918. This was my first time walking down this quiet street, lined with town houses and gardens, yet it felt familiar. Thanks to Google Maps, I had many times covered the 750 yards between Smolenskaya Place and number 5 Denezhny Lane—a nine-minute walk, according to Google's directions. I knew its details intimately from scrolling across facades on my computer, zooming in on the buildings' Art Deco details, and exploring the gardens behind the residences.

The old map of Moscow that has kept me company for years bears witness to this in its own way. It is blanketed with colored crosses, circles, and arrows that indicate important places where Blumkin had been between 1918 and 1929: apartments, literary cafés, and hotels, as well as Lubyanka offices and cells.

Denezhny Lane itself is underlined in red felt-tip pen—pink, actually, because the color has faded with time—like crime-scene tape around a security perimeter. The street doesn't just lead from one point to another on my map, which is wrinkled and papery from being folded and unfolded so often. It connects periods that overlap and straddle each other.

The "vertical" of transmissions and genealogies had yielded to the "horizontal" of adjoining and contiguous historic events. The historic division between freeze and thaw periods was no help in approaching this layering of eras, this intersection of destinies that all surfaced at the same time. "The main problem posed by the 1989–1990 events is no longer of a social or political order," writes historian Mikhail Epstein. "It is of an eschatological order: how to live after your own future, or, if you prefer, after your own death."

As I walked down the street, I had a strange feeling of stepping backward toward the past, approaching that July 6, 1918, around two in the afternoon, when a dark Packard convertible turned into this peaceful street and stopped in front of the entrance to the German embassy, which was guarded by a few Latvian soldiers.

The embassy occupied one of the most beautiful residences in Moscow. Before the Revolution, it had belonged to a sugar magnate, Sergei Pavlovich Berg. In 1897 he bought an old wooden house on the site and had a sumptuous neobaroque palace built to replace it. Each room had its own style, reflecting different architectural periods, from neoclassical to

Second Empire and Vienna Secession. Passing from one room to another, you had the feeling of crossing eras, of plumbing the depths of time. And Villa Berg was not just the most luxurious residence in Moscow; it was also the first to be lit with electricity. The society pages noted that when the place was inaugurated, aristocratic women discovered the effect of electric light on their faces for the first time.

Berg didn't have much time to enjoy his palace. He fled to Switzerland shortly after the fall of the tsar. Historic irony: having been the object of so much care, enlisting the talents of architects and hundreds of artisans—weavers, carpenters, painters, and decorators—Villa Berg fell into the hands of the Bolsheviks in the Revolution, and later became the seat of the German embassy. Count Wilhelm von Mirbach-Harff, the first German ambassador to Bolshevik Russia, moved in on April 25, 1918. But he didn't have much time to enjoy it, either. He was assassinated on July 6.

Across from the German embassy was the French commercial legation, and farther on, at number 11, the German consulate. The French mission was located at number 17, with the French naval attaché directly opposite, at 18. This proximity of enemy representatives in the elegant, short, empty street facilitated discreet, informal encounters and allowed for every possible intrigue. Victor Serge mentions the rumor that the French had assisted the attack on the German ambassador by giving the terrorists information about his habits. Others claimed they even procured the bombs for them. So the representatives of the powers that had plunged Europe into fire and blood in 1914 could run into each other daily, exchanging perfectly civil greetings, as if at the theater or racetrack. The fate of millions of men in the trenches depended on them. They could launch an offensive on the strength of a piece of information, cause a reversal of alliances, or—a highly unlikely but theoretically possible hypothesis—start work on a peace treaty.

On seizing power, the Bolsheviks unilaterally declared the end of what they called the "imperialist war." The peace decree was ratified by the Congress of Soviets on October 26, 1917. Speaking on the radio on November 7, Trotsky urged all the belligerents, whether Allied or enemy, to conclude a general peace. On November 22, the Bolsheviks signed an armistice agreement on all fronts, from the Baltic to the Black Sea, and called on the peoples of Europe to rise against their oppressors. In early March, the Germans occupied Ukraine. A month later, the Japanese landed in Vladivostok. The Revolution was completely surrounded. Reduced to the Muscovite grand duchy, the Soviets' homeland was now the prey of the White and Triple Entente armies.

Peace talks began on November 9, six weeks after the peace decree. December 28 in Petrograd saw a huge demonstration in favor of a democratic peace. At Brest-Litovsk the next morning, Germany laid out its demands in the names of the Entente powers.

Ten years later, when Blumkin visited Trotsky in exile on Prinkipo, he found him still obsessed by what he called "the Brest-Litovsk dilemma." He had undertaken to write his memoirs at the request of a German publisher, and had reached the pages devoted to the peace negotiations. Closeted with Blumkin in a first-floor room overlooking the Sea of Marmara, Trotsky paced while trying to pitch his metallic voice over the cries of seagulls that flew in through the open windows.

"We were facing two questions," he said. "Yielding to the German demands meant crediting the rumors started by the Whites and Allied propaganda that the Bolsheviks were merely the Kaiser's puppets. Some people claimed that German officers had directed the October insurrection. Sir George Buchanan, the English ambassador, even repeated the rumor that there had been six German officers at the Smolny Institute with Lenin. But rejecting the German conditions meant continuing the war when the trenches were empty, and betraying the promise of peace made to the soldiers in October. Would the Kaiser send his armies against a revolution that wanted peace? We couldn't answer that. We had to find the answer in the course of negotiations."

"To delay negotiations," said Lenin, "there must be someone to do the delaying." At his request,

Trotsky left for Brest-Litovsk, "as if I were being led to the torture chamber."

Up to then, Prince Leopold of Bavaria had treated the Soviet delegation as his "guests." The Germans ate meals with them, and in a friendly way tried to worm out whatever information they wanted. "The first delegation included a worker, a peasant, and a soldier," wrote Trotsky. "They were delegates by mere accident, and they were little prepared for that sort of trickery. The peasant, an old man, was even encouraged to drink more wine than was good for him. As the head of the Soviet delegation, I decided to break off the familiar relationships that had imperceptibly developed during the first period."

Wrote a Polish diplomat in his diary on January 7: "Before dinner, all the Russians under Trotsky's orders arrived. With apologies, they made it known that they would no longer share communal meals, and in general we no longer saw them. A wind was apparently now blowing that was not at all like before." Falsely friendly relations were succeeded by drily official reports.

After delaying, Trotsky terminated the negotiations. It would be "neither war nor peace." This was his reasoning: If German imperialism couldn't force its troops to march against us, it would mean we had scored a terrific victory, with incalculable consequences. On the other hand, if the Hohenzollern could still strike at us, we could always capitulate in time.

The Bolsheviks abandoned the battlefield and turned their backs on the Germans. "Let's see if they attack a peaceful revolution!" they blustered in the eyes of the world. The answer was quick in coming. The Germans launched a lightning war against the Soviets' power. Their objectives: to occupy Ukraine and launch a "brief and vigorous" strike to seize all the Soviets' artillery and supplies, thus preventing them from forming a new army. The German offensive encountered no resistance. The German troops did more traveling than fighting. They took the train. The front line rolled smoothly forward. "The socialist nation is in danger," declared Lenin on February 21, in the face of the German advance. A few days later, the Germans took Pskov, 150 miles from Petrograd. It was decided to move the capital from Petrograd to Moscow. "The Council of People's Commissars can't live and work within a two hours' march of the German army," said a sobered Trotsky.

On March 3 the Bolsheviks signed a peace treaty with Germany and Austria-Hungary at Brest-Litovsk with what the European press called "a knife on their throat" and "a gun pointed at their temple." In the face of the German offensive, Lenin had chosen to give up space to gain time. By refusing to make peace while rejecting war, which the Bolsheviks no longer had the means to pursue, they were forced to accept what Lenin dubbed an "obscene" peace treaty. Russia lost some 772,000 square miles in the west (Poland, Lithuania, parts of Belorussia and Latvia); it had to evacuate the Baltic territories (Livonia and Estonia), abandon Ukraine and Finland, and put part of the Caucasus in Turkish hands. It's been estimated that the Brest-Litovsk treaty cost Russia a third of its territory and population, but also nearly all (90 percent) of its wheat and sugar production, most of its energy sources, and two-thirds of its metallurgy industry. But there was still worse. The first proletarian revolution found itself deprived of its manpower: the industrial proletariat of the Donets coal basin, now occupied by the Germans. All of Europe watched for a dying revolution's last gasp.

Ambassador Mirbach moved into Villa Berg in April 1918, at about the same time Blumkin was recruited by the Cheka. Both got to work, one of them on Denezhny Lane, the other on Lubyanka Square: two crosses on my old Moscow map, separated by a few inches of yellow dotted line, like a pedestrian passage. Blumkin was assigned to the Cheka's department of counterespionage and put in charge of the surveillance and protection of the German embassy. For surveillance, he could be counted on. But protection was something else again.

Count Mirbach had participated in the peace negotiations right up to the signing of the treaty. He had been at the heart of the chess match that became a perverse game where the imperial cat toyed with the Bolshevik mouse until delivering the final swipe of its paw. Irina Kakhovskaya was a well-placed witness to the state of mind then prevalent in Russia. She belonged to the same Left SR party as Blumkin, and planned and executed the assassination of Field Marshal Hermann von Eichhorn in Ukraine in July 1918. "Count Mirbach in Moscow and Marshal Eichhorn in Kyiv were the two personalities that held the attention of all the workers in Russia," she wrote. "They were the first targets for the SR vanguard to attack. Using his diplomatic influence, Mirbach was preparing a repression that the other man was accomplishing with iron and fire. But above them loomed the silhouette of their lord and master, Kaiser Wilhelm."

Blumkin to Victor Serge again: "We knew that Germany, as disintegrated as she was, could not start a new war against Russia. We wanted to give her a stinging reverse. We were banking on the effect of this action in Germany itself. We were negotiating with German revolutionaries who asked us to help them organize an attempt on the Kaiser's life. The attempt fell through because we insisted that the principal actor should be a German. They didn't find anyone."

Once given his assignment, Blumkin went to work. He wanted to know about the embassy's daily operations, its official agenda, and the coded dispatches that Mirbach exchanged with Berlin. The information he sought was designed not just to inform Soviet diplomacy about a disloyal partner, but to eliminate it.

He soon had eyes inside the embassy, thanks to an electrician working for the Moscow power company. Like the angel Gabriel come to enlighten him, a certain Vaismann (or Fisman) providentially walked into his office. An electrician himself, Blumkin chatted for a while and, on hearing that he had access to the German embassy, promptly recruited him.

In the guise of checking electric meters, Vaismann was to see if the embassy had a store of weapons, how the building was guarded, what the staff's schedule was, etc.

Found in the Cheka's investigation report on the Mirbach assassination is a handwritten note from Blumkin to Vaismann listing the information to be gathered:

1. Check to see if the embassy has a store of
    weapons. According to our information it
    is located in one of the annexes: the stable,
    the garage, or the woodshed.
2. To find out:
    a) If there is a secret radio in the
        building.
    b) How visitors are received. (Does
        Mirbach receive visitors in person or
        is it his secretary? Who can schedule
        meetings with Mirbach?)

c) What room Mirbach works and lives in. Is there a safe in his office?
d) What is the profile of visitors to the embassy?
e) The composition of the staff (approximate number, qualities, functions).
f) Who is in charge of guarding the building? Are there Russians in the guard? In what proportion, compared to Germans?
g) Overall impression.

Over the next few weeks, Vaismann (or Fisman) proved an excellent detective. According to Blumkin's testimony during his trial, the electrician had diagrams of the building and its security system by June 25. He not only gave Blumkin the information requested, but also added a long (and not especially useful) description of the setting, mixed with observations on the political origin of the count's visitors. (The well-placed electrician alerted the services to the presence in Villa Berg of a group of monarchists conspiring with the Germans against the Bolshevik powers.)

Mirbach's code name was "Moby Dick," and Blumkin pursued his target with the same tenacity as Ahab in Melville's novel. He wanted to know everything about him. His family tree, his childhood, his studies, his culinary tastes, his reading.

As Blumkin wrote to an Odessa friend a few months later: "Mirbach didn't speak Russian, so I had to read in his soul."

Jacques Sadoul, the French military attaché, proved an equally valuable informant in describing "Moby Dick": "Tall, distinguished, youthful looking, Mirbach gives the impression of an active and intelligent man with a real personality. He is accompanied by a large staff of talented people renowned in Germany for their qualities as diplomats and technicians. Gone are the days of pomaded diplomats, brilliant talkers and skeptics, ignorant of everything about the country to which they are accredited, and uninterested in learning any of it."

The historian Yaroslav Leontiev, an associate professor at Moscow State University, is probably the best-informed person in Moscow about Blumkin. He was close to the late KGB historian Aleksei Velidov and released excerpts of the latter's unpublished Blumkin biography. Through Velidov, he got access to a number of classified sources in the KGB archives.

I had been corresponding with Leontiev for months and was eager to meet him. But he turned out to be almost as elusive as my hero. He was willing to get together but made me play hide-and-seek with him. The places he chose for meetings included an art gallery opening, a conference hall, even a church. But each time, either the interview didn't happen or it was cut short because of a delay, or he had to immediately leave for an important appointment, or he had chosen a café so noisy we couldn't hear each other. And Leontiev would leave, a backpack on his shoulders and sneakers on his feet. I concluded from this that he didn't want to share his information, and was probably saving it for a future book. I did see him one last time, coming out of his institute. As we walked along in the rain, the only thing he said, with regret, was that it was impossible to get an overview of all of the sources relative to the attack on Mirbach. Then he recommended the second edition of the *Red Book of the Cheka*, which anyone with an interest in the Revolution's first decade knows, and Irina Kakhovskaya's book, *Souvenirs d'une révolutionnaire* (Memoirs of a revolutionary), translated into French in 1926; I had found it at a book stall in the 1980s. As the rain fell harder and the water from Leontiev's umbrella soaked my shoulder, he added to his reading recommendations a brochure by a certain B. Leonov, "La dernière aventure de James Blumkine" (James Blumkin's last adventure), while stressing "its low historiographic level and a great number of spelling mistakes in first and last names." Then he wished me good luck.

We were in front of Villa Berg, which is now the Italian embassy. There was no way to get in, because of construction, so I walked along the front of the villa under the eye of the lone Russian policeman on duty. He seemed oddly indifferent to my comings and goings I paced out the length of the ballroom (about eighty feet). The residence is separated from the street by a small courtyard enclosed by a wrought-iron fence eight feet high. It was on this fence that the fleeing Blumkin's pants got caught. Standing on tiptoe, I tried to see into the room where Count Mirbach had collapsed, hit in the head by a bullet before a bomb shredded his body. Painters in white coveralls perched on ladders were delicately restoring the ceiling's gilt work, which framed a misty sky bordered by roses. They looked like scientific or technical police experts gathering clues at a crime scene. Two enormous chandeliers lit the bare room, where white shadows furtively passed and disappeared, as if absorbed by the red background of the walls.

The attack took place in the villa's Red Room, the main drawing room next to the grand ballroom. It was named that by the villa's former owner Sergei Berg, not as a reflection of the political winds but simply because he liked the color red, even though he made his fortune in sugar—"white gold." In Russian, the word for red comes from *krasny*, "beautiful," and the meanings of the two words are very close. Berg simply wanted this ballroom to be beautiful. At his request, designers composed a symphony in red, with an interplay between heavy, dark red brocade curtains shot with gold and silver threads, walls hung with purple silk, and oriental carpets glowing with orange and deep red tints.

So the red scarf around Blumkin's neck, which contrasted with the black of his jacket and the red of his accomplice's hair, matched the drawing room's dominant color, blending with the other hues like iron filings attracted by a magnetic field. Or like the blood that would flow from the unfortunate ambassador's skull and shattered chest, seeping into the deep pile of the carpet as his head rested in the center of a scarlet corolla. Years later, a diplomat who attended a ball in that very room told me that the bloodstain that had soaked through the carpet was still there, under the dancers' feet, indelible.

On July 4, 1918, before the evening session of the Congress of Soviets, Blumkin was called away from the Bolshoi Theater by a member of his party's Central Committee. The Left SR had decided to assassinate Count Mirbach to cause a rupture of the Brest-Litovsk treaty. When Blumkin was told to pass on all the information he had collected about the German ambassador, he volunteered to commit the attack himself. That very night, members of the Left SR Central Committee accepted the offer of services by Blumkin and by Nikolai Andreyev, a former Cheka photographer.

The Left SR committee member who ordered the attack has never been identified. Nor do we know the person to whom Blumkin addressed the will that he wrote the night before the attack. Two faceless, nameless individuals before and after the assassination—the classic structure of a plot. And yet the motivations of the Left SR were perfectly clear, and shared by a minority of Bolsheviks. The killings of Eichhorn and Mirbach, the twin avatars of the German invasion, had a double goal: spread panic in the enemies' ranks, and fire up the masses for a future popular guerrilla war. This was a message addressed to public opinion in Germany and Russia. The ambassador's assassination was to be the initial spark of a chain reaction, leading not to the Bolsheviks' peace or the pursuit of an imperialist war, but a war of partisans. An insurrection of the worker and peasant masses.

On the night before the attack, Blumkin wrote his will.

Sentence after sentence, the quarter hours chimed as the clock trailed its cortege of premonitions. History hesitated. "When it starts to shift from foot to foot, only poetry or war remains," wrote Mandelstam. Blumkin's will is not without a certain pathos, which can be excused by the hero's circumstances and age—he was only seventeen. It deserves to be quoted in full.

As an epigraph, Blumkin wrote, "You will win your rights in the struggle."

Dear Comrade:

You are probably surprised that I am writing this letter to you and not to someone else. We only met once. You left the party to which I still belong. But in spite of that I am closer to your opinion on certain things than that of my comrades in the party. Like you, I think that what is involved are not programmatic questions but something essential: the attitude of so-cialists toward war and peace with German imperial-ism. Like you I am particularly opposed to the separate peace with Germany that is so humiliating for Russia, and I think we must break that peace at any price, even at the cost of the individual act I am prepared to commit.

But my choice is not inspired by general and moral motives alone. Other considerations, which I not only do not want to hide but instead will par-ticularly stress, drive me to accomplish this act. I am Jewish and I do not deny belonging to the Jewish people, because I am proud of it. But I also belong to the Russian people. The anti-Semite members of the Black Hundreds, many of them Germanophiles themselves, have accused the Jews of being Ger-manophiles since the start of the war, and are now putting all responsibility for Bolshevik politics and the separate peace with the Germans on the Jews. For that reason, the protest by a Jew against the betrayal of Russia and the Allies by the Bolsheviks at Brest-Litovsk is especially important. As a Jew and as

*a socialist, I take responsibility for accomplishing an
act that expresses that protest.*

*I do not know if I will succeed in what I am
planning. Nor do I know if I will survive. In case of my
death, I want this letter to be a document that explains
my reasons and the meaning of my individual act. I
want people who read my letter to know that a Jewish
socialist was not afraid to sacrifice his life to protest the
separate peace with German imperialism. I want them
to know that I was not afraid to spill a man's blood to
wash away the shame of Brest–Litovsk.*

I give you my hand in friendship,
Yours,
Blumkin.

No night was ever so heavy with foreboding. In
his Villa Berg office, Ambassador von Mirbach sat
drafting a note for his ministry in Berlin, unaware
that it would be his last. The Bolsheviks' situation
was alarming, he warned. The ambassador cited
"the situation's increasing volatility" and predicted the Soviets' imminent collapse. The government was running short of material resources;
the Kremlin didn't even have enough gasoline for
its cars. The situation was worsening every day,
Mirbach reported. Famine stalked the capital, in-
security was rising, and the increasingly nervous
Bolsheviks were executing traffickers and plotters

by the hundreds. He described the internal conflicts within the Party. Feeling the end approach, some members were jumping ship. Others were in such despair, they were preparing to commit suicide.

The objective now, wrote Mirbach, was to ensure an inevitable "political transition." Comparing the Revolution to a dying man, he proposed to fill the power vacuum by creating a new government ready to ensure the transition that would be "composed of people entirely at our service." In short, the ambassador was preparing a coup d'état against the Soviets.

For his part, Blumkin was unable to sleep. Having written his letter, he reviewed the protocol he had established with his leaders. He was to go to the Cheka, type the mission order, forge Dzerzhinsky's signature, find his photographer accomplice, Andreyev, at the National Hotel, and go to the garage, where a service vehicle would be waiting.

As July 6 dawned, a slight breeze blew through windows, rustling curtains and carrying to Blumkin's Metropol room the songs of the worker and peasant delegations heading to the Bolshoi for the Fifth All-Russian Soviet Congress. More than a thousand delegates had come from all over the country: 673 communist Bolsheviks, 269 Left SRs, 30 Maximalists, and about a hundred delegates belonging to various other parties or to none. They crowded into the luxurious Bolshoi auditorium, filling the orchestra seats and a few seats in the balcony. Jacques Sadoul, the French military attaché, was in the hall. In a series of letters to communist deputy Albert Thomas, he described the surreal scenes of the Fifth Congress, "compared to which the stormiest sessions of our national Convention seem quite calm."

An initial speech by a representative of Ukrainian peasants to the Congress was "one long cry of despair, bitterness, and anger at the Germans," he wrote. The entire hall leaped to its feet, shouting "Long live free Ukraine!" "Faces turned to the diplomatic loge, where attachés of the German embassy were seated. Every sentence was greeted with applause. On the Left SR benches to the right of the crowd, indignation and fury were at their height. Shouts of 'Down with Brest!' 'Down with Mirbach!' and 'Down with Germany's lackeys' rang out everywhere."

Then it was Maria Spiridovna's turn to mount the dais. The leader of the Left SR was an old Narodnik populist who had led an armed fight against the tsar and paid for it with many years of prison and forced labor. In the debate over war and peace, she refused to take sides, instead attacking policies and people. She questioned Lenin and Trotsky's honesty, accusing them of sacrificing the peasant masses to benefit the working class. "Either this treacherous policy ends, or I will take up revolution again with a bomb in the hand that used to hold it." Emma Goldman, the deported American anarchist, once described her this way: "Though only thirty-three years of age, she was shriveled in body; a hectic flush was on her emaciated face, her eyes were feverishly brilliant, but her spirit remained unchanged and unfettered."

Trotsky gave two speeches in the course of that day. "He was tired and nervous," wrote Sadoul.

> His voice was drowned out by the shouts from the Left SRs calling him a Kerensky and a Mirbach boot-licker. Lenin, with his odd faun-like appearance, finally stood up, looking calm and sarcastic. He never stopped laughing, despite the curses, attacks, and threats raining down on him. At most, a sharper word or a more stinging jibe would briefly freeze his smile, which so galled and exasperated his adversaries. Lenin's lips would tighten and his gaze harden, as his eyes shot flames from under his slanted lids.
>
> Seated next to Lenin, Trotsky tried to laugh as well. But anger, emotion, and exasperation turned his laughter into a painful grimace. His lively, mobile face fell, faded, and disappeared beneath a terrify-ing Mephistophelian mask. Trotsky doesn't have his leader's sovereign will, cool head, and absolute mas-tery. Yet he is the better man, and I know him to be less implacable.

Indignant faces swung toward the German diplomatic loge. Spiridovna's emaciated face, Lenin's strange, faun-like figure, Trotsky's Mephistophelian mask...such was the ballet of faces in pure, hard, Bolshevism.

On that July 6, around two thirty in the afternoon, little Denezhny Lane was deserted. Summer had settled on gardens buzzing with insects. From open windows and their billowing curtains, snatches of Russian, German, and French conversations could be heard.

At two forty-five, a dark-colored Packard sedan (license number 2760) pulled up in front of Villa Berg. Two young men jumped out and hurried inside as if a storm had just burst above their heads. But the storm was yet to come, and they were bringing it. "Capitalism carries war within itself the way clouds carry a thunderstorm," declared French socialist Jean Jaurès in his final speech on July 14, 1914.

A witness entering the hall at that moment claimed to have seen the two men. One had long, dark hair and a beard and was wearing a black jacket. The other was slender, with an aquiline nose, reddish hair, and a little mustache; he wore a brown suit. They asked to see the ambassador on a matter of "extreme urgency," a matter that "concerned him personally."

They were made to wait in the hall as usual, but the expression "made to wait" isn't a mere convention of language. For those two young men, waiting appeared to be the hardest thing in the world. Anyone observing them today would see clear signs of nervousness in their behavior. The signs were so obvious, they should have caught the attention of the embassy staff, who had been warned several weeks earlier that an attack on the count was being prepared. But in that month of July 1918, with the Revolution hanging by a thread, everyone's face bore the same signs of a nervousness that arose not from psychology but from history: the times were out of joint. So the embassy's first secretary walking down the hallway toward the two waiting young terrorists would have been hard pressed to notice any unusual nervousness in their faces. To put it more trivially, diplomacy in those revolutionary times had lost its head; signs had started to diverge, seeking new content. In his memoirs, Maurice Paléologue, the French ambassador to Russia before the Revolution, spoke of the store of knowledge he had accumulated over decades of carefully studying people. At a glance, he could recognize the rank and importance of a person he was dealing with, by their clothing, their gait, the sound of their voice, a certain inclination of their whole person, their hierarchical rank and quality. But all that knowledge had lost its meaning. Signs were now detached from their bodies and wandering the streets, like Gogol's nose.

The linguist Roman Jakobson spoke of a "veritable crash of signs."

So the first secretary was blind to the obvious signs of nervousness in the two people he was dealing with. When one of them held out his mission order, his hand was shaking so violently that the secretary, forgetting all protocol prudence, put his hand on the man's shoulder to calm him, almost paternally. Still, he was surprised by how young they were, barely out of their teens. He had trouble taking them seriously until he saw the signature of Felix Dzerzhinsky, head of the Extraordinary Commission, at the bottom of the mission order (where Blumkin had forged it). The secretary, who had seen generations of diplomats go gray in harness over a quarter century, remarked to himself, "The way this is going, we will soon be negotiating with children!" Mastering his annoyance, he asked the two to follow him, as courteously as if he were dealing with ministers of the tsar.

The two men fell into step behind him, and the three entered a maze of hallways with padded walls and deep-carpeted floors that absorbed the sound of their footsteps, beneath a series of Italian chandeliers. Secretaries briskly cut across rooms, the quicker to deliver the files they jealously held under their arms. Chambermaids carrying piles of linen took unpredictable trajectories from which they seemed to want to escape by furtive and somewhat baffled glances. Butlers with lustrous sideburns oversaw comings and goings with a practiced eye. In short, an entire domestic activity that had its logic, but within an air bubble squeezed between two space-time continuums. The young men were led into a drawing room and again asked to wait.

Upstairs, the ambassador was quietly finishing lunch in the company of his staff, which included Dr. Riesler, Lieutenant Müller, and Karl von Bothmer, who four years later would write a memoir, *With Count Mirbach in Moscow.*

Another witness described the scene downstairs: "Blumkin and Andreyev came in the main entrance. They were led to an antechamber whose walls were covered with valuable hangings. The two men wanted to see the ambassador over a personal matter. They waited the time it took for us to finish having lunch. They were given seats in the antechamber with other visitors. Description of the drawing room: on the floor, priceless oriental rugs. The wallpaper was purple silk; heavy brocade curtains, soft cushions facing the window; a low sofa stood behind a table with a marble top and bronze ornaments (a very heavy piece that a man alone could not move). A chair at each end of the table; armchairs facing away from the window."

In light of the many warnings announcing an imminent attack, measures had been taken. Count Mirbach was not to meet the men from the Cheka alone. So he arrived accompanied by Dr. Riesler, who stood six feet four inches tall, and his interpreter, Lieutenant Müller, because the ambassador didn't speak Russian.

Blumkin was seated in an armchair facing the sofa with his back to the window. Riesler and Muller were on the sofa to his right. Andreyev sat farther away, near the door leading to the ballroom. Mirbach entered the drawing room through the door next to Andreyev and sat down at Blumkin's left.

Blumkin told him about the case of a certain Robert Mirbach, who he claimed was a nephew of the count who was accused of espionage and whose case Blumkin was handling. But the ambassador shook his head dubiously. He didn't know of any Robert in his family, he said. The affair was taking an unexpected turn.

"This doesn't concern me, Mr. Blumkin. My family has no connection with the officer under arrest."

"I think we should wrap up this conversation, Your Excellency," said the tall Riesler. "We can simply send the Cheka a written answer via the Commissariat for Foreign Affairs."

Andreyev, who had been silent so far, then said the phrase that was the signal for action: "Doesn't the count want to know the measures that the tribunal is considering taking against the named Mirbach?"

Blumkin promptly repeated the question: "Wouldn't you like to know, Mr. Ambassador?"

Mirbach nodded.

A year later, Blumkin described the scene to Victor Serge:

"I was talking to him, looking into his eyes, and saying to myself: I must kill this man. My briefcase contained a Browning among the documents. 'Wait,' I said, 'here are the papers,' and I fired point-blank. Wounded, Mirbach fled across the big drawing room, and his secretary flopped down behind the armchairs. In the drawing room Mirbach fell, and then I threw my bomb hard on the marble floor."

At this point, the various accounts diverge. Blumkin said the wounded ambassador fled into the ballroom, clutching his stomach. Other people claim that Blumkin was rattled and missed, giving the ambassador time to run away. But the two versions then converge again.

Mirbach ran from the drawing room into the ballroom. But Andreyev, who hadn't moved from his chair, fired at him with a small-caliber, highly accurate pistol. The bullet entered the ambassador's neck and came out his nose. He died instantly. Andreyev then threw a bomb at the body, but it didn't go off. Blumkin grabbed it and threw it again, hard. The explosion was deafening. It blew out the glass in the windows and chandeliers, littering the floor with shards of glass like pearls from a necklace. Sheets of plaster fell from the ceiling. The parquet floor was splintered, as was a bookcase whose scattered volumes briefly sent pages fluttering around the smoke-filled room. The bomb had blasted a foot-and-a-half hole in the floor. The count lay next to it in a pool of blood.

From Gustav Hilger, a second witness:

> Having finished lunch, most of us went back to our offices. I had just reached mine on the first floor when Sergeant Berkigt, who was typing next to me, went to the window and said, "It sounds like shooting outside." He had no sooner said this than an enormous explosion was heard, along with screams and the clatter of windows breaking. I grabbed my pistol from the desk and ran downstairs, meeting Henning on the way. Downstairs, two embassy workers appeared, one of them looking extremely agitated. "I think the count has been assassinated. We're going to get weapons."
>
> In the hall, the glass windows had shattered. A couple of servants grabbed a man they thought suspicious. In vain. The rooms were filled with smoke and dust . . . The explosion blew out all the grand ballroom's windows. Plaster and marble ceiling and wall ornaments lay strewn on the floor, which had been holed by the bomb's impact. A second bomb was found that hadn't exploded. It was one of those bombs that have played such a big role in Mother Russia's history: a metal sphere full of explosives with a protruding acid-filled glass tube. Henning, Schubert the military attaché, who had joined us, and I found Count Mirbach lying in a pool of his blood.

Blumkin and his accomplice, Andreyev, jumped from the windows facing the street. They left their hats, a pistol, documents, and a briefcase containing an unused bomb and a cigarette holder behind on the table. Among the pieces of evidence of the attack, the presence of the cigarette holder remains unexplained.

Blumkin was hurt when he jumped from the window, and may have been blown out by the bomb blast. As he struggled to climb the enclosure fence, a bullet fired from inside the embassy went through his left leg. Limping, he joined his accomplice waiting in the Packard.

A few minutes later, the car drove up to a town house occupied by the Popov Detachment headquarters and controlled by the Left SR. Blumkin was immediately taken in hand, his hair cut and his beard shaved. Dressed in a Red Army uniform, he was hospitalized as a soldier wounded at the front. Later, when he was on his feet again, he left his room and disappeared for several months.

CHAPTER

5

Our taxi, a big sedan with tinted windows, raced along the Moskva River docks. Atop the Kremlin walls, M-shaped crenellations formed a kind of temporal frieze connecting the Moscow of the Bolsheviks to the modern capital, invaded by the billboards of capitalism. On the GPS screen, a red arrow hovered over the dotted network of streets and the blue line of the Moskva. When we woke up on November 7, 2015, we learned that the Lubyanka building had been attacked during the night. Without waiting for breakfast, we jumped into a taxi and headed there.

Emmanuelle followed the taxi's itinerary with an eye on the GPS screen and a finger on a map of Moscow, trying to identify the palaces, churches, and museums along the way that we should visit later. I paid hardly any attention, unable to see the city without it being immediately overlaid with the 1918 sepia photographs of the Bolsheviks' capital.

Threatened by the German armies, the Bolsheviks discreetly left Petrograd from a freight train station during the night of March 10, 1918. They reached Moscow two days later, in time for the All-Russia Congress of Soviets, which had been urgently called to ratify the Brest-Litovsk peace agreement. I could imagine clumps of peasants and workers from all over Russia gathered in little groups under a red flag on the great square in front of the Bolshoi Theater, rifles slung and packs on their backs. On the other side of the square stood the Metropol. Requisitioned by the Bolsheviks, the hotel housed hundreds of bureaucrats, as well as the offices of the commissariat of foreign affairs. Commissar Georgy Chicherin received foreign emissaries in the middle of the night in a room there, amid a jumble of dispatches and newspapers. From the balconies, a few Bolsheviks raised their fists, saluting the delegates as they reached the square behind their red flags, the only touch of color in the sepia photos.

A few hundred yards farther, the Lubyanka building stood out against the sky like a yellow-orange cardboard model set in the shallow square. The statue of Felix Dzerzhinsky that once stood in the center of Lubyanka Square had been removed in 1991, leaving only its base, like a sundial without a gnomon. After the fall of the Soviet Union, there was talk of turning the Lubyanka into a museum, as was done with its equivalents in the Warsaw Pact nations. In the end, the building retained its original purpose. Having hosted the Cheka, GPU, and KGB, it was now the home of the FSB, the Russian internal security secret service.

Given that this was the wake of an attack, we were surprised not to see any police presence on the square, or even a single TV van sprouting antennas and parabolas. Most surprising of all, there was no visible sign of any attack. The Lubyanka reigned over its namesake square, immovable.

When I walked over to the heavy wooden doors, I noticed a few dark marks on them, but that was all. The supposed attack was the work of a dissident performance artist. During the night it seems he had splashed the building's entrance with gasoline and set it on fire. He then had himself filmed standing before the blazing "gates of hell." The gesture was a protest against the recent conviction of a Ukrainian filmmaker for terrorism, for setting fire to the doors of a small pro-Russian political party's headquarters in Crimea.

A quick search on our smartphones revealed that the artist was Pyotr Pavlensky, age thirty-one, and that this provocative "action," which he called *Threat*, wasn't his first. In *Seam*, in July 2013, he sewed his lips shut with scarlet thread in protest against the arrest of Pussy Riot. A year later, in *Carcass*, he was carried naked, wrapped in a coil of barbed wire, to the Legislative Assembly of St. Petersburg to protest the authorities' homophobic propaganda. For *Fixation*, he nailed his scrotum to the pavement in Red Square on November 10, 2013, Russian Police Day. Declared the artist: "It isn't the powers that have the people by the balls, it's the people who remain unmoved." Western journalists called it "a metaphor for the apathy, indifference, and political fatalism of contemporary Russian society."

After he consented to having the nail pulled from the freezing pavement, he was forced to undergo tests in a Moscow psychiatric institution. But the artist turned this into yet another performance. On the clinic roof he stripped naked as usual, and cut off his earlobe. He was photographed naked and streaming blood as a protest against the use of psychiatry for political ends.

In the video shot the night of our arrival in Moscow, Pavlensky appears wearing a black hood pulled around his face and carrying a jerrican of gasoline. The scene is lit only by the flames racing up the tall wooden door. A political artist known for inflicting physical suffering on his body in the name of art, Pavlensky is a kind of Christ 2.0 who carves the stigmata of repression into his flesh, and preaches by symbol instead of parable. To reporters who asked why self-mutilation was at the heart of his artistic work, he said, "The authorities' actions are violent, so I have to imitate their visual code in order to denounce them . . . I am very critical of any decorative art as an idea, the idea of ornamentalism and concealment. Everything that does the opposite, that brings things out and reveals how things actually are, this is what interests me." When *Vice* magazine asked Pavlensky if he thought violence had to be fought with violence, he answered: "There's a philosophy of endless carnage; it's a willfully self-turning mechanism of violence, and if you can get in the works you can bring it to a screeching halt. Then you have the opportunity to stop it for good."

Pavlensky's performance only lasted a few seconds, but was guaranteed a kind of posterity when it was shared by thousands of Internet users. "Burning doors sometimes turns into terrorism," he said when he was arrested. He demanded to be treated as a terrorist, and told the court that if this were not done he would remain silent, ignoring what he called their "judicial rites." Putting his words into action, he then fell silent. Like all Russian terrorists since Sergei Nechayev, Pavlensky believes in "propaganda by fact."

"The fire is in the minds of men and not in the roofs of houses," wrote Dostoyevsky in *Demons*. Pavlensky's performance was the latest flame, flickering and a bit laughable, of the fire that has been burning in minds for the last century. I decided to take this performance, which coincided with our arrival in Moscow, as a welcoming gesture.

———

In mid-April 1919, a man with a face covered with bruises, his head wrapped in a wide, bloody bandage, showed up at Cheka headquarters in Kyiv. He was wearing a jacket and patched pants that looked too big for him. To the sentinel guarding the door at 5 Sadovaya Street, the man opened a gap-toothed mouth and said, "My name is Blumkin, Yakov Blumkin. I am wanted for killing the German ambassador, von Mirbach." After a pause to catch his breath, he asked to see the head of the Cheka. The guard gestured for him to wait, and ran inside the building.

This was the first time since the attack on July 6, 1918, that Blumkin had spoken his real name.

He had successively been Grigory Belov in Moscow, Averbach in Petrograd, and Grégoire Vishnevsky in Kyiv, changing his identity and appearance and inventing a new personality for himself at every stop in the theater of warring armies that Russia had become in the Civil War. After nine months of clandestine existence, he had decided to come in from the cold. Nine months of hopping from one city to another, sneaking across Civil War fronts, using fake passports and real photographs, where he appeared made up and unrecognizable. Having given his name to the Cheka sentinel, Blumkin was now naked—as naked as Pyotr Pavlensky on the roof of the psychiatric hospital—his body covered with the stigmata from his successive metamorphoses. Masks were about to fall, and he would have to account for himself in the ambassador's murder.

To appease the Germans, the Bolsheviks announced Blumkin's execution even as they were letting him get away. Publicly, Lenin called Blumkin and his companion "scoundrels." But in the hours after the attack, he said, with his usual humor, "Look for them! Look for them! But don't find them!"

To some, Blumkin was a traitor being manipulated by the Anglo-French services; to others, a Chekist in the pay of the Bolsheviks. According to the first group, the attack had been ordered by the Allied powers, who had every reason for reviving the conflict with Germany and would exfiltrate Blumkin and shelter him until war's end. According to the second, Lenin and Dzerzhinsky had known all about the SRs' planned attack and let them go ahead. Some people even claimed that Trotsky had recruited Blumkin and sent him to Ukraine to launch terrorist attacks behind White Army lines. Finally, there were all those who saw him as a hero who had sacrificed himself to defend the nation's honor.

From July 6, 1918, when he dropped off everyone's radar, until mid-April 1919, when he surfaced, ragged and toothless, at the Cheka's door in Kyiv, Blumkin's biography shows only nine long months of silence. Dozens of stories have been told about him, tales of heroism and betrayal, plots hatched by enemy secret services and sordid complicities with Bolshevik authorities, brilliant actions and memorable scenes lit by courage, conversion, and redemption. There is no lack of sources about this period;

what is disconcerting is their multiplicity. Blumkin's biography floats off the solid ground of established fact and supporting evidence to lose itself in a fog of rumors and gossip. But by cross-checking sources, I have been able to re-create his trajectory during those nine months.

Given the political and administrative chaos of summer 1918, Blumkin would have had no trouble slipping through the net in the hours and days following the attack, as he had accomplices in the Left SR establishment. He was hospitalized under the name Grigori Belov, a soldier wounded in fighting Left SR rebels, but left the infirmary after receiving first aid. Given a Red Army uniform, crutches, and a fake identity as one Averbach, he climbed into the train to Petrograd. The word was to lie low for a while. Some say that Blumkin, alias Averbach, hid out in Rybinsk; others, in Gatchina near Petrograd. But all agreed in describing him bent over a school notebook, conscientiously drafting a report on the July 6 attack. Here was an example, rare enough to be worthy of note, of a terrorist trading his still-warm weapon for a memoirist's pen. He had just turned eighteen. According to the verbatim transcript of his interrogation in April 1919, he told the Kyiv Cheka: "After July 6 I lived in the environs of Petrograd. I devoted myself to a strictly literary task, which consisted in gathering documentation and writing a book about the events of July 6."

In one of his few letters to his mother, Blumkin spoke of his filial devotion and tried to reassure her, while also justifying his crime: "Mother, I am safe here, or at least as safe as one can be in these times. After the Brest-Litovsk peace, I had to accept the responsibility of taking another man's life. I did it for our country, Russia, but also in the name of Jews, who are so often accused of betraying the Russian nation to benefit Germany. My life has since split in two and I can no longer go back. I embrace you."

Every two days, a messenger from his party brought him news about Ukraine. In early August, his comrade Andreyev visited to discuss a new project, an attack on General Pavlo Skoropadsky, the Ukrainian head of state who briefly governed the country with German support from April to November 1918.

On some evenings, Blumkin could be seen on the banks of the Neva, in defiance of his comrades' security protocols, gazing at the enormous bridges rising against the pale screen of the sky. A Kronstadt sailor claims to have recognized him one day in the Baltic fleet's conference room, dozing on a chair. Apparently it was there that he first heard the word Shambhala, a lost country bordering Tibet, Afghanistan, and India. At the end of one talk, according to a Cheka informant, Blumkin approached the speaker, a certain Alexander Vasilyevich Barchenko. A biologist who had strayed beyond the frontiers of his science to dabble in parapsychology, Barchenko claimed that the Shambhala people had discovered the secret of telepathy.

At night, Blumkin would sometimes compose a poem or two "by the light of an oil lamp," writes one of his biographers. He had a map of Russia facing his desk and used pins to track the positions of the armies attacking or defending the country. The news about the front that reached him in dribs and drabs was vague, contradictory, and sometimes overtaken by events. (The news sometimes came with the food he was brought each morning by a "party comrade with a childish face framed by pigtails, and the heavy breasts of a wet nurse," *dixit* Blumkin.) In the north, enemy armies had crossed the Finnish frontier. In the east, the German front stretched in a straight line for four hundred miles from the Gulf of Finland to Ukraine. The southern front was a tangle of Red, White, and Green forces, an inextricable snarl.

But those colors designated more than the flags of the armies fighting over Russia; they were signs you had to decode when traveling the country. Sharpened by circumstances, people's minds were alert to this task of identification. The whole country was one vast interrogation room where people came together to make signs speak.

Double agents, crooks, speculators, and ordinary refugees all carried a variety of safe conducts in their wallets and used them as circumstances dictated, the way a secret agent carries a choice of passports. A single word could condemn you or set you free. The frontier was now everywhere: behind very hill, around every turn, sometimes at every street corner.

Writes Victor Serge:

> White officers from the Romanian front (for example Drozdovsky's forces) kept crossing Ukraine in order to get to Kuban. The Czechoslovak legions were at large in the heart of the country, under orders from the Allies to retreat before the German advance and take up positions on the Volga. The German settlers in the region were in revolt. Petlyura's nationalist commandos, or haidamaks, held various points in the countryside. Villages bristling with machine guns defended themselves fiercely against all comers. Local republics were inaugurated, such as that of the Donets workers. Red brigades, totally undisciplined, often drunk, often commanded by adventurers who later on had to be shot, discredited the authority of the Soviets with the local populations. Shooting, looting, and assassinations went on everywhere. Sometimes strong formations retreated before the enemy without firing a shot; magnificent resistance came from odd handfuls, like the thirty-five Red fighters who held back two German regiments at Putyvl. At the rail junction of Lozavaya, a whole unit, the Lenin Battalion, was wiped out covering the Reds' retreat. Amid such frightful chaos, the revolutionary struggle demanded an uncommon strength of personality.

Amid this chaos, all of Blumkin's attention was focused on Ukraine, where his Combat Organization comrades were preparing an attack against Field Marshal Eichhorn, the commander of the German troops occupying Ukraine. He was the SR's second target after Ambassador Mirbach. A young woman, Irina Kakhovskaya, was the leader of a dozen disciplined terrorists. Blumkin was eager to join them, but for the moment his instructions were clear: lie low. Every day, he waited for news of his friends and scanned the newspapers for news of Eichhorn's execution.

Fortunately, we know more about those events than Blumkin did, thanks to Kakhovskaya's book, *Souvenirs d'une révolutionnaire: souvenirs sur l'attentat contre Eichhorn* (Memoirs of a revolutionary: on the Eichhorn attack), which was published in France in the 1920s. "In the Ukrainian workers' eyes, Eichhorn was the hangman, the murderer of the worker and peasant proletariat," wrote Kakhovskaya. "On the margin of a report about the elimination of a peasant township, where 8,500 people had been killed, peasants to be hung had been held, and seventeen gallows were erected in a single village, Eichhorn had written, 'Good.' Though brief, his domination of Ukraine lasted long enough for him to litter that prosperous country with gibbets and unhallowed graves."

When Kakhovskaya's group reached Kyiv, it faced the usual difficulties in this kind of enterprise: scouting the area, surveilling the target, observing his habits, and studying his timetable. Catherine Street, where Eichhorn lived, was a veritable armed camp. Every house was occupied by members of the high command, and German agents were everywhere. It was impossible to walk down the street more than once without being noticed. Studying the terrain required multiple changes of clothes and disguises. "The tasks of reconnaissance, doing makeup, caring for the horses, maintaining our quarters, running errands by coach, assembling the bombs, and making daily trips from the countryside into town took up all of our time." And no sooner did the group learn enough about Eichhorn's habits than he would disappear abroad for a few days or go inspect his troops. The attack would have to be put off, and everything started all over again. Hours were spent carrying a box of candies or a food basket, while waiting for a coach to drive by. The old surveillance techniques took months and tied up dozens of informants while remaining vulnerable to a last-minute change of route or habit that would ruin a long-prepared operation in a few seconds.

In his hideout near Petrograd, Blumkin was getting impatient. He was dying to go into action. He had been ordered to keep a low profile so as not to raise German suspicions before Eichhorn's execution, but the inactivity was taking an increasing toll.

Privately, he raged against the Left SR's archaic terrorism methods, which were inspired by those of nineteenth-century anarchists. Blumkin felt it was time terrorism underwent a true technological revolution. Terror needed engineers to calculate trajectories and speeds, skilled tacticians to choose actions, psychologists to predict a target's behavior, logistics managers to move people and explosives, and experienced journalists to anticipate editorials that hadn't yet been written. It was now possible to detonate explosives at a distance or fly a blimp over a palace and bomb it; a brilliant engineer in Munich had already drawn up the plans. All that was lacking was the money to move to the operational phase. But in the meantime, under Civil War conditions, you had to make do with what you had: one or two working bombs and a few brave people.

"Every day [Boris] Donskoy bid farewell to his friends and went off to accomplish his dreadful deed," writes Kakhovskaya in her book. "We would accompany him as far as the street corner, and stay for the hour that Eichhorn spent at his headquarters. Then he would go, and we would wait for the sound of the explosion." Several times Donskoy came back, distraught over his failure. Either a coach had driven by just as he was about to throw his bomb, or some children were playing too close to the general. Once, the top of his thermos-bomb came off and rolled right over to Eichhorn's feet.

Keeping his cool, Donskoy retrieved the top without arousing suspicions.

On July 30, Donskoy finally saw Eichhorn leaving his circle of officers. He followed him, got within eight steps, and threw his bomb. The field marshal's body was blown to bits. "When I saw the bomb explode, I stepped aside and surrendered to the German soldiers," said Donskoy. "I wanted them to take me prisoner. I wanted it to be known why I had killed Eichhorn with premeditation."

Condemned to death, Donskoy was hanged on August 10 at five in the afternoon. A witness described the execution to Blumkin:

> The executioner, a Lukyanivska Prison inmate with a shaved head and wearing a gray coat, stood next to the telephone pole. Attached to it was a strap of braided cables and a big sign that read, "Killer of Field Marshal von Eichhorn." Boris Donskoy walked over to the pole perfectly calmly, and with his bound hands took off his cap so the executioner could put the rope around his neck. A German soldier yanked the stool out from under him... They left the body hanging there for two hours. That night it was taken down and carried to a chapel by a criminal prisoner. Without the warden's knowledge, he picked a few flowers in the garden and put them on the coffin.

In his last days, Donskoy had written this to his mother: "Give me your blessing, Mother, and do not feel sorry for me. I am as happy as if I were seeing heaven." The letter wound up in the hands of a German examining magistrate, and Donskoy's mother never received it. Wrote Kakhovskaya: "That man of the law could not understand that a son might ask his mother for her blessing for a murder."

The French writer Romain Rolland, who read her manuscript before publication, wrote this to the translator: "Thank you for sending me Kakhovskaya's memoir. I condemn its ideas, but the account is of striking human (or inhuman) value; it's a psychological document of the first order." In his letter, Rolland stressed "the narration's absolute simplicity, its gift of objective vision that is so typically Russian, and the incredible energy expended . . . So much heroism, patience, and total self-sacrifice, how many treasures of the soul and of humanity spent for monstrous and absurd ends."

A month later, on the morning of August 30, Moisei Uritsky, the head of the Petrograd Cheka, was assassinated. The killer was quickly arrested: a young poet, Leonid Kannegisser. At twenty-two, he was well known in Petrograd's literary circles and a friend of the poets Sergei Esenin and Marina Tsvetaeva. A poet and a terrorist. A kind of Blumkin twin, but with the political profiles reversed. Two jacks in the deck of cards being played that summer of 1918.

Lenin dispatched Dzerzhinsky to Petrograd to decide what measures needed to be taken. Increased checkpoints, arrests in opposition circles, a search of the British embassy. The Bolsheviks feared that the murder would be the signal for the Allies to attack the Soviets' forces in Petrograd. But Dzerzhinsky turned around and hurried back to Moscow two hours later. An SR named Fanny Kaplan had shot and wounded Lenin. The Revolution was hanging by a thread.

A Red terror was unleashed. Hundreds of hostages were executed on the night of August 31. Barricades were set up at street corners. Now in danger of being arrested at any moment, Blumkin had to flee Petrograd. The city's Left SR network swung into action, to exfiltrate him to a safe hiding place far from the two capitals. At two o'clock in the morning, as dawn was breaking, Blumkin was jerked awake. At the foot of his bed stood a pair of militants holding out a Red Army uniform and a passport in the name of Vishnevsky. He was driven to a suburban station and put on a train.

The train crossed landscapes devastated by war, skirted smoking cities, and passed crowds of gaunt, ragged, bewildered refugees huddled on the platforms. To Blumkin, everything he had experienced since the July 6 attack felt unreal. "My story will end in rubble," he suddenly thought. In the history books he would just be the man who assassinated the German ambassador. All the rest would be erased, overshadowed by his crime. At seventeen, he was already posthumous.

The trip was eventful. At one point he had to jump from the speeding train to escape Latvian riflemen who had recognized him. Continuing on foot, he reached Kimry, a little city on the Volga a hundred miles north of Moscow, from which convoys of wheat were shipped. Kimry was far from everything, and a safe distance from the Red terror unleashed in Petrograd. As "Vishnevsky," he was hired by the local agricultural commissariat. Wearing a black leather coat and an officer's cap without insignia, he oversaw the wheat convoys, one hand resting on his Browning.

Between dispatching two convoys to Moscow, Blumkin contacted his SR comrades. A question had been haunting him ever since Boris Donskoy's death. He put it to Ilya Ehrenburg in early 1921 when the latter was preparing to go to Paris. "Is there any chance you will run into Savinkov?" he asked. "If so, ask him what he thinks about leaving after the action." Ehrenburg didn't quite understand what he meant, so Blumkin put the question this way: "Should a terrorist try to escape after committing an action, or should he pay for the crime with his blood?"

Savinkov had gone over to the Whites, but he had led the SR Combat Organization under the tsar, and Blumkin respected him as his teacher in terrorism. For Savinkov, terrorism was a kind of church composed of believers who each pursued their own earthly aims but who all shared the same faith, an apostolic mission of death with its codes of honor and very strict rules. A terrorist's voluntary sacrifice was part of that—the price to be paid for transgressing the biblical law "Thou shall not kill." "For people like him," concluded Ehrenburg, "terror was not a weapon in the political struggle, but a world of its own."

In early November 1918, Blumkin was in Ukraine, where he reconnected with the party's Combat Organization. He was no longer alone, and his reunions with comrades were warm ones. Eager for details of the attack against Eichhorn and about Boris Donskoy, Blumkin peppered Irina Kakhovskaya with questions. The plan to assassinate the puppet Ukrainian leader Pavlo Skoropadsky was soon back on the table again. The attack was planned for November 26, when the target was due to attend the funerals of officers killed by rebels, but it was pushed back. No doubt the armistice signed at Rethondes, France, on November II had something to do with this. The Germans had lost the Great War. All they wanted now was to leave Ukraine and go home. Skoropadsky was overthrown, and the assassination plan abandoned. A White general, Anton Denikin, took his place on the Combat Organization's blacklist. Blumkin was elected a member of the clandestine Kyiv soviet and battled the new Directory that governed Ukraine until the nationalist Simon Petlyura seized power in February 1919. At about the same time, he was elected secretary of the Kyiv Left SR Committee headed by Irina Kakhovskaya.

On Christmas Eve, Blumkin was in Rostov. As machine guns chattered around the city, church bells tolled, calling the faithful to midnight mass, celebrated with Denikin in attendance. When the tsarist general arrived with his personal guard, wrote Kakhovskaya, the little group passed through the porch from which hanged men dangled, instead of Christmas tree ornaments.

> In the distance, I saw a white shape above the crowd in front of the cathedral, possibly an orator speaking from a dais. As I got closer, I saw that it was a man hanging from a tree, with a sign on his chest that said, "Deserter." People stood around, studying the spectacle. On the other side there was another hanged man with the word "Bolshevik," and farther on a woman labeled "Talked too much." Seeing the first hanged man, the woman had apparently voiced her indignation and been strung up herself. Unaware of its import, children were describing the scene. "Over on Ekaterininskaya Street, there's a lady hanging with her daughter. And there are four guys near the station." And they dragged each other off to go see these novelties.

Denikin sat in the front pew, smoothing his famous mustache. His closed eyes hid a weary gaze, a vague piety, and probably memories of the happy Christmases of his childhood, which he confused with a so-called golden age of tsarism. At the cathedral entrance, a beggar with a big hood hiding his face watched Denikin come in. It was Blumkin, who could study the man to be shot at leisure and count the bodyguards accompanying him. These details are mostly beyond our ken, but are essential elements in the machinery of an assassination.

Next day, Blumkin boarded another train, for a destination known to only to him. Wrapped in a long gray Red Army coat, he crossed regions that Denikin had just devastated, stopping in ravaged cities. Over the following weeks, his presence was successively noted in Podolia, where he worked to restore Soviet power, and around Zhmerynka, where he organized the rebel peasantry against Petlyura's followers. In Vinnytsia, he helped a certain Lisovik, the president of the local executive committee, get out of jail. In March, he was in Yelisavetgrad, two hundred miles southeast of Kyiv. There, he organized the city's defense against the anarchist detachment led by Marusya Nikiforova, which had been fighting in the streets for the previous two weeks.

From the train rolling across the endless Donets Basin steppes, Blumkin saw desolate landscapes, steaming vegetation black with coal dust, huge factories and roaring blast furnaces in a dying world. At night he would stretch out near the luggage net and smoke cigarette after cigarette while reading Jack London novels by the dim light of the compartment lamp.

In March 1919, his walkabout came to a sudden end. While crossing the forest near Kremenchuk in a horse-drawn cart, he ran into one of Petlyura's armed detachments. Without even knowing him, they recognized Blumkin for the Jew he was and the Chekist he was no longer. A chase ensued, but their horses were faster than his wagon. Though held and tortured all night long, Blumkin didn't talk, and was left for dead next to a railroad track. He was naked, his body covered with bruises and scars, his neck marked by the ropes he'd been strung up with, and his jaw broken. Straining to remain conscious, Blumkin managed to crawl along the tracks to a crossing guard's cottage, where he was taken in and cared for. Next day, the guard drove him in a handcart to the nearest train station, where he was hospitalized for a month. When he got out, he decided to surrender to the Cheka in Kyiv.

The news of Blumkin's surrender was a sensation in the Cheka ranks and spread like wildfire from Kyiv to Kharkov and Moscow. When Martin Latsis, the head of the Cheka in Ukraine, got the word, he immediately alerted Trotsky in his armored train with its sealed windows, who in turn informed Lenin and Sverdlovsk at the Kremlin. Latsis was quickly dispatched to Kyiv to interrogate Blumkin in person. The two men knew each other well. In July 1918, Blumkin had dealt with Latsis when Dzerzhinsky suspended him from his functions at the Cheka following Mandelstam's complaint. A Latvian Old Bolshevik, Latsis had gone underground after the aborted 1905 revolution, helped shape the seizure of power by the Bolsheviks in 1917, and was one of the founders of the Cheka.

Latsis assumed his position on April 10, 1919, and Blumkin turned himself into the Kyiv Cheka in mid-April—a striking coincidence. Blumkin, who knew Latsis very well, probably felt that he could trust him. For his part, Latsis needed committed revolutionaries to help him reform the Cheka, and Blumkin fit the profile. The debriefing took several days, with neither restrictions nor pressure. Blumkin was well treated. Given medical help and decent food, he quickly recovered his strength, and actively cooperated. So many stories had been told about him that he was eager to explain himself.

Germany's defeat by the Allies, signed in November 1918, had erased the humiliating Brest-Litovsk treaty. By the same token, it eliminated the main point of disagreement between the Bolsheviks and the Left SRs. In Ukraine, Belarus, and the Baltic countries, the restoration of Soviet power was underway. On March 2, 1919, the founding congress of the Third International was held in Moscow. The next day, responding to a call by the German Communist Party, the Berlin workers councils launched a general strike. On March 21, Béla Kun took power and declared Hungary's Republic of Councils, modeled after the Russian soviets. Blumkin, who had devoted his life to the Revolution from his earliest days, could no longer stay on the sidelines.

Blumkin's deposition at the Kyiv Cheka in April and May 1919 was recorded in the *Red Book of the Cheka*:

> *The events that have unfolded since July have changed the political situation. The German revolution, which is just beginning, broke the chains of Brest-Litovsk, and the attitude of the Soviet authorities toward us is no longer relevant. When power in Hungary passed into the hands of the workers and the peasants, it clearly showed the outline of world revolution, to which Mirbach's head was dedicated. Yet I, who have committed myself to social revolution and who proudly served its cause during its worldwide offensive, was expected to remain hidden on the sidelines. This was a deeply abnormal state for me. I was burning with the desire to really work for the cause of the Revolution, so I decided to come to the Cheka, an authority of Soviet power, in order to escape that abnormal state.*

When the initial interrogations were finished, the Kyiv Cheka sent Blumkin to Moscow. A special judicial commission was convened that interviewed him at length. On May 8, 1919, he declared: "I decided to come to the Cheka to clear up the confused situation that was created after the Mirbach assassination by my party's Executive Committee's refusal to hand me over to the police."

After several interrogations, the special judiciary commission presented its report on the Blumkin affair to the presidency of the Central Committee. On March 16, 1919, taking into account Blumkin's voluntary appearance and his detailed explanations of the circumstances of the German ambassador's assassination, the president of the Central Committee took a spectacular decision: Blumkin was amnestied.

The Red Book of the Cheka contains the main reports on the Blumkin affair. Under the title "After the Verdict," Appendix X contains the following materials:

Pages 367–382: Deposition of Blumkin at the Kyiv Cheka (April–May 1919).
Pages 382–386: Deposition before the Commission of Inquiry.
Pages 387–389: Report by the Special Commission of Inquiry on the Blumkin affair.
Page 389: 16 May 1919 decree by the Presidium of the All-Russia Executive Committee ordering the freeing of Yakov Blumkin, [signed] Yenukidze.

One point remained to be cleared up. In the course of his interrogation, did Blumkin make amends? Did he ask his judges to forgive him? Not at all. With his first deposition in Kyiv on April 17, 1919, the young man made this preliminary declaration: "It would be a serious mistake to interpret my surrendering as a giving up. I do not regret the act that I committed, and I stress the significance we wanted to give that act in the context of the Brest-Litovsk treaty. I am still a member of the Socialist Revolutionary Party, and I still disagree with the Soviet authorities' policy."

In answering his judges' questions, Blumkin was aware that he was testifying before history, and not just before the Bolshevik authorities' institutions. He was speaking to posterity, to future generations of the Party, to all those who one day would be adolescents and like him want to change the world. The Mirbach assassination inscribed his name next to those who had fought the tsar's autocracy with bombs: Boris Savinkov, Egor Sazonov, and Ivan Kalyayev.

That was the same Kalyayev who inspired Albert Camus's 1949 play, *The Just Assassins*. When I was a sophomore in high school, I remember our old French teacher pacing the dais, a chalk-dusted arm outstretched, declaiming in his quavering voice:

"I threw the bomb at your tyranny, not at a maaaaan!"

To which Camus answers, in the voice of the police chief:

"Perhaps. But it was a living human being whom it blew to bits."

Our teacher walked back to his desk, brushing chalk dust from his sleeves, pleased with the effect of the lines on his young audience—his "dear blond heads," as he called us. Our votes were split between the terrorist's heroism and the police chief's rough common sense. I sided with the first group.

CHAPTER

6

Whether it involves an artist, poet, statesman, or revolutionary hero, the writing of a legend always seems to draw from a shared well of recurring representations and heroic images. The "real" and "truthful" episodes that mark Blumkin's biography follow a pattern common to any biography of an unusual person, including the scene where the hero is initiated. The future knight goes down on one knee with the sword resting on his shoulder, and pledges fealty to his prince. This medieval scene is so familiar to us that it becomes part of many tales of apprenticeship. In Blumkin's case, he was knighted and pardoned in the same event, under the aegis of Leon Trotsky.

As the story goes, the head of the Red Army asked to meet the young terrorist and, after spending a night talking, forgave him and took him into his service. But versions differ as to the place and time of the meeting. It has been variously set on July 6, 1918, on the very evening of the attack; or a few months later in fall of the same year; or in the spring of 1919, after Blumkin's surrender to the Kyiv Cheka. As for the meeting's locale, some mention Trotsky's office in the Kremlin; others, Blumkin's cell in the Lubyanka. Finally, one version reconciles the time and the place of the meeting by having Blumkin brought to Trotsky's famous armored train at the little Sviyazhsk station shortly before the capture of Kazan, in other words in the fall of 1918.

I would dearly love for the meeting to have happened in Sviyazhsk, the crossroads where the wave of the revolutionary offensive began to break. Having Blumkin and Trotsky meet at that time and place in the Civil War when the future of the Revolution was being decided, would have forged a junction between individual and collective histories. The start of Blumkin's second life, which he spent at Trotsky's side, and the rebirth of the Russian Revolution at the battle of Sviyazhsk, which opened the Red Army's path east to the Urals, south to the Caspian Sea, the Caucasus, and the borderlands of Persia, and north to Archangel and Poland.

"Planes came and went, dropping their bombs on the station and the railway cars; machine guns with their repulsive barking and the calm syllables of artillery drew nigh and then withdrew again," wrote Larisa Reisner, whose beauty was praised while her courage and intelligence were overlooked. She was Boris Pasternak's inspiration for Lara (Larissa Antipova) in *Doctor Zhivago*, but the original was much more interesting than the copy played by Julie Christie in David Lean's film.

Larissa wasn't a devoted nurse, the role women are usually relegated to in wartime; she was a warrior, and Trotsky pays homage to her in his autobiography, *My Life*. With Kazan occupied by the Whites, she disguised herself as a peasant and made her way into the city to spy on it. She was arrested but managed to escape, taking advantage of a break during an interrogation. She was a scout for the Red Army and participated in battles on warships. But Trotsky blurred her image with too many heroic metaphors and references to mythology: "This fine young woman flashed across the revolutionary sky like a burning meteor, blinding many. With her appearance of an Olympian goddess, she combined a subtle and ironical mind and the courage of a warrior." Then he lays it on even thicker. "But after coming unscathed through fire and water, this Pallas of the Revolution suddenly burned up with typhus in the peaceful surroundings of Moscow, before she was even thirty."

Is it really so hard to describe a female warrior without enlisting the goddesses of mythology? When Reisner died, her second husband, Karl Radek, asked Pasternak to write a poem about her.

He did so, as he told Varlam Shalamov in a conversation in Moscow in 1953, and its four verses included the line: "Descend into the depths of legend, heroine..."

As a writer herself, Reisner carefully avoided the trap of lyricism. She could describe industries in the Urals or a worker insurrection in the Ruhr. Her writing about the Civil War is as good as John Reed's much-vaunted *Ten Days That Shook the World*, which sometimes sinks to pathos. In describing the battle of Sviyazhsk, she resisted the impulse to write an epic. How could you describe an entire people's battle by focusing on individual destinies? "Up till now history has always solved this problem with imposing but moth-eaten theatrical tricks," she writes. "It would summon to the stage some individual in a 'tricorn hat and a gray field uniform' and he or some other general on a white horse would cut the revolutionary blood and marrow into republics, banners, slogans."

It's a shame that Blumkin and Trotsky's meeting couldn't have happened at Sviyazhsk, because Blumkin might have met Reisner there. That's a scene I would have loved to write.

Nor could the scene have taken place on July 6, the day of the Mirbach attack, or in the days immediately afterward, because Blumkin was first in the hospital, then quickly discharged and bundled onto a train to Petrograd. The theory doesn't hold water. Also, why would Blumkin have gone to the Kyiv Cheka in April if he had already been pardoned by Trotsky six months earlier? And why would he remain hidden from the fall to the next spring?

Result: three improbable versions of the story collapse at once.

So the only possible date for the meeting has to be after Blumkin's surrender in mid-April, when he was sent to Moscow after Martin Latsis's initial interrogations at the Kyiv Cheka were conducted and transcribed.

Which leaves us the choice of the meeting place: Kremlin or Lubyanka? I opt for the Kremlin, even though the Lubyanka offers advantages from a dramatic point of view. The Lubyanka and its executioners, its secrets, its bureaucrats, its death-row cells... The Lubyanka excites the imagination. A conversation under a bare light bulb between the head of the Red Army and a young fanatic would pack a punch. Now imagine that same scene in a movie, with sound techs mimicking the drip of unseen water, lighting and makeup specialists artfully limning pale faces, and set designers and painters creating a crack in the ceiling here, an ominous stain on the wall over there.

Alas, the Kremlin is the more rational choice. Trotsky was a man of action; his time was precious. In the middle of the Civil War, dispatches from the front landed on his desk day and night, and sometimes required immediate answers. So he must have summoned Blumkin to his office.

That's the opinion shared by the Cuban writer Leonardo Padura, who describes the scene in his novel *The Man Who Loved Dogs*, though without specifying a date. His account is dense with improbabilities, however.

> *Twelve years before, when the new head of the Red Army, Lev Trotsky, had called for him in his office, Blumkin was a callow youth—like a character out of Dostoyevsky—who faced charges that the military tribune would penalize with a death sentence . . . The evening before the trial, after reading some poems written by the young man, Lev Davidovich had asked to meet with him. That night they spoke for hours about Russian and French poetry (they shared an admiration for Baudelaire) and about the irrationality of terrorist methods (if a bomb could solve everything, what was the good of parties, of class struggle?), at the end of which Blumkin had written a letter in which he regretted his action and promised, if he was forgiven, to serve the Revolution on any front to which he was assigned. The influence of the powerful commissar was decisive enough to pardon his life, while the German government was informed by official means that the terrorist had been executed. That day Yakov Blumkin's second life had begun, thanks to Lev Trotsky.*

The scene is clearly made up, and the threat of a death penalty is pure invention. Blumkin was in no danger of being condemned to death. He had already been convicted in absentia on November 27, 1918, by the Revolutionary tribunal and sentenced to three years in prison at hard labor—a relatively light penalty, considering his crime could have dragged Russia into a new war with Germany. But the German menace vanished at the eleventh hour of the eleventh day of the eleventh month of 1918. Blumkin didn't risk being executed, so Trotsky didn't have to save his life. As for the conversation about Baudelaire, it's doubtful that Trotsky, who was busy repulsing White and foreign armies, would have had the leisure to talk poetry for hours with him.

We can mock novelists' imagination (Padua) or the taste for moral paradoxes detached from concrete context in which people speak and act (Camus), and set the stubbornness of facts against seductive fictions. But we could also accept imagination, rumor, and fable as a kind of self-defense by historic reason that spontaneously fills gaps in a narration and never accepts the silence of facts. In the trunk that held my Blumkin Project archives, I found a few sheets of paper in a blue folder labeled, "Meeting between Jacob Blumkin and Leon Trotsky." Those pages held my own version of the famous scene. So I too had yielded to the temptation to use fiction to fill the gaps in history.

Persuaded by Trotsky to join the Bolsheviks, Blumkin enjoyed an amnesty. But he didn't fully commit to the Bolshevik Party right away. Instead he quit the Left SRs to join the Union of SR Maximalists, an organization midway between the Bolsheviks and the Left SRs. The Maximalists recognized Soviet authority, but intended to fight counterrevolution by terrorist actions and expropriations—the ideal structure for Blumkin. The Bolsheviks disapproved of individual terror in principle, but didn't stop others from using it. Sometimes they even helped, when the struggle was against a common political adversary.

In May 1919, Blumkin was sent to Ukraine with the Bolsheviks' blessing. His mission: to create a terrorist cell to prepare the assassination of Admiral Kolchak, the head of anti-Bolshevik forces during the Russian Civil War. On May 28, an order was drawn up in Blumkin's name whereby "all Soviet institutions in Russia and Ukraine are asked to collaborate with him." Blumkin reached Kyiv triumphantly in a headquarters train car. Within two months, the exhausted fugitive who had knocked on the Kyiv Cheka's door was in favor with the Bolsheviks and had been assigned a secret mission by the highest state authorities. He needed to account to just one man, the regime's number two, the head of the Red Army, Trotsky.

Blumkin's former Left SR comrades didn't view it that way, however. He had been seen entering the local Cheka building several times, and they accused him of betraying them. On the evening of June 6, three of his former comrades made a date to meet Blumkin in a Kyiv suburb to discuss political matters. The conversation ended abruptly when the conspirators pulled out their guns. Despite a hail of bullets, Blumkin somehow managed to escape. It is said that his first love, Lidia Sorokina, was among the attackers.

The very next day, Blumkin wrote the left SR Central Committee this:

> In the night of the 6th to 7th instant, three members of the Party tried to kill me. Without going into the details of this attempt at summary justice, I will only say that they acted with neither declaration nor warning, in secret, in silence, and in an unexpected way. I am fully aware that this attempted murder is the punishment that revolutionary political parties only impose on traitors. I am no traitor. The Executive Committee's decision to eliminate me, without a prior inquiry and based only on suspicions known only to itself, is a tragic error. For a revolutionary and a terrorist, an accusation of betrayal is the most terrible. For that reason I am putting myself at the disposition of the Left SR Party's Executive Committee so as to be proven innocent of this accusation.

Blumkin barely had time to mail his letter before he faced his former comrades' bullets for a second time. He was sitting on a café terrace on

Khreschatyk Street when two terrorists attacked, emptying their clips into him. Music covered the sound of the gunshots, and the two conspirators strolled away without attracting attention. People at a nearby table only saw a man collapsed next to them, apparently dead drunk except that his head was bleeding. Blumkin was taken unconscious to the hospital and put in intensive care. As he was slowly recovering, his attackers returned a few days later and threw a bomb through the window of his hospital room. He tossed it back out.

This following appeared in the Ukraine Central Executive Committee's *Izvestia* on June 20, 1919:

> *The third attack against Comrade Blumkin took place three days ago. This time the terrorists didn't even show any pity for the other patients in the adjoining rooms. During the night, an unknown person threw a grenade into Blumkin's room. It was only by luck that there were no victims. Nor was Blumkin wounded. This was the third attack against Blumkin in 12 days.*

Blumkin proposed convening an arbitration tribunal composed of members of the various terrorist parties (Maximalists, anarchists, Left SRs, etc.) to fully explore the accusations of betrayal. The hearing was held in a room of the National Hotel in Moscow and lasted two weeks. Witnesses were called, and both sides submitted written documents. Blumkin affirmed that he had never betrayed his party and that he had surrendered to the Cheka to exonerate his former party of the accusation of insurrection against the Bolsheviks. This, however, did not convince his opponents. According to D. G. Maximov, who published his remembrance of the Blumkin trial abroad in 1980, the tribunal, after examining all the documents, didn't think the evidence supported the accusation of betrayal against Blumkin. But Maximov said that the tribunal's decision was so vague it neither quite supported nor dismissed the accusation. Blumkin claimed that Irina Kakhoskaya exculpated him and apologized in the name of the left SR Central Committee, while denying any responsibility for the attacks against him.

Wars are sources of images and tales of atrocities. Blood has been flooding people's minds ever since the invention of photography and the cinema. "The movie theaters reopened," wrote Kakhovskaya, "and all the overexcited public saw were fantastic images of executions and torture. Deceit invaded everything; volunteer spies listened to everything and stuck their noses everywhere, poisoning relationships between people . . . I had to take the little train to the Svyatoshynskyi district every day, and by the time I got there I was sick to death of having to listen to monstrous, bloody-minded conversations on the way."

French historian Thomas Chopard was able to study the archives of the Kyiv Cheka. His book *Le Martyre de Kiev* (Kyiv's martyrdom) illuminates the spiral of violence operating on all sides. The city's population was hostage to guerrilla warfare, anti-Semitic persecutions, and health crises. In giving voice to witnesses, Chopard traces the confrontations raging in Ukraine during the years of the Civil War—an earthquake that shook all Russia, but whose epicenter was Kyiv. The city would lose a third of its inhabitants. Between 1918 and 1922 Kyiv would go through some twenty governments, and each time a new regime took power, a new chapter of reprisals would begin. The dictatorship of the proletariat, which made every bourgeois responsible for all the evils of war, would be followed by anti-Semitic violence that considered every Jew to be a Bolshevik. Cheka summary executions would be succeeded by mass killings of "revolutionaries" and the blind savagery of pogroms.

The Cheka rolled into town in Red Army train cars in February 1919 and moved into the governor's former mansion at 5 Sadovaya Street. This was the heart of Kyiv's old linden-tree neighborhood, and it still has government and ministry buildings today. On the same street, Ilya Ehrenburg and Osip Mandelstam had found work with Kyiv's social security services, in an artistic education institute for "moficient" (so-called morally deficient) children, a neologism that included juvenile delinquents and "children with problems." The moficient institute was in a town house next to that of the Cheka. Only a fence separated the writers from the Chekists. On one side, people were taught. On the other, they were charged, interrogated, and tortured.

Kyiv was surrounded by all sorts of armed groups, and while strategists discussed whether Petlyura or Denikin's army would enter the city first, Ehrenburg says the writers worked at their "projects." They discussed the date to deliver the third volume of Chekhov's works to the printer, the best place to erect a monument to the glory of the Revolution, the assignment of tasks among artists charged with decorating the streets. They held conferences on Marxism and delivered safe conducts and certificates.

Martin Latsis was the head of the Ukrainian Cheka, and is known as a hard case. But he mainly was a thinker who tried to put into practice what European theoreticians of the transition to socialism had called "the dictatorship of the proletariat." The expression is credited to Marx, who sometimes used it, but it was actually coined by a Frenchman, Louis Auguste Blanqui. Latsis translated it literally. In a December article in *Pravda*, he wrote: "Don't bother finding incriminating evidence to prove that a prisoner had participated in a rebellion against the Soviet government by speech or deed. Just ask him what class he belonged to, and about his origins, his education, his profession." "In those days," writes Chopard, "Latsis understood the liquidation of the bourgeoisie as a class to mean the liquidation of the bourgeois themselves." Lenin reproached Latsis for this, writing on June 4, 1919: "The Cheka brought a multitude of evils with it to Ukraine, establishing itself too soon and admitting a number of parasites into its ranks." To which Latsis answered: "You press me to purge the Cheka, but I have been doing that since my first day at work. All our problems are due to the fact that we don't have anything to build on." Regretting the impossibility of ending summary executions, he confessed his impotence: "Death has already become much too common."

On August 31, Petlyura's nationalists and Denikin's Volunteer Army both entered Kyiv. Before pulling out, the Cheka shot the hostages it was holding. The cellars where they had tortured and killed were overflowing with corpses. Nadezhda Mandelstam remembers looking out the window and seeing a horse-drawn cart full of naked bodies being driven out of town. "They were crudely covered with a canvas tarp, and the arms and legs of the dead stuck out on all sides."

The Cheka's summary executions were followed by mass massacres and pogroms committed by the Whites and Petlyura's nationalists. "The week of October 14–20, 1919, was the apogee of collective violence," writes Chopard. "In the following days, 488 bodies were counted; with those thrown into the river, at least six hundred Jews died in a week."

A woman witness gave this account: "We hunted the Reds down. We killed a lot of them. First we threatened the sailors. Those idiots stayed where they were. 'We're on the water,' they said, 'we can live with the Whites too.' Everything went well. We dragged them to the other side of the pier and made them dig a ditch. Then we lined them up at the edge of the ditch and shot them one by one with a revolver. The bodies fell directly into the ditch. It was unbelievable. They twitched like crayfish down there until we filled the ditch. And even later, the ground kept moving."

Testimony by a Kyiv inhabitant also quoted by Chopard: "A young lieutenant in uniform was guarding the room where I was. He was particularly courteous, wore a well-cut coat, and had the manners of a gentleman, dropping French words into his speech. As he carefully searched a girl who was shaking with terror, he reassured her: 'Don't worry, miss.' He took the rings, earrings, and other jewelry she tremblingly held out to him, and gallantly thanked her. His job done, he sat down, waiting for his companions to finish 'working' in the other rooms. Then he took out a file and started doing his nails."

Notes historian Orlando Figes: "Shulgin, a fervent anti-Semite, confessed that he was bothered by the mood of medieval terror that reigned in the streets, and that the 'terrifying screaming' of 'yids' in the night was 'heartbreaking.'"

The writer Ilya Ehrenburg remembers: "In 1919, the executioners hadn't yet come up with the idea of gas chambers. The cruelties then were quite rudimentary: carving a Star of David into a forehead, raping a little girl, tossing a baby from a window."

Kyiv, spring of 1919. In the old linden-tree neighborhood, a pair of lovers are chatting on the first-floor balcony of the Continental Hotel. A stone's throw from the cellars where the Cheka used to torture and kill, love has bloomed. The man wrote his first happy line of poetry in a long time: "A fresh breeze blew, from a young girl's rounded brow..."

Suddenly a cavalcade sweeps down Nikolayev Street. At its head is a rider wrapped in a black cloak, followed by his mounted escort. As he approaches, the horseman looks up and, seeing the couple, turns around in his saddle and aims his Browning at them. The man on the balcony instinctively recoils, but then catches himself. Recognizing the rider, he leans over the edge of the balcony and gives him a big wave. All this lasts only a few seconds, "less time that it takes to tell it."

The rider in the black cloak was Blumkin, "the man who shot Mirbach." This was his first public reappearance in the archives since the attack on the German ambassador on July 6, 1918. The couple on the balcony watching them pass? Nadezhda Khazina and Osip Mandelstam. She was a beaux arts student in the studio of Alexandra Exter, one of the most notable artists in the Constructivist movement, who would immigrate to Paris in 1924. Nadezhda described herself as "spontaneous and always looking for provocation, which corresponded to the spirit of the age; definitely on the side of the Revolution, hungry for adventure, with a strong appetite for life and a great thirst for change." She was nineteen and had just discovered love in the poet's arms. Mandelstam was nine years older than her and had reached Kyiv only a few weeks earlier. Nadezhda and Osip barely knew each other. They met on May 1 at Khlam, the celebrated cabaret in the basement of the hotel where Osip had a room. Kyiv's artistic bohemia would gather there in the evening while the sound of gunfire echoed around the Ukrainian capital.

In a 1973 interview, Nadezhda spoke candidly about that initial encounter, when she and Osip slept together that first night. "It simply happened," said the old lady in English with an irresistible Russian accent.

Nadezhda Mandelstam's stories usually deserve to be taken on faith. Hadn't she often railed against the lies that émigrés to the West told, embroidering their recollections to please gullible readers? But the balcony scene is hard to believe. When I shared my doubts with Thomas Chopard, he agreed. The pairing of the cavalcade with the black cape struck him as highly unlikely, for two reasons: One, there weren't any horses in Kyiv at that period; the Chekists traveled by car. Two, Blumkin's black cape wasn't part of a Chekist wardrobe. Archival photographs always show them in their famous leather coats, or wearing suits and ties when working in an office. The black cape was closer to the dandy's costumes worn by his Imaginist friends than to a Cheka uniform. But who really knows?

Osip Mandelstam was repulsed by terror and violence in general but not because he was a frail poet, as was often said, or because poetry would be naturally opposed to terror. It was because Mandelstam himself, frail poet though he was, had felt the lure of terror. According to his wife, he bought and read many books and brochures devoted to terrorism. Indeed, the poet was fascinated by it.

As a teenager, Mandelstam had tried to join the Left SR's Combat Organization. In *The Noise of Time*, he describes a trip to Finland where he went to a remote dacha in Raivola to sign up. In the book, he remembers that adolescent voyage: "The wet wings of glory strike at the window... The midnight sun in a Finland blind with rain... *War and Peace* lived on— only the glory had moved elsewhere... Glory was in the Central Committee, glory was in the 'fighting organization,' and feats of valor began with a novitiate as a propagandist." But Mandelstam was too young, and they turned him away.

"I was troubled and anxious. All the agitation of the times communicated itself to me. There were strange currents loosed about me—from the longing for suicide to the expectation of the end of the world." In 1905, he wrote, boys were joining the Revolution "with the same feelings as Nikolenka Rostov had on going into the Hussars: it was a question of love and honor. To both, life seemed impossible unless it were warmed by the glory of one's age; both thought it impossible to breathe without valor."

Those young people all projected their desire for intrigue and their quest for glory onto "action." Youth without a story to tell stood on the threshold of the century, champing at the bit. Terrorism offered them a possible narrative; it redeemed their lost biography. Impatient youths were an easy prey for "literati in Russian blouses and black shirts [who] traded, like grain dealers, in God and the Devil." All of provincial Russia, all of the schoolchildren, was consumed with sympathy. "The 'periphery' seethed with novels."

CHAPTER

7

Since killing Count Mirbach a year earlier,
Blumkin had disappeared. To appease the Germans, they were told he'd been executed. In fact, he
was allowed to slip away to Ukraine to carry out clandestine operations behind White Army lines. His
daring gesture had turned the seventeen-year-old
terrorist into a patriotic legend. So when he reappeared at the Poets' Café on Tverskaya Street one
evening in July 1919, people couldn't believe their
eyes. They'd thought him dead, yet there he was
standing among them, covered with scars, like some
sort of Bolshevik Christ. People examined him,
touched him. Having heard the rumor, a clutch of
Chekists in their leather coats gathered at the door.

When the poet Mayakovsky saw him come in, he
interrupted himself and thundered ("We Will Proclaim a New Myth"):

No more literature, no more cant!
Shut up, you orators.
The floor is yours,
Comrade Mauser!

Looming over Blumkin by a couple of heads, Mayakovsky embraced him, stroking his head and affectionately calling him "Blumochka." Then he picked him up ("To raise up a man, he makes him a Mayakovsky," Trotsky quipped) and leaped onto the stage. There, he plopped "Blumochka" down and shouted, "Comrades, here is 'Zhivoi'! He's alive!"

Futurists threw their caps and top hats in the air; others shot out the chandeliers in a tinkling of glass. People drank more than usual that evening, and Blumkin was celebrated as he never had been before, and probably never would be again. He was the hero who had come to satisfy a crowd hungry for romantic adventures, the survivor who had looked death in the face. A long scar running from his skull to his gap-toothed mouth testified to the ordeals he had undergone.

"Death didn't want me," he told his friends gathered around the table. After a pause, he added theatrically: "Every Jew has nine lives. As long as I haven't lived them, I can't die! There's no point in trying to kill me!"

I don't know where the variation of a saying about Jews that is usually ascribed to cats came from, but under the effects of alcohol, nobody contradicted him. But whether about cat or Jew, Blumkin's nine lives metaphor is very useful for putting some order in his tangled biography.

Blumkin's first life was his childhood in Odessa, caught between the social misfortune of being from a poor Moldavanka family, the 1905 pogroms, and the death of his father when he was six. It was also learning from Mendele Mocher Sforim, the grandfather of Yiddish literature. Call it a fable of the awakening of Jewish consciousness.

His second life was the school of the streets. Mensheviks, Bolsheviks, People's Will populists, and SRs clashing in the harbor's Greek bistros. At home, his brother was an anarchist and his sister, a Social Democrat. Between the two, Blumkin chose the Socialist Revolutionaries. An awakening of social consciousness.

Blumkin's third life was war, and meeting "Mike the Jap," who inspired Isaac Babel to create Benya Krik, the king of Odessa's gangsters. Blumkin also encountered Odessa's literary elite, Jewish self-defense groups, poetry, war, literary cafés, and Moldavanka's criminal underworld. An apprenticeship in violence and bravery, the awakening of a political consciousness.

His fourth life began with the October Revolution. The young Chekist prepared the attack on Mirbach while spending his nights at the Poets' Café. Here, the themes of his three earlier lives coalesced. Jewish, social, and political consciousness all merged to inspire an act that transgressed the prohibition against killing. The terrorism stage.

In his fifth life, Blumkin went underground. Living as a fugitive, he wandered from Petrograd to Kyiv, crossed a Ukraine ravaged by the Civil War, dodged White, Green, and Black armies, going through a kind of purgatory. And finally a conversion to Bolshevism and forgiveness not by a rabbi, but by a soldier-monk, the head of the Red Army.

Which brings us to the threshold of his sixth life.

During the second half of 1919, Blumkin was a member of the small group of advisers that accompanied Trotsky in his armored train. He made himself invaluable, taking every available task: from organizing the train's security to writing and printing its newspaper, from leading espionage missions in enemy territory to translating and encoding information. On some evenings Trotsky would call him to dictate a note for the Politburo or a few pages for a theoretical essay he was writing. During the few calm moments of the war, they would talk poetry: Baudelaire, Esenin, Mayakovsky. Blumkin would occasionally suggest a nighttime sortie with his fellow fighters. Trotsky agreed, while urging caution and specifying the time for them to be back. On those nights, you would hear explosions behind enemy lines: a bridge had been blown up, an ammunition dump was ablaze, a telegraph network or a

telephone exchange demolished. All bore the hall-
marks of Blumkin and his comrades, who trudged
home at dawn like drunken sailors after a night of
shore leave. As always, steam was up in the locomotive. The train would take off, quickly vanishing
into the darkness.

Trotsky's train was no mere convoy for inspection
trips. It was the Red Army's mobile headquarters, a
propaganda train, and a combat unit that carried
a store of matériel and one or two cars of machine
guns—the only cars that were armored, along with
the two locomotives. When it stopped, one of the
two engines would be used for quick side trips. The
other one was always kept under steam. The walls of
the cars had been lined with steel plates, and sand-
bags stacked in the windows. Dozens of sharpshooters manned the machine-gun nests on the car roofs
around the clock. The train carried rifles, machine
guns, and grenades. Several cars had been turned
into garages, including a gasoline tank car with a
number of trucks and small cars. These could carry
a team of twenty to thirty men, including riflemen
and machine gunners, on reconnaissance missions.
That way, they could travel away from the tracks
and go deep into the countryside. The train was
equipped with a recreation room, a galley, and a car
stocked with spare food and clothing. It had everything needed to sustain some fifty fighting men
whose leather coats, said Trotsky, gave them heft
and made them look imposing.

The train organized the troops, educated often-illiterate soldiers, tried deserters, and resupplied the army, though ammunition was always in short supply. The Red Army had no reserves. "Shirts were sent to the front direct from the workshop," wrote Trotsky in *My Life*.

> *Out of bands of irregulars, of refugees escaping from the Whites, of peasants mobilized in the neighboring districts, of detachments of workers sent by the industrial centers, of groups of communists and trades-unionists—out of these we formed at the front companies, battalions, new regiments, and sometimes even entire divisions . . . We were constructing an army all over again, and under fire at that . . . on all the fronts.*

The train was also a mobile government unit with its own means of communication: a telegraph station, a printing press, and a radio station with a tall antenna that was raised on the roof during long stops. In this way, it could receive not only Radio Moscow but also a dozen European broadcasts (including from the Eiffel Tower) and stay informed of day-to-day developments of events in the world. *En Route*, the train's daily newspaper, reprinted and editorialized on dispatches from the four corners of the world. People communicated from one train car to the next by telephone and visual signals. In war zones where information was sketchy and hard to get, or where radio and telegraph equipment was lacking, the train was "a messenger from other worlds."

Trotsky had the tsarist railway minister's private car remodeled for his personal use. A long table ran the length of the compartment. A map of Russia hung—and swayed—above it. A wide variety of books filled the shelves of a big bookcase: encyclopedias, technical works, novels, even collections of poetry in several languages. You could find both Antonio Labriola's *Essays on the Materialist Conception of History* and Mallarmé's *Vers et Prose* in the Perrin edition with the blue cover.

In his train car, Trotsky received military and local civilian authorities, read telegrams, and dictated orders and articles. With war raging and the train crossing steppes and deserts, stenographers took dictation from him in shifts, day and night. "In those years I accustomed myself to writing and thinking to the accompaniment of Pullman wheels and springs," he wrote.

In the Civil War, the train soon became legendary. It was credited with the success of the Red Army and ascribed quasi-supernatural powers. The train was worshipped like a god of war, and its saga told as if about a hero. It was awarded the Order of the Red Banner for its part in fighting White leader Nikolai Yudenich. Lenin claimed that the train's appearing at the front had a magical effect on the soldiers and the army as a whole. Diplomat Alexander Barmine wrote of "the surge of energy it brought everywhere in tragic moments." A situation that had been catastrophic the night before was suddenly and miraculously resolved with the train's arrival. The pages that Trotsky devotes to the train in his autobiography bear witness to the popular infatuation with this magical train. He writes as if it were a living being: "Sometimes the train was cut off and shelled or bombed from the air. No wonder it was surrounded by a legend woven of victories both real and imagined." Word that the train was coming galvanized Russian soldiers. "The news of the arrival of the train would reach the enemy lines as well. There people imagined a mysterious train infinitely more awful than it really was... The train earned the hatred of its enemies and was proud of it."

After the end of the Civil War, an exposition was organized in the train's honor that drew many visitors, according to the newspapers. Trotsky asked Blumkin to arrange it, but it may have been Blumkin's own idea. He gathered all the documents connected to the train's history: posters, proclamations, orders, flyers, photographs, films, books, speeches, etc. The train was displayed in a huge hall, and visitors could walk through the cars in small groups. The great antenna that allowed the train to connect with the rest of the country and the world was raised on the roof. On the sides of one car, instead of destination signs, a diagram was painted that showed the trips the train had made during the war. It had covered a distance equal to five and a half times around the world: Samara, Chelyabinsk, Vyatka, Petrograd, Balashov, Smolensk, back to Samara, Rostov, Novecherkassk, Kyiv, Zhyrovyr . . .

In the Russian Civil War, 1919 was a pivotal year. For the first six months, White Armies encircled the Soviets' republic, threatening Petrograd and Moscow. Fighting had destroyed the country's industrial infrastructure. Natural resources were drying up, and the occupation of Baku deprived the Bolsheviks of the oil that is essential to a wartime army. The cars that Bolshevik commissars drove ran on a mix of turpentine and alcohol. Lacking kerosene, airplanes filled up with a pharmaceutical mixture concocted by chemical engineers. Pistons and connecting rods were lubricated with castor and cotton oils. Marine diesel fuel was rationed, and steam engines were fed dead fish and animal carcasses.

The White Armies led by Denikin, Kolchak, Yudenich, and Wrangel were gaining ground everywhere, backed by the French in the south and west, and by the English in the north and the Urals. The French supported Pilsudski's Polish troops and Denikin's army in the Caucasus and the Black Sea coast. The British supported Yudenich and Kolchak in the Urals. Denikin's soldiers occupied Baku. The Reds lost Kharkov on June 24, and Ekaterinoslav on June 27. Tsaritsyn (the future Stalingrad, the "Red Verdun") fell under pressure from British artillery and air strikes.

Denikin launched the White Armies' big offensive on July 3, making no secret of his objective. "We were already choosing which horses we would ride for our triumphant entrance into Moscow," remembers a British lieutenant who served under Denikin.

The intervention by Allied armies in Russia would reach its greatest intensity in 1919. By the summer, few people were betting on Lenin's survival. Newspapers in New York, London, and Paris announced Red Army defeats daily. Whether true or not, the reports lent credence to the promise of an imminent victory over Bolshevism.

Every Western government had its wartime hawks, but Winston Churchill, the United Kingdom's young secretary of state for war, was one of its most rabid. Even Prime Minister Lloyd George was concerned: "He is obsessed by Bolshevism, and absolutely wants to go fight in Russia." The British press, most of which opposed intervention, spoke of "Mr. Churchill's personal war." But Winston stuck to his guns. To the prime minister, who listened with alarm, he declared, "Of all the tyrannies in history, the Bolshevist tyranny is the worst, the most destructive, and the most degrading." In the House of Commons he proclaimed, "Bolshevism is not a policy; it is a disease... Civilization is being completely extinguished over gigantic areas, while Bolsheviks hop and caper like troops of ferocious baboons amid the ruins of their cities and the corpses of their victims." He called them "a league of failures, the criminals, the morbid, the deranged and the distraught" . . . sustained by "typhus-bearing vermin."

In fighting that "vermin," Churchill wanted to pull out all the stops. Researchers at the Porton Down military laboratory had just perfected a secret weapon dubbed Device M: a shell that released a toxic gas derived from arsenic when it exploded. It was intended for use against the rebellious tribes of northern India. The general in charge of its development called it "the most effective chemical weapon ever devised."

Many voices in His Majesty's government were raised against using such a barbarous weapon in Russia, either on principle or for fear of public reaction if word got out. Churchill was unmoved. "I am strongly in favor of using poisoned gas against uncivilized tribes," he declared in one secret memorandum. "Why is it not fair for a British artilleryman to fire a shell which makes the said native sneeze? It is really too silly."

On August 27, 1919, British air strikes began against the garrison in Yemtsa south of Archangel, in Russia's northern forests. Reported a survivor: "Not knowing what it was, ground troops ran in the cloud. Some died before they managed to get out, others staggered a few more steps, then fell down dead." According to a medical report, soldiers were seized by dizziness, bleeding from the nose and ears, then vomiting blood and suffocating. The air offensive continued for all of September. The War

Ministry reported that 2,718 Device Ms were used against Bolshevik positions. One village was hit by 183 toxic gas shells. When chemical warfare was finally abandoned, some fifty thousand unused shells remained. Because they were too dangerous to transport, they were thrown overboard in the White Sea. They remain on the seabed, 240 feet down.

But as 1919 drew to a close, the fighting finally turned to the Bolsheviks' advantage. In October, Yudenich was driven from the outskirts of Petrograd. By November, Denikin's army was in retreat. Kolchak evacuated Siberia. At the end of November, Ukraine and the southern provinces of European Russia were liberated. The Red Army retook Kharkov, Kyiv, and Rostov. The Whites were chased out of Astrakhan. The French departed Odessa for good. Churchill was out of favor, and Lloyd George put an end to British intervention, choosing to negotiate with the Bolsheviks instead.

Directed from Trotsky's armored train, the Red Army now went on the offensive on every front. It was during 1920, the last year of the Civil War, that the trips were the most risky, and most often directed to the southern front, which was the most persistent and most dangerous.

In the summer of 1919, Trotsky had an insight of genius: the path of world revolution leads east. In his armored train, he started hatching all sorts of plans. Late into the night, he dictated to Blumkin notes that showed an ambition worthy of Napoleon. Trotsky wanted to create an industrial basis in the Urals to make the Soviets independent of the strategically vulnerable Donets Basin; open a revolutionary academy in the Urals or Turkestan in order to train military leaders to direct the struggle in Asia along with technicians, planners, linguists, and other specialists. A "serious military man" suggested a plan to Trotsky for the formation of an expeditionary cavalry corps to serve in India. Blumkin edited as he took dictation, suggesting this or that measure, such as the creation of a Red Army in Azerbaijan. When Trotsky went to rest in his cabin, Blumkin carefully encoded the secret memorandum before transmitting it to the Politburo in Moscow.

Trotsky was asking for a "radical reorientation" of Soviet foreign policy. Up to then, the Bolsheviks had hoped and waited for the workers' movements in Europe to pick up the revolutionary torch. And events seemed to be proving them right. In Britain's Clyde region, more than a hundred thousand workers went on strike in January 1919. In March, after a series of strikes, worker councils seized power in Hungary. In Poland, the Dombrowa miners did the same. Other attempts occurred in Austria and in Switzerland; they would be brutally repressed.

The secret memorandum that Blumkin encoded read as follows: "There is no doubt that our Red Army is an incomparably more powerful force in the Asian terrain than the European one. There, we have a clear possibility of deploying our activity, instead of a long and tedious wait to see how things evolve in Europe."

This line of thought wasn't firmly rooted in Trotsky's own mind, wrote his biographer Isaac Deutscher. "It came as an impetuous reflex of his own brain in response to an exceptional set of circumstances." But Deutscher failed to note that this reflex was shaped by Trotsky's contact with a generation of young Bolshevik commissars who were fascinated by the East. For someone like Blumkin, Persia was the gateway to Asia. It opened the way to India and China, but also to the Middle East, Europe, Palestine, and Mesopotamia. In his imagination, Blumkin could see himself as a Bolshevik Lawrence of Arabia in a long white tunic, riding a camel through the desert, bivouacking in oases and taking sleeping cities by storm. This thinking didn't reflect only geopolitics or ideology, but an intellectual climate. Poets like Esenin and Khlebnikov and painters like Yakulov all shared this Orientalist inclination.

The "Orientalization" of Bolshevism's political and intellectual climate would prove to be a stroke of genius. Writes Deutscher: "The road of the revolution to Peking and Shanghai, if not to Calcutta and Bombay, was to prove shorter than that to Paris and London, and certainly easier than the road to Berlin or even to Budapest."

And on that road lay Persia—and Gilan.

CHAPTER

8

"'My Persian tale'? There were a few hundred of us ragged Russians down there...One day we had a telegram from the Central Committee: 'Cut your losses, revolution in Iran now off.'...But for that we would have got to Tehran."

For a long time, those few lines that Victor Serge quotes in his *Memoirs of a Revolutionary* were all I had to go on in tracing Blumkin's footsteps in Persia. Four months of combat and political intrigues summed up in just four sentences, about forty words—the only thread connecting me to him. A slender thread, but a reliable one. As far as I know, Victor Serge has never been shown to be mistaken, even after the Soviet archives were opened in the 1990s. "Blumkin then lived next door to Chicherin in a freezing room at the Metropol," he wrote. "In 1920–21 he was sent to

Persia to start a revolution in Gilan on the Caspian coast with Kuchek Khan."

But Serge interrupted Blumkin's account in two places, indicated by those ellipses. They covered a part of the intrigue I was trying to figure out. What could Blumkin have told him? I couldn't imagine Serge censoring important information about the expedition to Persia. As it turned out, the reason for those cuts was purely literary. The passage was part of a long portrait, a kind of elegiac biography, a register that excludes digressions, and in which wanderings and intrigues are secondary. In writing it, Serge was concerned with just one thing, "that this powerful figure of a warrior not be forgotten." Serge had been my ally from the very beginning of the Blumkin Project, for years the best source I had.

In Moscow, I booked a room at the Metropol. At the front desk, I didn't ask for Blumkin's room, since obviously no one would remember him, but for the room next to the one that had been occupied by the celebrated Georgy Chicherin. The name of the former Soviet foreign affairs commissar appears in the hotel's guest book. I knew that Blumkin had been in the room right next to his, so I had a fifty-fifty chance of being in the right one. I could then describe the scene of the meeting between Blumkin and Serge in the Metropol's "freezing" hotel room, and maybe even re-create snatches of their conversation.

It was a waste of effort. The hotel had been completely renovated and seemed to have lost even the memory of its revolutionary period. Walls may have ears, but rooms have no memory. It was pointless to imagine Blumkin and Serge in these luxurious, well-heated and richly furnished rooms. When the Bolsheviks first requisitioned the hotel, its rooms were open to the four winds, panes were missing from the windows, and people slept wrapped in heavy army coats. We always ascribe more to places than they can deliver. Most of the time their indifference to the past disappoints us. Like servants accustomed to changing households, they devote themselves to their new masters.

But books are less forgetful than hotels; they retain the living evidence of those they have sheltered. To track Blumkin, I would do better to rely on Serge's *Memoirs*. I knew entire passages of it by heart. I had even picked up some of his language tics, along with the rhythm and construction of his sentences. At times, when I reread my old notebooks, I couldn't tell my sentences from his. The ellipses he had inserted in the Blumkin account inspired me more than the Metropol's drapery and Italian chandeliers. They opened (and closed) doors to barely glimpsed landscapes. They were like collapsed walls whose trace remains on an archaeological site. Broken columns whose aligned pediments let us imagine the capital they once supported.

In 1919, Persia was no longer Alexander's or Genghis Khan's Persia, but it hadn't yet become Iran. Russia wasn't quite itself either. The tsar's empire had sunk with all hands in the shipwreck of the war, and as 1919 began, nobody gave the Bolsheviks much of a chance as they lost ground to White Armies sustained by the occupying power of fourteen nations. Great Britain was marking time. It was in the victors' camp, of course, and its colonial empire was intact, but it doubted itself. It was threatened within by spreading strikes, and led by a government split between supporters and opponents of military intervention in Russia. It seemed "psychologically paralyzed," as Correlli Barnett wrote in *The Collapse of British Power.*

The shadow cast by empires across the world map was breaking up. War had shifted the tectonic plates of power, opening faults and creating collision zones that shattered the lines of settled frontiers. The German, Russian, Austro-Hungarian, and Ottoman Empires had been dismembered, and their conquerors were divvying up the remains. Nations were being erased from the map as others appeared. Syria, Iraq, and Transjordan rose from the ruins of the Ottoman Empire. A Jewish homeland was recognized in Palestine under British mandate. In places where the aftershocks from the upheaval of World War I were still being felt, entire zones remained unattributed, to be decided later by revolution or war. One of these was Persia.

Located at the edges of the Russian and British Empires' zones of influence, Persia had been the theater of confrontations between the two powers since the start of the nineteenth century. The Russians coveted the road to the Persian Gulf and the Indian Ocean. The British were determined to keep control of commercial land and sea routes to India. This was what Rudyard Kipling called "the Great Game" in his 1901 novel, *Kim*.

The new age of oil now complicated the deal. In 1901 Russia produced 233,000 barrels a day, compared with 190,000 for the United States. With more than 3,400 wells, Baku was the planet's principal oil-producing region, pumping half of the world's crude. Though rich in coal, Britain totally lacked any petroleum resources at a time when oil was becoming the key to world power. It imported more Russian oil than American. If Britain wanted to maintain its dominant role in the world through its fleet, it needed to control its own oil. So Persia, where oil had just been discovered, became a major focus of British strategists. No need to launch an expensive war of conquest, they reasoned, when you could gain mastery of the oil by paying off the local authorities. In 1901, William Knox D'Arcy acquired exploration rights to a territory twice the size of Texas from the Kajars, the corrupt dynasty reigning in Tehran. The sixty-year concession was a major trump card for the Crown in its domination of Central Asia. The first wells were drilled in 1908. A year earlier, the Russians and the English had signed the Anglo-Russian Convention, which divided Iran into two zones of influence, with Russia in the north and Great Britain in the south. This ended a century of conflict, temporarily suspending the Great Game.

The October Revolution and the Russian Civil War reshuffled the deck. Russia and England, who had been allies until 1918, now clashed again. But Russia, caught in the chaos of civil war, had other concerns than conquering territories—it first had to preserve its own. So Persia became a de facto British protectorate. For the Russians, this meant starting all over again.

By early 1920, the Civil War was ending. Nikolai Yudenich, the White general who got so close to Petrograd that he could see its glittering domes and spires, was driven back to the Baltic countries, where he booked a train ticket for Paris and abandoned his army to its fate. The Whites and the English were driven out of Archangel, which they had blanketed with Churchill's poison gas. Defeated in Siberia, Kolchak was arrested and executed by firing squad. His corpse was thrown in the Angara River, where it sank under the ice. On the same day, the Bolsheviks triumphantly entered Odessa, occupied the Don and Kuban, and signed an armistice with Estonia.

In February 1920, the Bolsheviks occupied Krasnovodsk in Turkmenistan. In April, the British were driven out of Baku. On April 15, the Azerbaijan government fell to local Bolsheviks. The Revolution was going from strength to strength.

A "Red Persian Army" was assembled in Tashkent, the capital of Uzbekistan. Victor Serge described it as "two to three thousand partisans chosen from among soldiers who had fought in the Russian Civil War, many of whom didn't speak the country's language." It was neither an international brigade nor an army of Persians in exile; it was a Russian militia infiltrating Persian territory. In the spring, Fyodor Raskolnikov, who commanded the Volga-Caspian flotilla, was in Astrakhan, scoring a series of crucial victories north of the Caucasus. He left Astrakhan to celebrate the new Soviet republic and entered Baku on May 1. Denikin's White Fleet fled across the Caspian with the British. The Soviet fleet pursued them, crossing the Caspian north of Persia in turn. On May 17 it encircled the port of Anzali.

Gilan lies on the border between Russia and Persia, a narrow band between the Caspian Sea and the Elburz mountain range stretching from the border of Azerbaijan in the northwest to the borders of Turkmenistan and Afghanistan in the east. One of Iran's twelve old provinces, Gilan borders two empires, making it the Alsace-Lorraine of the Russo-Persian conflict. On a map of Iran, Gilan is shaped like a comma. But this comma is in just the right place, between the Caspian Sea and Persia, on the Tehran-Baku commercial route. In the early 1920s, that comma nearly changed the course of Iranian history.

At the time, the port of Anzali was the only access to Baku; the coastal road that would be built later didn't exist yet. In the north, Anzali was the linchpin that opened the way to Baku's oil. In the south, it gave access to Tehran, the capital. The linchpin was surrounded by dense beech and chestnut forests, and dominated by the high plateaus of the Elburz range, which rise to 18,250 feet. In his wartime diary British general Lionel Dunsterville marveled at the variety of plant species he encountered in Gilan, describing river-laced mountainsides with "primrose, scented violets, snowdrops, and strawberries in quantities." When you descended toward the Caspian, he noted, the land turned boggy, and green with rice fields.

Four actors battled over this narrow strip of land: London, Moscow, Tehran, and the Jangali ("forest warriors") liberation movement led by Kuchek Khan, who intended to rid Persia of the other three. But those actors were themselves divided.

The British government was split between the supporters of Prime Minister Lloyd George and those of his fire-breathing secretary of state for war, Winston Churchill. The first wanted to turn the page on the Civil War and sign a commercial agreement with Russia. The second hadn't given up on confronting the Red Army, and pursued military interference on various Russian fronts.

The Soviet government was even more divided, between the supporters of a western offensive through Poland and those who wanted to consolidate the Revolution in the east. The first were led by Lenin and Stalin, the second inspired by Trotsky. The Bolsheviks on the ground were divided between "reformers," who supported the Jangalis' nationalist line, and "radicals," who pushed for a true communist revolution.

Churchill feared Bolshevik contagion in Persia. Lloyd George was frightened by Churchill's anti-Bolshevik passion. Lenin distrusted Lloyd George, who in turn doubted Lenin's peaceful intentions. Kuchek Khan didn't trust the Bolsheviks, who returned the favor. The Jangalis were divided among those who, like their leader, wanted to consolidate a revolution in Gilan based on an alliance between merchants and peasants, and those who wanted to make a communist revolution and march on Tehran.

In the capital, Ahmad Shah, the last sovereign of the Kajar dynasty, was in the twilight of a rule marked by the growing power of army chief Reza Khan, who would seize power in a coup d'état in the night of February 20–21, 1921.

Four actors, but with at least eight factions with opposing interests and strategies tugging every which way.

In the spring of 1920, the situation abruptly became simpler. The Soviets entered the port of Anzali and drove out the British and Denikin's troops. A Soviet socialist republic was declared at Rasht, the capital of Gilan. The weakened central government in Tehran didn't object. This republic would survive for a year and a half before falling apart under the combined pressure of a London-Moscow-Tehran triad. At the heart of the Persian imbroglio, two men would play a central role and influence the course of events: Yakov Blumkin and Kuchek Khan. Blumkin headed the so-called Red Persian Army assembled in Tashkent. Kuchek Khan led an army of a few hundred partisans in the Gilan forests. Coming from Azerbaijan, the Red Army crossed over the border into Persia as the partisans hurried to meet them on the Elburz plateau.

The whole affair was straight out of a Hollywood screenplay, a geopolitical mare's nest brought to life and incarnated by two heroic figures: the secret agent and the guerrilla, archetypes that would enduringly dominate the twentieth-century imagination. Blumkin spent about four months in Iran, from the spring to mid-August 1920. Some question remains about the exact nature of his mission. Was it a simple information-gathering survey or a clandestine military operation? How often does an intelligence officer show up with a thousand-man army? What is certain is that his engagement at the side of the Gilan revolutionaries went well beyond his initial assignment.

In his autobiography, Blumkin tells how he directed the defense of Anzali while sick with typhus, running a high fever and suffering splitting headaches. Comrades described him giving orders in a typhus-induced fog, his face flushed with fever, pointing out some strategic point on the map in a kind of haze. The next day he was seen walking Anzali's muddy streets, which were crowded with camels and decked out with yellow roses. Others saw him riding horseback through empty bazaar alleys, setting fire to merchants' stalls and caravansary stables.

The local communists disclaimed the attack, but the identity of the man giving orders was in no doubt. Blumkin was Trotsky's special emissary, and his instructions were clear: "No military intervention under the Russian flag. No dispatching a Russian expeditionary corps. We must absolutely stress our nonintervention, underlining Moscow's demand that Russian troops and the Red fleet be withdrawn from Anzali, so as to avoid arousing suspicions about our ambition for conquest." It's not surprising that Blumkin's assignment in Persia was surrounded by mystery. It was one of those black ops designed to leave no trace—the secret services' stock in trade.

In short, the premises were confused and the actors conflicted, while events unfolded in their own way, defying the scriptwriter's demands. The outcome would be a complete mess.

Confirmation of Blumkin's mission order in Persia would await the opening of the foreign affairs commissariat archives in the 1990s. A letter by L. M. Karakhan, Chicherin's deputy, dated July 17, 1920, states: "In response to the request by Kuchek Khan, relayed by Comrade Raskolnikov, to be sent competent revolutionaries as counselors in building socialism, we are dispatching Comrade Blumkin, in whom we have total confidence."

So Blumkin had been sent to Gilan supposedly as an expert to help Kuchek Khan build socialism in Persia. That's absurd, because Kuchek Khan had absolutely no intention of building socialism; quite the contrary. Nor did the Bolsheviks have any illusions about the nature of the revolution underway in Gilan. It was a democratic revolution whose sole aim was to drive out foreign invaders and establish democratic rule in Tehran. In fact, one of the heads of the Gilan operation, Comrade Sergo Ordzhonikidze, made that perfectly clear: "We knew that there was no proletariat in Persia, and the peasantry were ignorant, downtrodden, and passive." Kuchek Khan's was a movement of national liberation that expressed the interests of the commercial middle class.

What would be the sense of a proletarian revolution without a proletariat? A Soviet republic without soviets? As Blumkin wrote in his first report: "Even if Kuchek Khan and his partisans' support for certain fundamental principles of socialism were proven, the masses that support him are either absent or at most evanescent."

The way was wide open for intrigues: plots, official state lies, and a palace revolution.

At the other end of the spectrum from Blumkin stood Mirza Kuchek Khan (1880–1921)—a hero in spite of himself. He was the first twentieth-century guerrilla, a Persian Che Guevara whose Sierra Maestra cradle and grave were the Elburz Mountains.

Born in 1880 at Rasht, Kuchek Khan—also spelled Kouchik, Koochek, Kuchak, Kuchik, Kouchak, Koochak, and Kuçek—received a traditional religious education completed by theology studies, which he pursued until he was twenty-one. In addition to Arab and Islamic theology, he studied classical Persian poetry; he knew many poems by heart and loved Ferdowsi's *Book of Kings*. Introduced to politics through the Constitutionalist movement that gave Iran its first constitution, he experienced hunger, exile, and prison. Banished from his home city of Rasht, he went underground, seeking refuge in Gilan's mountains and forests. There, he and a few young fighters created the Jangali movement.

During World War I, Kuchek Khan launched guerrilla operations against the British, the Russians, and the corrupt Tehran authorities. The Jangalis were the first of those national liberation movements that would mark the twentieth-century history of decolonization in Africa, the Americas, and Asia.

At the head of a group equipped with a dozen rifles and a few bullets, he attacked Russian troops occupying Gilan. The operation was no more than a mosquito bite for the tsar's soldiers, but word spread that a group of homegrown revolutionaries had gone into action. This was the spark that would fire Kuchek Khan's popularity among a people seething at Russian oppression. All through the war, the Jangalis set multiple ambushes in the Gilan mountains. Despite their small numbers, they were able to launch lightning strikes thanks to real-time information given them by supportive peasants.

One episode of this guerrilla war has become legendary. After fresh troops landed in Anzali, the Russians decided to strike a major blow. They organized an expedition of five hundred heavily armed Cossacks against some sixty Jangalis. But the Jangalis moved through the forest the way fish move through water, and Cossacks were used to operating in the steppes. The Jangalis drew them into the forest, where they ambushed and decimated them. News of their defeat brought jubilation to Gilan inhabitants and fury to the Russians. The Russian consul fomented a plot to assassinate Kuchek Khan. It failed.

Kuchek Khan's contemporaries described him as a tall, athletic man. His face revealed an iron will, "even when he smiled." A biographical portrait drawn by the British intelligence services—which he harried mercilessly—described him as "inconstant" and "suspicious" but recognized his great honesty. He was noted for his courtesy and "enlightened asceticism." An abstemious man, he used neither alcohol nor tobacco, and his secretary claimed he was so shy that he only married two years before his death at forty-one. According to the French military attaché in Tehran, he had a soft, compelling voice and incarnated "an apostolic figure beloved of the peasants, who saw him as a savior."

The qualities in Kuchek Khan most often mentioned are loyalty, tolerance, and moderation. During his entire life, he seems to have been driven only by patriotism and a love of justice. Nothing was lacking in his legend: not courage, or the daring of his fighters in the forest, not even the role of a woman. That would be the brave and beautiful Bolour Khânon. A bold fighter from Manjil, she ambushed some British and Russian troops and relieved them of a supply of munitions, which she gave to Kuchek Khan.

Kuchek Khan hated the spirit of vengeance, and preferred to counsel rather than punish. Some thought he didn't have the boldness required of a revolutionary leader. Victor Serge, who didn't know him personally, was probably relying on Blumkin in describing him as "a very thin man, with glasses, who looked like a European intellectual...I have every reason to believe that he was sincere in his militant idealism. His photographs were long displayed in the museums of the Revolution."

A lover of poetry, Kuchek Khan could recite great swaths of *The Book of Kings*, the longest Persian epic written by a single poet: Ferdowsi, "the reviver of the Persian language." In a biography published in 1920 in the *Revue du monde musulman*, Kuchek Khan is described as "the new prophet in the land of the Jangalis," and "a man of the north: tall, with a long black beard, bright, deep-set eyes, a steely gaze that expresses a will of iron. Kuchek Khan has always been a visionary...A nationalistic dreamer and a poet of freedom and his country." He is said to have learned very young to disdain everything that Western oppression represented.

As a good Muslim, Kuchek Khan always started his day by praying. Awakened at dawn on May 18, 1920, by the sound of Soviet planes bombing Anzali, he invited Blumkin, who had come to inform him of the Bolsheviks' intentions, to join him in prayers. Blumkin, who didn't have a moment to waste, skipped the niceties. He said he never prayed, and that "if you want to be friends with the Bolsheviks you would do well to quit praying." An exchange that didn't augur well for future relations between the Russians and the head of the Jangali rebels.

Yet everything had started so promisingly. For the first time in the history of relations between Russians and Persians—especially in Gilan, a Russian frontier region—their interests converged. Having rid themselves of the White Armies, the Bolsheviks wanted to secure the Caspian Sea coast and the port of Anzali. The Jangalis were glad to see the Bolsheviks drive out the British troops and what was left of the White Army. An alliance of circumstance, certainly, but one that would carry the new partners much further than they could have imagined: the proclamation of an independent, socialist, Soviet republic. There wasn't so much as the shadow of a soviet in Gilan, of course, and the Bolsheviks were under no illusion about the nature of the ongoing revolution.

For his part, Kuchek Khan distrusted the Russians, even when done up in fresh red paint and animated by the best of intentions. He had struggled against the imperial pretensions of this awkward neighbor all his life and wasn't about to hand the reins of his revolution to some new converts. But the situation got away from him, as it got away from the Bolshevik leaders.

On May 17, 1920, the Soviet Caspian fleet commanded by Raskolnikov sailed into the port of Anzali. It had come from Baku, and its mission was to seize the ships of Denikin's forces and secure

Persia's Caspian coast. The idea was to take control of the ships without damaging them. These were tankers that had been converted into warships, and the Bolsheviks urgently needed them to carry oil from Baku.

A group of commandos from Raskolnikov's fleet, perhaps including his wife, Larisa Reisner, planned to steal aboard the ships and take them without firing a shot. Blumkin was part of the group.

Would the failed meeting between Yakov and Larisa suggested in the previous chapter finally happen in Anzali on May 17, 1920? The reader will remember that in June 1918, when Osip Mandelstam told Reisner about his run-in with Blumkin at the Poets' Café, she went to Dzherjinsky to denounce the young Chekist. Nearly two years had now passed. I had been dreaming of the two of them meeting and having it out once and for all. Blumkin, whose ordeals had certainly marked him, would have apologized, blaming the incident on his immaturity. Reisner, who so admired Trotsky, would have easily forgiven his protégé. She would have appreciated Blumkin's courage. He would have been seduced by her culture and beauty. Alas, I have to stick to the facts. Nothing like that happened. And yet the encounter might have happened, without their knowing or realizing it.

At dawn, a team of a dozen fighters with swim fins slipped into the sea and silently headed for the White fleet ships. For obvious reasons of security, the identity of the commandos participating in the operation was kept secret. In particular, no one on the swimming team would be told if Larisa Reisner was along; she would have been an invaluable hostage for the Whites and the British. Blumkin had already changed his name. On land, he had assumed the identity and nationality of one Ehsanollah Khan, a Jangali, but there is no way to know whether he participated in the operation under that name. The team members all spoke Persian, German, and English without an accent. In case of capture, nothing could connect them to Russia. They belonged to those armies without uniforms or flags, directed by shadowy forces and fighting in the name of interests that are no less shadowy. In their wet suits, Yakov Blumkin and Larisa Reisner may have swum through the waters of the port like two shadows, with neither memory nor future, daggers on their hips, preparing to board the ships.

In just one day, the Reds captured all of Denikin's ships, four British torpedo boats, weapons, radios, and transmission material. At seven o'clock the next morning, the cruiser *Rosa Luxemburg* began shelling the British headquarters. Witnesses reported that when the first shells hit the building, the surprise was such that officers ran away in their underwear. They were operating on London time, and for them it was 4:30 a.m. The Brits couldn't imagine that anyone would dare attack at such an early hour. It wasn't even a battle; the British just retreated to the interior. Was it a rout caused by a time difference? Hard to believe. Maybe people opted for this explanation as a way of minimizing the effect of a defeat that permanently damaged the empire's prestige in the region.

According to Raskolnikov, the people of Anzali greeted the Bolsheviks as liberators. Other accounts suggest more muted enthusiasm. The people's joy at seeing the British flee was most likely doubled by the excitement that accompanied the arrival of Kuchek Khan.

In her journal, Larisa Reisner described May 18, 1920, this way:

> *The first marvel that stirred the consciousnesses in Gilan was the defeat of the English. The second was Kuchek Kahn's appearance in Anzali and his visit to the Russian battleship. He was the talk of the town long before his arrival. Merchants left their shops, devout Muslims abandoned their prayer rugs, beggars and the poor gathered, all forming a human mass of thousands. Shoeshine boys stood barefoot on their red boxes for a better view. Beggars took over street corners. Everyone knew that Kuchek Khan had arrived. Old men threw themselves in the dust at his feet to kiss his long, righteous hands. The English had put a price on his head: a bag of gold. And that esteemed head was now right in front of them.*

The city was decked with red banners and tri-colored flags in the national colors. The bazaar shops had been spruced up, hung with lanterns and carpeted with Persian rugs. The Red Army orchestra played "La Marseillaise" and "The Internationale" as demonstrators shouted "Long live free Iran!" and "Long live the Soviet Union!"

Kuchek Khan crossed the city in a kind of waking dream, surrounded by the crowd, carried by the fervor of his people, who saw in him less a revolutionary than a saint or savior. At his side, Blumkin tried to shield him from the fervor of his most enthusiastic supporters, who were determined to touch the hem of his tunic or his hands and hair. He weighed the popularity of this discreet, almost shy man walking through the crowd, smiling. That evening, he wrote to Trotsky: "Given Kuchek Khan's special situation and the glory that surrounds him, we risk dozens of Kuchek Khans popping up. Sooner or later we will have to fight them, and that will demand many sacrifices."

They soon found themselves before the Soviet destroyer *Kursk*, where the Bolshevik military staff stood lining the gangway. Bowing to each member, Kuchek Khan came aboard, acclaimed by the crowd.

Raskolnikov explained that he had landed at Anzali only to recover Denikin's Russian fleet and to clear the Caspian Sea of the White Army. That mission accomplished, the Red Army would withdraw from Anzali. Kuchek Khan stated that he had no intention of copying the model of the October Revolution in Persia. Above all, he wanted to preserve the unity of his people as they fought the British presence and the autocracy in power in Tehran. Anyone hoping for a rapid sovietization of Persia was disappointed. The Jangali leader wouldn't even discuss the issue of land reform.

Blumkin, who had remained silent up to then, asked to speak. Intrigued, everyone turned to him, knowing that he was in regular contact with Trotsky. He suggested to Kuchek Khan that they immediately proclaim the Socialist Republic of Gilan as the only way to prove the revolution's absolute independence in the eyes of the world. In fact, this idea hadn't just popped into Blumkin's head. He had previously discussed it with the progressive wing of the Jangalis, who now loudly acquiesced. Raskolnikov and Kuchek Khan exchanged a puzzled look. They didn't seem to realize what was going on. Finally Raskolnikov added that in that case, of course nothing would be done in the name of Soviet Russia, only with its tacit support. Kuchek Khan agreed, while pondering the implications of his decision. By aligning himself with the Soviets, he might be able to contain their influence while benefiting from their military support. The proposal accelerated his timetable but took advantage of the Soviet fleet's presence in port, which would dissuade Tehran and the English from intervening.

One of his counselors present at the table stated in his memoirs that Kuchek Khan had "turned socialist" during the encounter for one simple reason: "If he had not taken the leadership of the revolution at that moment, his more radical rivals would have done so in his place. Kuchek Khan made his choice with a heavy heart."

The people greeted the news with cheers, and the Jangalis marched the twenty-five miles south to Racht, the capital of the province, to establish the new republic and form a provisional government. Meanwhile, Trotsky suggested that Raskolnikov "grant the rebels all possible military power while giving Kuchek Khan the territories we have occupied," but also "secretly work to establish significant Soviet propaganda and organization in Persia."

Forgotten in the euphoria of declaring the Republic of Gilan was the fact that the revolutionary movement comprised a mosaic of divergent interests sharpened by ambition and divided between reformers and revolutionaries. This was due to the movement's history and sociology. Some of the militants had grown up in exile among the thousands of migrant Persian workers in the Russian Caucasus. They joined local Georgians and Azerbaijanis in founding the Hemmat (Determination) Party, which would give rise to the Iranian Communist Party in June 1920. Those Marxist militants had little in common with the Jangalis. Neither side agreed on the nature or pace of reforms, or on the important question of extending the revolution to the whole country. The Jangali leader planned to first unify the entire Persian people before launching an attack on Tehran and undertaking social reforms, which would start with land reform. Persia had a huge number of agricultural workers. His opponents wanted to reverse those priorities and start with social reform, which would enlarge the movement's social base, while military victories would swell the ranks of the Persian Red Army.

The arrival of the Soviets in Gilan had forced a fusion of those two currents. The divergences had been papered over in order to form a government, but the disagreements quickly became visible. It didn't take more than two weeks for cracks to start to appear in the beautiful facade of the Soviet Socialist Republic of Gilan.

The notes that Blumkin sent Trotsky were unambiguous. "When I got word of the government manifesto that accompanied the proclamation of the Soviet Republic of Persia, I tore my hair out," he wrote.

> I gathered my comrades and we started thinking about what we should do. If Kuchek Khan took his inspiration from this manifesto to govern Persia, it could only collapse. We spent three hours with Kuchek Khan, and I tried to prove to him that you couldn't have a

revolution without fighting the ruling class and the feudal powers. Kuchek Khan answered by saying, "You are forgetting that in Persia many people, revolutionaries but also merchants and religious figures, have fought the Shah. Why should we turn away from them?" I demonstrated point by point that those landowners had opposed the Shah because he taxed them too heavily. I proved that the Shah and the imperialists were allies. It was hopeless! Finally, I made one last try. "Put out a resolution in support of unions!" I said. "What good would that do?" he asked. I tried to explain that the workers needed a union to defend their interests as a class. His answer convinced me that we would never understand each other: "If a worker needs something, he should come see me, I will be happy to help him."

In the following weeks, occasions for conflict multiplied. Land reform, repression of religious figures, taxation of merchants, military offensives against Tehran, all were stumbling blocks in the government factions' path. Everything was a pretext for conflict. Each measure taken became a provocation. Kuchek Khan's political line and authority were challenged. His rivals considered him a Persian Kerensky. So as not to further poison the situation and divide the movement, the Jangali leader decided to retire to the Gilan forest.

The republic had been proclaimed, and the Russian fleet left Anzali, as promised. But the government had lost its titular figure, and the essence of its legitimacy. Power was vacant. In Moscow the leadership worried about the developing situation. On the ground, communists planned a coup d'état. The date was set for July 31, and its execution entrusted to Blumkin, the only one of the conspirators with real military experience.

At one o'clock in the morning Blumkin led the insurrection with about a hundred men, and occupied the city's military and civilian administration buildings, starting with that of the republic's government. They met no resistance. In the morning, shops opened as if nothing had happened. "When we woke up yesterday morning, power had changed hands," wrote an inhabitant in his diary. "Kuchek Khan had been overthrown and a new government formed without his supporters. Otherwise, everything went on as usual." In the afternoon a communiqué was broadcast from Anzali on all radio frequencies, announcing the successful coup d'état. "The provisional government of Kuchek Khan proved itself incapable of leading the revolutionary movement in Persia. It was unable to successfully fight the English imperialists or to satisfy the urgent needs of the working masses." Kuchek Khan, who had been praised by the Bolsheviks a few days earlier, had become an "enemy" and a "traitor" overnight.

The flip-flops of Soviet politics in Persia can't be understood without taking into account the Anglo-

Russian negotiations in progress at the same time in London. At stake in those negotiations was the suspension of the blockade that had been strangling Soviet Russia for the previous two years. For the blockade to be lifted, the Bolsheviks had to agree to give up their military operations against the shah in Persia, and generally stop fomenting anti-British rebellion in the Middle East, Afghanistan, and India.

On August 3, Chicherin wired his instructions to the Soviet representative in London: "The pace and intensity of our policies in the Middle East are subject to our English policy. In the course of a conversation, try to get the English to understand that besides a few pinpricks on the margins, we could severely damage all the English positions in the world if we deployed the means at our disposal in the Middle East. They can't fail to understand this, given their shock at our thrusts in the Middle East."

In a telegram dated June 4, the very day that the Soviet Republic of Gilan was proclaimed, Trotsky made the Bolshevik strategic position perfectly clear. A Soviet coup d'état in Persia and the other Middle Eastern countries bordering Russia would cause the Bolsheviks "the greatest possible difficulties," he wrote. "Even in Azerbaijan, the Soviet republic is not able to stand on its own feet." It had been sustained by Red Army bayonets, if not occupied. Trotsky concluded that "the main interest of a Russian revolution in the Middle East is as a diplomatic bargaining chip to play against England."

In London the Bolsheviks had been negotiating their economic survival since the spring. "That scoundrel Lloyd George is fooling you in the most vile and shameless manner," Lenin wired his negotiators. "Don't believe a word, and fool him threefold."

On July 7 the foreign affairs commissar let it be known that to achieve peace quickly, Moscow was prepared to "abstain from any military action or propaganda susceptible to encourage the peoples of Asia to act against British interests." Yet three weeks later Blumkin would occupy the capital of Gilan and overthrow Kuchek Khan's government.

Had Blumkin acted on his own initiative, against instructions for Moscow? Was there a divergence of a line or a lack of coordination between Bolsheviks? It's possible, but hard to believe. For Gilan to be a bargaining chip in negotiations with the British, the Bolsheviks would have preserved and if possible helped it prosper, so as to be able to use it at the right time. Thus the "double blind" of Soviet policy in Persia: official nonintervention in Persian affairs, but hidden support to local communists who wanted to march on Tehran.

Radek answered the Iranian regime's protests against Russian activities in Persia in the pages of *Izvestia* on June 10, 1920: "There are no Soviet ground forces in Persia. But Russian ideas, and the ideas of communism, have entered Persia." Radek failed to add that along with "ideas of communism," Soviet forces led by Blumkin, Trotsky's closest collaborator, had entered Iran. Yakov Blumkin—that disciplined artisan of Soviet foreign policy—was one of the two irons that the Bolsheviks kept in the fire throughout their difficult negotiations with the English. Victor Serge outlined the chain of command that the Blumkin operation in Persia depended on: "Blumkin and his commissars obeyed orders directly from Moscow. Not those from the Executive Committee of the Communist International, which theoretically was the only competent authority, but from the Central Committee of the Russian Party, of which they were faithful members."

Before leaving Persia, Blumkin wrote Trotsky: "The Persian problem must be settled one way or another: either attack them or make peace with the Shah's government and abandon Anzali."

With the negotiations in London on the point of succeeding, the Central Committee decided to pull out of Gilan. Blumkin was recalled to Moscow. "The insurrection ended the way it began," wrote Serge. "The Russian partisans re-crossed the border or boarded feluccas and sailed back to Baku. Kuchek Khan and his Persian friends refused to obey, and the question of killing them was discussed. I actually don't know how Kuchek Khan ended up, but Blumkin told me that the decision was taken to kill him if he persisted in his refusal to disband the movement."

That turned out not to be necessary. Kuchek Khan, who had not capitulated and took refuge in the forests with a few dozen fighters, died of cold in the mountains in December 1921. The Persian Che Guevara was forty-one years old. His body was decapitated, and his main comrade in arms brought his head to the authorities. He was awarded a colonel's epaulets by the minister of war, the future dictator Reza Shah Pahlavi. Kuchek Khan's head was displayed as a trophy in the Gilan capital.

Despite the efforts made under the shah's dictatorship to erase Kuchek Khan from Iranians' memory, he remains a patriotic fighter for them, and the Gilanis continue to revere him as a "rare example of honesty" among Iranian politicians. The new regime in Iran has managed to graft a religious dimension onto the mythologies surrounding the Jangali movement. Followers of Khomeini saw Kuchek Khan as a martyr who had raised the banner of Islam against the West, and who died fighting monarchists and communists. Iranian television produced a fourteen-hour miniseries honoring the "revolutionary mullah." But Kuchek Khan was no mullah. He had simply studied theology, as all students did in those days. The Islamic Republic has honored him with stamps and posters, and schoolbooks devote whole chapters to him. Streets have been named and statues of him raised in parks in his honor.

The Soviet Republic of Gilan has long been misunderstood. Its history belongs to the domain of rumors and legends, but not only to "the romantic mythology that shrouds the deserts of the Arabian peninsula," in the words of Fred Halliday, an old Mideast hand. Attempts to install workers in power in Berlin, Munich, and Budapest in 1919, and in the Turin soviets in 1919–20, have left a deep mark on collective memory. The same can't be said of the insurgent republic created in Gilan province in northern Iran in June 1920. Blumkin was one of its founders. The official history of this republic, which lasted a year and a half before being dismantled by the joint efforts of the London-Moscow-Tehran triad, was written by the very people with an interest in making it disappear.

CHAPTER

9

The train is crossing a barren landscape of eroded hills, stunted vegetation, and rolling desert sands. The locomotive is a Baldwin, as freshly painted as a stolen car and flying flags that are so red, they seem to have just come from a dye shop. The same red recurs on the engine's tubes and pipes, on the coaches' trim, and in the giant murals that cover the sides of the train cars. All freshly painted, several weeks' worth of work. Red connecting rods drive the wheels, which are also painted red. Rolling in tandem, they give an exaggerated impression of speed, since the train isn't going more than thirty miles an hour. The smokestack sends puffs of black smoke to dissolve in the blue of the sky.

Behind the locomotive, an open car is filled with Red Army soldiers, Kalashnikovs slung on their shoulders. Blumkin was in charge of the train's security, and I find it easy to imagine him sitting on an ammo crate, telling the young soldiers about his adventures in Persia. Following that car are a dozen coaches, their sides painted with scenes from the Civil War and the Revolution. Seen from afar, the train looks like a toy model wending its way through papier-mâché hills studded with plastic bushes.

The daylight fades, and lights come on in the compartments. The train is now driving through the night, with a big red taillight and windows lit by flickering yellow lamps. Inside, a man is sitting, looking exhausted. He holds a glass of water in one hand while searching an inside jacket pocket for his medicine, which he dissolves in the glass. This is John Reed, author of *Ten Days That Shook the World*, the famous account of the October Revolution. A flyer from an American labor union falls from his pocket. He picks it up. On the back are a few hand-written lines to his wife, Louise Bryant, who at that moment is far away in Petrograd, desperately looking for him.

Day and night and day
You cannot think one bitter thought away,
That we have lost each other.

Dawn breaks on a prairie seared yellow by drought. Scenes unfold, one by one. Another night. Then it's morning again, with the train traveling in a valley along a wall of mountains. A scattering of white houses is visible in the distance. Soon a camel appears alongside the train, then two camels, then a whole cavalcade of horses, their riders in tunics and turbans, waving sabers at the train. At the compartment windows, the delegates wave to the galloping riders, as the first Bedouin tents appear, then the old city's ruined ramparts and Moorish gates carved out of Styrofoam. When the train stops, Reed climbs down, drained by the heat. His eye lights on three dangling effigies: Woodrow Wilson, Lloyd George, and Alexandre Millerand, the American president and the British and French prime ministers, recognizable by their top hats and national flags. They are in flames.

Those are the images that came to mind as I prepared to describe the circumstances surrounding the first Congress of the Peoples of the East that met in Baku in the late summer of 1920, and in which Yakov Blumkin played such a large role. They are from Warren Beatty's film *Reds*, a three-hour-plus epic that tells John Reed's story. He was sent to Baku with other leaders of the new Communist International to participate in the congress. Blumkin, who had just come back from Persia, was also on the trip. The train sequence comes toward the end of the movie. I saw *Reds* when it first came out in 1981, as I was starting to take an interest in Blumkin, and hadn't thought of it since.

Before I start writing a chapter, I'm in the habit of putting up photos of the main characters, maps of certain cities or neighborhoods where the action takes place, etc., on a blackboard that covers one of my office walls. Once the chapter is finished, I file these documents in an archive box. I then repeat the same operation for the next chapter, the way a detective does at the start of a new investigation. For this chapter, the left side of my board was occupied by a pyramid of portraits topped by Grigory Zinoviev, the president of the newly created Communist International. Below him were the trio of Karl Radek, Belá Kun, and John Reed, respectively representing Germany, Soviet Hungary, and the United States at the congress. This was followed by a clutch of lesser leaders. Beside the head of each delegation, I wrote in chalk the number of its delegates, broken down by nationality. The right side of the board was filled with snapshots from various archival sources: the armored train with its black locomotive; photos of a vast Baku oil field; reproductions of posters bearing the Islamic crescent and the red star of the Revolution; and a facsimile of the brochure containing the actions taken by the Baku conference, published in 1971 by François Maspero.

For Russia, creating an organization that would embrace all the nations of the East was no small task. Delegations came from China, Persia, Japan, and Turkey. Lenin conceived of the conference toward the end of June, but it was a long way between concept and realization. Originally, the idea was to assemble just the Turks, Persians, and Mesopotamian

Arabs. As enthusiasm grew, the target was widened to all of the peoples of the East and representatives of the colonial powers. This call went out: "Spare no effort to ensure that as many as possible may be present on September 1 in Baku. Formerly you traveled across deserts to reach the holy places—now make your way over mountains and rivers, through forests and deserts, to meet each other."

Hundreds of messages of support poured in from cities and villages in Asia. One proposed sacrificing a hundred sheep and cattle in honor of the people's liberation, and asked the conference for help transporting them to Baku. Proposals for resolutions came from everywhere. In a single dissenting note, Manabendra Nath Roy, an early proponent of Indian communism, chose to ignore what in his memoirs he would call the "Zinoviev circus."

The date for the conference was first set for August 15, 1920, but had to be delayed by two weeks to give time for Blumkin to return from Persia and ensure the train's security. The Bolsheviks were afraid that it would become a target for peasant fighters or a White Army detachment. Crowned by his military exploits in Gilan, Blumkin outfitted the train with field guns, machine guns, cars, and horses, and recruited sharpshooters and expert riders. The heavily armed train headed east with a hundred brave men aboard. Standing on the footsteps, hair blowing in the wind, Blumkin scanned the steppes with binoculars, looking for a black dot on the horizon or a cloud of dust raised by a troop of Cossacks.

Aboard the train were Frenchmen, Englishmen, Germans, and Dutch, along with five Poles, three Hungarians, and 104 Russians. Baku, which until then had attracted only the greed of capitalists, had become the lodestar of all the oppressed peoples of the East. Converging on the city were 157 Armenians, 235 Turks, and 192 Persians. Some had set out on foot or on camelback weeks before. Others had shipped aboard freighters as deckhands or as stowaways in the holds, hiding under sacks of spices. They arrived at the conference hall trailing hints of pepper, ginger, and cardamom, which were soon overpowered by the stench of oil that permeated the city despite falling production. The congress's stenographers included 3 Koreans, 14 Indians, 8 Chinese, a dozen Uzbeks, 35 Turkmens, 8 Kurds, 82 Chechens, 41 Israelis, 7 Avars, 2 Tekesians, 9 Khabards, 13 Ingushes, 25 Lezghiens, 12 Jamshids, 10 Kojars, 10 Sarts, 47 Kyrgyz, 61 Tajiks, 1 Horvat, 33 Kumyks, 17 Ossetians, 2 Abkasians, 1 Bashkir, 3 Arabs, 3 Kalmyks, and 11 Khazars.

To no surprise, some of the delegates decided to "take advantage of the trip to Baku to conclude various commercial transactions," as Elena Stasova, a congress organizer, put it. "Comparing weapons and selling products they had brought from home interested them far more than the conference debates," reported the British intelligence service, which sent observers after doing its utmost to pre-vent delegates from reaching Baku. A steamship from Persia was fired on. Turkish delegates prepar-ing to cross the Black Sea were intercepted by ships from the British fleet. Several Persian delegates bound for Baku turned up dead at the Azerbaijani border.

"The trip was full of interest and without dan-ger," wrote the French delegate Alfred Rosmer in his memoir *Lenin's Moscow*. "It allowed us to see at first hand the vast extent of damage done by the Civil War. Most of the stations had been destroyed, and everywhere the sidings were full of the half-burnt wrecks of coaches. When the Whites had been beaten, they destroyed everything they could as they retreated . . .

"On the station platforms peasant women of-fered us eggs, and even little roast chickens, things which were rare or quite unknown in Moscow. All the length of Caucasia there were appetizing piles of fruit—grapes, pears, figs, dates, every va-riety of melon and watermelon. John Reed often came to talk with us and traveled alongside us. Every time the train stopped, he rushed up to the hawkers with their baskets and came back with his arms laden with fruit. After Petrovsk, the track ran along the shore of the Caspian Sea, and if there was an extended stop, he would run off to swim in the sea. He was enjoying the trip, as one would expect from a young American. Once, in his haste to get dressed again, he tore his trousers—a tragic event, since of course he didn't have any others with him."

In his memoir, Rosmer also recalls talking with the man he calls "Bloomkine."

> *He was returning from a mission that the government had entrusted him with. He had lived for some time in Paris and spoke a little French. He asked me about the socialist movement in France and about its leaders, some of whom he had known, notably Jean Longuet, whom he was quite determined to see guillotined. Several times he would interrupt himself, and saying "Longuette," he would make a gesture in imitation of the blade of the fearful machine coming down on the neck of Karl Marx's unfortunate grandson—a quite undeserved fate—and then he would burst out laughing. He was a typical embodiment of the mixture of heroism and puerility which was common among Socialist Revolutionaries.*

In fact, Blumkin did not know Longuet or any other socialist deputies, and it's hard to see when he could have gone to Paris in his short and already crowded life. Maybe he was just showing off for Rosmer. What he said about Longuet merely parroted Trotsky's opinion. Speaking in the French parliament, Longuet had affirmed that "the noble sacrifice" of dozens of Tunisian soldiers killed or wounded during World War I gave them the right to more justice and more liberty.

Trotsky was outraged. In *The First Five Years of the Communist International*, he wrote: "The poor, unfortunate Arabs of Tunisia, whom the French bourgeoisie flung into the fiery cauldron of war, this black cannon fodder, fell...at the Marne and the Somme, perishing along with the imported Spanish horses and American steers." This revolting smear on the sordid picture of the Great War, he wrote, "is depicted by Jean Longuet as a supreme and honorable sacrifice which ought to be crowned with the gift of freedom...as if it were a tip to be thrown to its slaves by the sated and magnanimous Bourse, at the request of one of its parliamentarian brokers."

When the train pulled into the Baku station during the night of September 1, heat and humidity greeted the passengers. Wrote Rosmer: "From the station we went to the theater where a meeting had been called. By the end of the journey the train was running late, and the theater had been packed for more than an hour by the time we got there."

After being welcomed by Nariman Narimanov, the president of Revkom, the Azerbaijan Soviet government, the members of the Comintern Executive Committee, "the headquarters of world revolution," began to speak.

I was able to see a video of the Baku conference at the Center for Russian, Caucasian and Central European Studies in Paris. At sixty-five minutes, it's the longest video of the event preserved. There are long shots of the delegations. John Reed at the dais. Scenes of daily life accompany images of the congress: landscapes, markets, street scenes, festivals, dances. You can hear a short excerpt of Zinoviev's speech calling for "holy war" and various steps in favor of "the emancipation of women."

"The auditorium was extremely picturesque," wrote Rosmer. "All the Eastern costumes gathered together made an amazingly rich and colorful picture." Picturesque! The word occurs again and again in the Frenchman's account: "The town was picturesque and highly attractive. The sun, beating down mercilessly, offered extraordinary lighting effect in the alleyways—the blacks and whites were equally vivid."

On the dais stood Grigory Zinoviev, Karl Radek, Alfred Rosmer, and Béla Kun. Zinoviev spoke first: "We don't want to look like the Second International... There are other people in the world besides the white race, those Europeans who are its exclusive focus." Radek, whom Victor Serge described as "simian and sarcastic," called for battle in the "villages and cities of Asia" alongside the "proletariat in revolt," while hitching up his pants, which were so loose they kept slipping down. Then it was the turn of Béla Kun, who was briefly the president of the Republic of Councils in Hungary, and whose constant blunders Lenin used to mock in French as "*béla-kuneries.*"

Tom Quelch, the British delegate, began his speech with a quotation from Karl Marx, who wrote, "The British working class would be free only when the peoples of the British colonies were free." Alfred Rosmer savaged his country's imperial aims: "Why did France, which said it was fighting against German barbarism, oppress and hold down Morocco, Tunisia, and Algeria and other Muslim countries? And why is France now carrying on a war in Cilicia and Syria in order to enlarge her empire by adding a piece of Asia?"

As for Zinoviev, he asked, "What sense does it make to a Georgian peasant if [the country's rulers] sing like nightingales about the 'independence' of Georgia, when the land remains as before the property of the old landowners, when the same old oppression continues, and when at any moment some British general can trample with his jackboots on the throat and on the chest of the Georgian peasant and worker?"

The choice of the congress's official language was the subject of thorny negotiations. Reed pointed out that most of these peoples had been under British colonial rule, so English seemed the most practical solution, the only language that could unite them. Others proposed French, the language of the Revolution of 1789. Zinoviev wound up imposing Russian, as the language of the great October Revolution. So that everyone could follow the debates, dozens of interpreters called out translations in the four corners of the hall, which made for a huge cacophony. People were hearing for the first time Asiatic languages that had been forbidden under the tsar. Blumkin, who spoke several Eastern languages, ran from one group to the other, here translating a word that stumped a translator, there catching snatches of a phrase on the fly or a slogan chanted by half the hall while the other half stood puzzled and mute. "When I was about to speak," remembers Rosmer, "Blumkin came with me and absolutely wanted to translate my speech."

According to congress organizer Elena Stasova, most of the delegates appeared to be illiterate. The speeches therefore had to be translated into various dialects for those who did not have access to a written language. In this way the audience's attention was split into dozens of linguistic channels, contained by the narrow dikes of translation, briefly spilling over in a flood when the delegates, most of them Muslims, finally recognized themselves as a single people engaged in the same struggle. The audience would leap to its feet. Some applauded; others waved their weapons. Witnesses reported that people shouted "Jihad!" "Long live the resurrection of the East!" and "Long live the Third International!" Zinoviev, who quickly grasped the magical impact of certain words, drew huzzahs when he ended his speech by shouting, "Brothers! We summon you to a holy war, in the first place against English imperialism!"

John Reed, with his gift for understatement, drew laughter when he started by addressing the participants in his few words of Russian: "Do you know how to say Baku in American? It's pronounced *oil!*" He then started reading a long speech that dealt with workers in the Philippines, the people of Central America, and the Caribbean islands and the Yankees who oppressed them. But could anyone understand him? His speech had been translated from English to German and then into Russian before being dispersed in a cacophony of languages and dialects mixing Arabic, Persian, Turkish, and Cantonese. At the end of his speech, Reed called on the delegates to pursue class struggle worldwide. Suddenly his plea drew applause from the crowd, which started yelling slogans that he didn't understand. Standing next to him, Blumkin explained: "They're cheering your call to jihad!"

Once again, fiction intrudes into my account. Not a gratuitous fiction of my invention, but a scene from Warren Beatty's film. The real John Reed in the black-and-white archive photographs speaking at the congress tribune has been replaced by Beatty the actor. The images of Reed's speech that I saw in the video at the center didn't fade completely, but were overlaid by scenes from the movie. Actors mixed with historical characters the way gate crashers mingle with guests at a reception, and their images are so vivid that the historical characters pale beside them.

One scene in *Reds* takes place in the train's dining car during the trip back to Moscow. Zinoviev is having lunch with his colleagues when Reed bursts in, furious because he just learned that Zinoviev has edited his speech. A violent argument breaks out between the two men.

> *John Reed: Zinoviev, did you do the translation of my speech?*
>
> *Zinoviev: I supervised it, yes.*
>
> *John Reed: I didn't say "holy war," I said "class war."*
>
> *Zinoviev: I took the liberty of ordering a phrase or two.*
>
> *John Reed: Yeah, well, I don't allow people to take liberties with things I write.*
>
> *Zinoviev: Aren't you propagandist enough to write what people need the most?*
>
> *John Reed: I'm propagandist enough to utilize the truth.*
>
> *Zinoviev: And who defines this truth? You or the Party? Your life is dedicated to—*
>
> *John Reed: You don't talk about what my life is dedicated to!*
>
> *Zinoviev: Your life? You haven't decided what your life is dedicated to. You see yourself as an artist and at the same time a revolutionary. As the love of your wife but also as the spokesman for the American—*
>
> *John Reed: Zinoviev, you don't think a man can be an individual and be true to the collective, or speak*

for his own country and for the International at the same time, or love his wife and still be faithful to the Revolution. You don't have a self to give.

Zinoviev (calmly): Would you be willing to give yourself to this Revolution?

John Reed (shouting): You separate a man from what he loves most, what you do is purge what's unique. And when you purge what's unique in him, you purge dissent. And when you purge dissent, you kill the Revolution! Dissent IS revolution!

Almost hoarsely, Beatty repeats, "You kill the Revolution." The characters' faces are lit by the setting sun. No sooner has Beatty spoken those words than a violent explosion behind him shakes the car. An armed White detachment has attacked the train. People jump from the windows to the ground, crawl over the ballast, and take cover behind the cars. But resistance is organized very quickly. Blumkin, who doesn't appear in the movie, launches a counterattack and repulses the assault.

The train had been specially configured against just such an attack. Cars could be uncoupled while the train was underway. Some compartments were equipped with ramps so that horses could run down and gallop in pursuit of attackers. In the film, a mounted cannon fires. Snipers shoot from the tops of the cars. Very quickly, the Whites flee in disorder. The attack on the train turns into a cavalcade, a furious chase with dozens of horses and riders, who had spent weeks rehearsing it. The movie's production archives say that a hundred fifty extras were used for that single scene, most of them Arabs. When they learned how big the film's production budget was ($35 million), they promptly went on strike. Fittingly for a movie about the Revolution, they got satisfaction.

As it happens, the argument in the train between Zinoviev and Reed reflected another disagreement, a real one this time, between Beatty and his screenwriter, Trevor Griffiths. The two men couldn't have been more different. Beatty was a beloved son of Hollywood who wanted to tell a love story against an epic tale of war and revolution. But he also was committed to the realism of the situations. Which is why he chose Griffiths, an English screenwriter known for his extreme left-wing views—a "hard-core Marxist," in Beatty's phrase. Griffiths had caught the enthusiasm of May 1968 and written *Occupations*, a play about Italian revolutionary Antonio Gramsci and the occupation of the Fiat factories in the 1920s. Griffiths believed in the battle of ideas and saw his screenwriting as a weapon in that struggle, which he called the "strategic penetration" of minds.

The two men shut themselves away in a London hotel room to work on the *Reds* script. But when they reached the train scene, a disagreement arose.

"Do we really need the scene of the attack on the train?" asked Beatty.

"What really matters," said Griffiths, "is the argument between the two men, not the attack on the train."

For Griffiths, the heart of the film was John Reed's dilemma: the conflict between art and revolution, between the individual and the collective.

"But you have to realize something," said Beatty. "In a movie, one bullet from a revolver is worth thousands of words."

"That was terrible," remembered Griffiths years later, "because I was the writer and I only had words at my disposal. Beatty got angry, and so did I. So I picked up my things and left the room, and we never saw each other again." Exit the hard-core Marxist. But Beatty didn't need him anymore. By then he had the outline of the script and could go on to develop the plot's central love story between Louise Bryant and John Reed.

It took Beatty years to get *Reds* made. The project was born in the mid-1960s amid demonstrations against the war in Vietnam, and was completed in 1981, when neoliberalism had triumphed in the United States with the election of Ronald Reagan. A heroic saga, the movie faced the challenge of bringing to the screen issues as complicated as the birth of the American labor movement, Marxism, and the Russian Revolution, but also the anarchic Greenwich Village utopia. "Marxism, feminism, free love—these subjects might have assured box-office success in the late Sixties, when Beatty first considered filming the life of activist reporter John Reed," wrote *Rolling Stone* in 1982. "Releasing this movie in the Reagan Eighties would seem to be professional suicide." Added *Vanity Fair* in 2006: "The mood of the times had definitely changed. Ronald Reagan was president and it wasn't at all chic to be radical."

Reds was a worldwide success anyway. Reagan, who saw the USSR as the "Evil Empire," invited Beatty to the White House for a private screening. The president liked the movie. His only regret was that the hero dies at the end. Reagan would have almost brought him back to life, if he could. The Hollywood actor couldn't resist the seduction of a *Love Story* in the land of the Soviets.

Gradually, my curiosity began to shift from Blumkin's life to Reed's, and from the fierce debates at the Baku congress to the making of *Reds*. I wanted to learn all the secrets of the making of the film, from script to cinematography and locations. I wanted to move away from history writ large, which swallows images like a black hole, leaving only written evidence of lived events, to the black screen of the movies, where those events reappear as ghosts.

On my office blackboard, images from *Reds* joined the black-and-white archive photos. A map of southern Spain, where the film was shot, now covered that of Azerbaijan. Rising from war-ravaged

Baku was an imaginary city that looked somewhat like Seville or Granada. Two parallel universes overlapped, one real, the other make-believe. Fiction was injecting its images and its myths into reality. The present of the movie was taking over the event from the past. After all, those hundreds of extras obeying the assistant directors' shouted orders were just as real as the delegates to the Baku conference, who were given the word and shouted the slogans suggested by the organizers. Hadn't the Baku master of ceremonies directed his congress the same way Beatty directed his movie? And wasn't the "Zinoviev circus" as carefully scripted as the scene shot in Andalucía?

I decided to go on location, if only in my mind. Not to Baku, but to Almería in Andalucía. I had spent time in the area in the mid-1990s, and still had friends there. I imagined that Fernando met me on the train platform along with a film historian who posted videos on YouTube under the pseudonym Nollito. Within half an hour, we were in the middle of the desert. The ruins of a few sand-swept ranches bore witness to the golden age of the great Hollywood shoots that Andalusians are so proud of: Sergio Leone's *Once Upon a Time in the West*, and David Lean's *Doctor Zhivago*.

The train sequence in Beatty's movie had been shot on an abandoned track in the Andalusian countryside. But the train didn't have to cover the fifteen hundred miles that separate Moscow and

Baku, just a few dozen miles between Guadix and La Calahorra. The vast Russian spaces crossed by the train were in reality not much bigger than the small Tabernas Desert around us. We drove along a weed-choked road to an abandoned warehouse whose walls were sheets of cellophane snapping in the wind. On two rails stood the famous Baldwin locomotive. It was covered with cobwebs and a translucent tarp through which you could just make out its former colors, now faded with time. I had the feeling of having snuck into a scene from the movie, the way you step into a museum.

Warren Beatty always liked Henry Ford's dictum "History is bunk!" because, he said, "we all rewrite our history to make it bearable." Of *Reds*, he said, "In writing the film we tried to be faithful to the facts in the chronology, but I'm not sure that was really necessary." Beatty advertised in newspapers all over the country for people who had known John Reed and Louise Bryant. He got thousands of responses and interviewed the best-known "witnesses," like Henry Miller, Rebecca West, and Roger Baldwin, who co-founded the American Civil Liberties Union. But on-screen they're not identified, not even Henry Miller, the most famous of them. They testify anonymously about another time. Filmed against a black background, we see them straining to remember, talking about the tricks their memories play. "No, I won't mention any names," says one. "I'd forgotten all that!" says another apologetically. "It never affected my private life," snaps a third. "I like baseball."

"Why did you choose to film them against the same black background?" I asked *Reds* cinematographer Vittorio Storaro in his suburban Rome studio. "I got the idea thanks to a new system that allows you to redevelop the image after an initial development," he said. "On top of the initial colors—red, green, and blue—you can overlay a fourth layer: black." So in *Reds*, black acquires an unusual depth and density. It isn't only one of the four base colors, but the depths from which memories arise. "Memory comes back in black."

"Storaro sees things that other people don't," wrote a film critic, "and Storaro shows things that nobody can forget." It's certainly true that when I sit down to describe those days in Baku, what comes to mind are Storaro's images, and not the archive photographs that cover my office blackboard. While generally faithful to the chronology of events, Beatty's movie doesn't present any new information about the Russian Revolution, but it helps to clarify it, to give it shape and colors. The audience thinks it is watching a political convention, but it is actually being invited to an encounter of colors, a conspiracy of colors. And unlike what one might think from the movie's title, the main character in this conspiracy isn't red, but black.

A train pulls into Madrid's Atocha Station, which serves the cities of Andalucía. It is June 27,

1980, and very hot. The station has been cleared of its electric wires and urban furnishings, and its walls plastered with Bolshevik-era posters—as was also done when David Lean's film *Doctor Zhivago* was filmed here. In the trunk that held my Blumkin Project archives, I had found an article from *Rolling Stone* dated January 21, 1982. The piece is illustrated by a photo of the shoot where you can see Beatty wearing the white tunic he wears in the film. Around him, members of the camera crew are listening to his instructions. Nuns and women in headscarves await the next take. The director says "Action," and a crowd of extras fills the station platform. Diane Keaton, who plays Reed's wife, Louise Bryant, tries to make her way among the extras, who have been instructed to block her path. A stretcher carrying a corpse passes in front of her. The train is emptying itself of passengers. Still no John. Finally, she glimpses him after a series of cleverly scripted delays. Following their long separation, the two lovers embrace. This will be the movie's poster.

A similar train pulled into Kazan Station in Moscow in mid-September 1920, on a cold rainy day, like the one John Reed encountered on his first trip to Moscow in the fall of 1917. From it, Reed hurried to Bryant's hotel and entered her room, calling her name. They were finally together again, but it would only be for a week. Reed was sick with typhus and would soon be hospitalized. The reunion became a farewell tour. They saw Lenin,

Kamenev, Enver Pasha, and Béla Kun. Reed told Lenin about his disappointment in the Baku conference, and about Zinoviev's contempt for Asian peoples. Lenin didn't seem surprised. "We'll never get over that 'Great Russia' mindset. It's infiltrating our own ranks!"

Louise Bryant liked Lenin. John Reed liked Lenin. Lenin liked John Reed. Together they talked about Jack London and "Love of Life," which Lenin felt was his best story. Louise agreed with Lenin, as did John. On this point, they were perfect Leninists. With them, Lenin showed himself open to idealism, a rare commodity when you're in power. He had read *Ten Days That Shook the World* and written a preface in which he "unreservedly" recommended it "to the workers of the world." Only an American, he felt, could have expressed the epic meaning of the Revolution. "Here is a book which I should like to see published in millions of copies and translated into all languages," he wrote. "It gives a truthful and most vivid exposition of the events so significant to the comprehension of what really is the proletarian revolution."

Next day, Blumkin, who had met Reed on the train to Baku, knocked at their hotel room door. He was there to bring them to see Trotsky. Before the war, the Red Army chief had spent time in Greenwich Village, the so-called republic of dreams. They discussed Dos Passos and Hemingway and his stenographic prose. Trotsky mentioned Eugene O'Neill, and Louise wondered if he knew that she'd had an affair with the playwright. John gave her a reassuring wink.

In their reunion, Louise realized how much John had changed. "I found him older and sadder, and grown strangely gentle and aesthetic." Reed was so impressed with the suffering around him, she wrote, that he would take nothing for himself. "I was shocked, and almost unable to reach the peak of fervor he had attained." That evening they attended a performance of *Prince Igor* at the ballet.

It was a stolen week, during which Bryant surrendered to the kind of happiness you can accept only when you know that it won't last. She had traveled for weeks trying to find Reed. She had skirted Finland and sailed for twelve days in the Arctic Ocean. To avoid the police, she and a Finnish officer and a German, both under sentence of death in their own countries, hid in a fisherman's shack. When she reached Moscow, Reed was in Baku, at the other end of the country. Civil war was raging in Ukraine. A military convoy took Reed in and brought him to Moscow in an armored train. "On the morning of September 15 he ran shouting into my room," she wrote. "A month later he was dead."

Reed's funeral on October 17, 1920, marked the end of the Revolution's lyrical age. "In Moscow, a sad piece of news greeted us," wrote Alfred Rosmer.

*John Reed, who had returned in advance of us, was
in the hospital, ill with typhus. No effort was spared
to save him, but it was all in vain and a few days later
he died. His body was displayed in the great hall of the
Trade Unions House. On the day of the funeral, winter
had already arrived and snow was falling. We were
overwhelmed ... During the journey we had seen him
full of youth and vigor, yet with sudden periods of sad-
ness. His interventions in the Congress, frank, sometimes
even brutal, had made him liked by all ... A burial place
was found for him in the Kremlin wall, in the section
reserved for heroes who had fallen in the Revolutionary
struggle. The words of farewell were spoken by Bukharin,
for the Central Committee of the Communist Party,
by Kollontai, and by his comrades from the Executive
Committee. Louise Bryant, who had arrived only to see
him die, was there, completely shattered by grief.*

Reed's old friend Emma Goldman, the anarchist
deported from the United States, was there too.

*I accompanied Louise when the procession started
for the Red Square. There were speeches—much cold
stereotyped declamation about the value of Jack Reed
to the Revolution and to the Communist Party. It all
sounded mechanical, far removed from the spirit of the
dead man in the fresh grave. One speaker only dwelt
on the real Jack Reed—Alexandra Kollontai. She had
caught the artist's soul, infinitely greater in its depth
and beauty than any dogma. She used the occasion*

*to admonish her comrades. "We call ourselves Com-
munists," she said, "but are we really that? Do we not
rather draw the life essence from those who come to us,
and when they are no longer of use, we let them fall by
the wayside, neglected and forgotten? Our Communism
and our comradeship are dead letters if we do not give
out of ourselves to those who need us. Let us be aware
of such Communism. It slays the best in our ranks. Jack
Reed was among the best." The sincere words of Kollontai displeased the high Party members. Bukharin knitted
his brows, Reinstein fidgeted about, others grumbled.
But I was glad of what Kollontai had said.*

As Emma Goldman wrote, Louise Bryant "had
fallen in a dead faint and was lying face downward
on the damp earth. After considerable effort we got
her to her feet. Hysterical, she was taken in the waiting auto to her hotel and put to bed. Outside, the sky
was clothed in gray and was weeping upon the fresh
grave of Jack Reed. And all of Russia seemed a fresh
grave."

A few days later, having barely recovered, Bryant
described Reed's last days in a long letter to their
American friends:

*Of the illness I can scarcely write—there was so much
pain. I only want you all to know how he fought for his
life. He would have died days before but for the fight he
made ... Five days before he died his right side was paralyzed. After that he could not speak. And so we watched*

through days and nights and days hoping against all hope. Even when he died I did not believe it. I must have been there hours afterwards still talking to him and holding his hands. He was never delirious in the hideous way most typhus patients are. He always knew me and his mind was full of poems and stories and beautiful thoughts. He would say, "You know how it is when you go to Venice? You ask people, 'Is this Venice?' just for the pleasure of hearing the reply." He would tell me that the water he drank was full of little songs. And he related, like a child, wonderful experiences we had together and in which we were very brave.

Some days later, Bryant returned to Red Square to visit her husband's tomb. The soldiers guarding it had taken off their hats. Among them was Blumkin, who had befriended Reed on the train to Baku. "He was a good comrade," he said. "He came all the way across the world for us. He was one of ours." Did Bryant hear those comforting phrases? She wrote: "I have been there under the stars with a great longing to lie down beside the frozen flowers and the metallic wreaths and not wake up."

We are now on the threshold of Yakov Blumkin's seventh life—the longest and most mysterious one. It stretches from the winter of 1921 to the middle of the decade and appears as a series of events distorted by rumor. Its one fixed point is Leon Trotsky, the pivot of the story. Trotsky's account is easy to check. Most of his archives were given to Harvard's Houghton Library shortly before his assassination, where they were safe from the censorship that erased Trotsky from Soviet history in the 1930s.

In 1937, Trotsky was interviewed in Mexico by the Dewey Commission, created to investigate Stalin's charges against him. Trotsky described his relationship with Blumkin this way: "After the revolution in Germany and the denunciation of the Brest-Litovsk peace treaty, he appeared before us and said, 'I am now a Bolshevik; you can test me.' He was sent to the front, where he was a very good fighter and a very courageous man." During the Civil War, Trotsky employed Blumkin in his military secretariat, reporting directly to him. He also had him edit his military writings and organize the exposition of the armored train, which proved a big success. Trotsky sent him to the military academy in Moscow he'd founded and gave him a number of dangerous missions, which Blumkin was always willing to carry out. "When I needed a courageous man, Blumkin was at my disposal."

The academy archives describe Blumkin as a serious student with a gift for languages. (He would learn Hebrew, Turkish, Arabic, Chinese, Mongolian, and Persian.) Classes went from nine in the morning until ten at night, with one-hour breaks for lunch and dinner. At the academy, Blumkin studied principles of strategy and tactics, military geography, the structure of the Red Army, military psychology, and six economic and social topics, including the philosophical and sociological principles of Marxism and the political economy of the transition.

Trotsky breathed new life into the military academy in Moscow, where former tsarist generals taught as professors and lecturers. He worked to modernize the teaching system and free it from "the pedantry typical of senior military thinkers." He railed against the academy generals and their traditional tsarist "pseudo-historical style," to which he opposed French military writers who knew how to combine historical research and the study of contemporary warfare with its sociological context.

Behind these questions of form lay a basic disagreement on the concept of war. Academics viewed the Civil War with a certain contempt, as a bastard child of grand strategy. Trotsky, to the contrary, thought that "the Civil War, with its highly mobile and flexible fronts, opened a fantastic field for real initiative and military art." He contrasted the revolutionary warfare of movement with trench warfare, which had shown its limitations during World War I. Victor Serge says Blumkin subscribed to his mentor's concepts and published articles on French generals Joffre and Foch in *Izvestia*.

Blumkin's stay at the academy was often interrupted by military missions. In particular, he fought Antonov's partisans in the Tambov Rebellion, an episode in the Civil War that Lenin called "the greatest threat the regime ever faced."

Outraged by the requisitions of wheat, peasants killed thousands of Bolsheviks, leaving a trail of bodies nailed to trees with crosses branded on their chests and foreheads, bodies with ears cut, tongues and eyes ripped out, arms legs and genitals cut off, and stomachs slashed open and stuffed with wheat. At the head of the 79th Brigade, Blumkin restored order "with an iron fist," says an article in *Pravda*.

A few days later, Alexander Barmine, a Soviet diplomat who would later flee to the West, encountered Blumkin on a train to Baku, watching over the drunken friend sitting next to him, the poet Esenin. "They took to each other tremendously and never went to bed sober," Barmine wrote. "[Esenin] made a painful impression on me. His youth had been early blighted, and he was now suffering from overindulgence in alcohol and women and from the orgies to which he had treated himself after writing his poems, which remain some of the most moving in the Russian language. His face was pale and puffy, his eyes tired, his voice husky. He gave the impression of someone who had completely lost all moral sense. Blumkin, whose soldierly temperament always saved him from excess, had saddled himself with the job of 'pulling him around.'"

In the summer of 1924, Blumkin helped put down the peasant insurrection in Georgia launched by Mensheviks and Georgian nationalists. Under orders from Stalin and Sergo Ordzhonikidze, the Red Army and the GPU killed thousands. "We may have gone a bit too far," conceded the latter, "but we couldn't stop ourselves." It's impossible to know Blumkin's contribution to this massacre, which is often compared to Kronstadt, but his superiors' reports show that his work was properly appreciated. V. Menzhinsky once reminded Mikhail Trilisser, the head of the Foreign Department, to mention

Blumkin's mission in Tbilisi in a report on his performance.

During the 1924–25 winter, under the name I. Issakov, Blumkin served with various frontier commissions (Irano-Soviet and Turko-Soviet) and oversaw the fortification of the border with Iran and Turkey. At the head of several hundred men, he liberated the city of Bagram-Tape, which had been occupied by the Iranians in 1922. The victory would open the path to irrigating the Mugan Plain in Azerbaijan.

By the age of twenty-five, Blumkin had already won several medals, and the three stripes on his uniform sleeve showed he was a member of the Red Army's high command. But in the summer of 1925 he decided to return to civilian life, probably weary of being continually in combat since 1917. We find him at the commerce commissariat wearing one of those blue serge suits with square shoulders that Bolshevik commissars wore when they worked in diplomacy or import-export. A sign on his office door gave this job description: "economic consultant," a title that hardly fits him. Officially, he ran an interdepartmental commission responsible for evaluating mechanical agricultural construction, and headed the "standardization office." Had Blumkin settled down? Whatever the case, he worked in several areas with the same energy he brought to fighting the Whites during the Civil War, and everywhere preached the militarization of work propounded by Trotsky. In the autobiography that Blumkin wrote at the end of his life he claims to have held twelve positions in this commissariat, but it isn't clear if those were real jobs or covers for more secretive activities. Fighting against sabotage? Investigating corruption?

In the fall of 1979 I interviewed Boris Bajanov, Stalin's former secretary in exile in Paris, who told me this:

> In 1925 Trotsky was visiting factories with the commission charged with production quality control. At the time he was trying to set up systems for production and transportation. Blumkin had been assigned to that commission despite his lack of experience, but Trotsky had no doubt about his ability within the commission. At one point, Blumkin wanted to present a report to a commission meeting, but Trotsky interrupted him, saying, "Comrade Blumkis is the Party's eye there, and, given his vigilance, we have no doubt that he has accomplished his mission. So we are going to hear the reports from specialists on the subcommission instead." Looking vexed, Blumkin said: "First of all, my name is Blumkin, not Blumkis. You should know your Party history better, Comrade Trotsky. And secondly—" But Trotsky slammed his fist on the table, and said, "I didn't give you the floor." When Blumkin left the commission, he was a bitter enemy of Trotsky.

Bajanov continued:

To make use of Blumkin's hatred of the opposition, the GPU tried to find him a slot by assigning him to Kamenev as a counselor when Kamenev was named commerce commissar in 1926. But Blumkin's situation generated howls of laughter among Kamenev's secretaries. They showed me a formal protest that an unhappy Blumkin had written him. It began this way: "Comrade Kamenev! I ask you: Where am I, what am I, and who am I?" He had to be reassigned from that position as well.

For anyone who knows how close Blumkin and Trotsky had been since 1918, the anecdote told by Bajanov is surprising. Trotsky had a phenomenal memory, so how could he misremember the name of one of his closest staffers? And how could the Central Committee ask Blumkin to spy on Trotsky, knowing the ties that connected them? I shared the anecdote that Bajanov told me with Trotskyist historian Pierre Broué, who wrote: "Frankly, this account casts doubt on his entire testimony." When I told Bajanov this, he refused to accept the evidence and stood by his story. It was obvious that he was lying, but I was just a young researcher; what was my point of view worth compared with the testimony of a former secretary of Joseph Stalin? Eventually, I pretended to agree with Bajanov and asked him to confirm his version in writing so that I could quote it in my book. A few days later I was surprised to receive a letter from him. Much later I found it in my Blumkin Project trunk. It is dated September 24, 1979.

Monsieur,

You asked me for a few details about Blumkin. He was an adventurer of a certain stature, very vain, who always wanted to play leading roles. His path was very tortuous, but don't forget that he joined the Cheka in the very beginning of the Bolshevik Revolution, and remained a Chekist to the end.

Did he have sympathies for Trotsky's Opposition (which dated from 1923)? If he did, they remained well hidden. In 1923–1924, one could very freely take positions in the Party, yet he remained on the side of (anti-Trotskyist) power and continued to be trusted by Stalinist authorities in 1924 when he was assigned to surveil Kamenev (as in 1925 to spy on Trotsky). In 1925 Trotsky considered him an agent of Zinoviev and Stalin, and disliked him, leading to the incident that I described.

For me, the "Blumkis" incident is completely authentic. It was confirmed to me not only by Stalin's secretary Kanner, who received a GPU report on the subject, but also from Blumkin's cousin Maximov, with whom I traveled in 1928 (in Europe). But it is certain that in 1927–1928 Blumkin went over to the Opposition, while carefully hiding his feelings from the GPU.

Best regards,
Boris Bajanov

The opening of the Trotsky archives at Harvard a few months later, in 1980, completely demolished Bajanov's version. It confirmed that of Victor Serge, who wrote, "Blumkin belonged to the Opposition, without having any occasion to make his sympathies very public. Trilisser, the head of the GPU's secret service abroad, Yagoda, and Menzhinsky were well acquainted with his views."

This didn't affect Bajanov's credibility with the French press, however, and his account continued to be taken for gospel. Blumkin and Trotsky were long dead, and French journalists in the early 1980s lapped up the old defector's words without seeking to contradict him. A complete rewriting of history was under way, and those who claimed to be fighting the Stalinist falsification of history didn't trouble themselves with nuance or complexity. The Berlin Wall was still standing, and the Soviet archives hadn't yet begun to speak.

Nor was Bajanov questioned about his meeting in Berlin with high Nazi leaders in June 1940, a few days before Hitler launched his offensive against the Soviet Union. Yet he didn't hide this in his memoirs, any more than he hid his political opinions. He had been one of the founders of the right-wing National Front, and former NF chief Jean-Marie Le Pen paid him homage on the organization's fortieth anniversary. I tried several times to interview Le Pen about Bajanov, but received no answer to my letters.

What Boris Bajanov had *not* told me was something I discovered thirty years later thanks to Anya Shapovalova, a Russian PhD student who was a great help when I was writing this book. While doing research in the French national defense archives in Vincennes, she stumbled across a Sécurité Nationale report on Blumkin. The file's summary page said that the intelligence had been gathered from a high-ranking official who had left Russia on January 1, 1928—the very day that Bajanov fled to the West. So Bajanov had been given political asylum in France in exchange for revealing the OGPU's hierarchy and its main agents to the French secret services.

Here is the summary page about Blumkin in file number F/7/13499:

> *Bloumkine (or Blumkin), Jacob Grégoréivitch (former socialist revolutionary, assassin of Count Mirbach, the German ambassador to Moscow). Served as an agent from winter 1923 to summer 1924 in the Near East section of the OGPU. Has traveled to Turkey, Palestine, Syria, and Egypt to spy and organize networks of Soviet agents. To enter Turkey and Palestine, he carried a Soviet passport in the name of "Moïse Gourfinkel" an emigrant to Palestine. From that region he continued his travels using false passports. On the photograph in his first passport, Blumkin is clean-shaven, but when he left for Palestine (about two months after that passport was issued) he had a mustache and long beard. In Jaffa he*

opened a laundry, where agent reports were encoded and forwarded to the Soviet consulate general in Constantinople, from which they were sent home by diplomatic pouch.

In 1919, Blumkin was attached as a counselor to the revolutionary Persian bandit Kuchek Khan. In 1924–1925, under the pseudonym Issakov, he headed the Cheka's frontier forces in Stancaucasus [sic] and took part in repressing the uprising in Georgia. In 1926 he was assigned to the Outer Mongolia OGPU station.

Description: looks forty years old, though he is only thirty. Fat, average height, a degenerate's large forehead and black eyes that make him look somewhat like Yevno Azev (according to a photo of Azev taken in 1907–1908). Distinguishing mark: twisted left hand. His address in Moscow is the following (Arbat, 35, apartment no34, tel 4-67-65). The address of his wife (Tatiana Issaevna) is Afanasyevsky Street no. 35; teleph. 4-71-15. In the phone book, Blumkin is listed as "Man of letters."

In Moscow I went to the address listed on the Blumkin file summary sheet. It was an Art Deco building on Denezhny Lane in the heart of the old Arbat neighborhood. A plaque on the facade stated that People's Commissar for Education Anatoly Lunacharsky lived in the building until 1929. The plaque didn't mention Blumkin, who had a service apartment on the third floor, on the same landing as Lunacharsky, where he stayed between missions. Victor Serge, a frequent visitor, described it: "He stayed in a small apartment in the Arbat quarter, bare except for a rug and a splendid stool, a gift from some Mongol prince; and crooked sabers hung over his bottles of excellent wine."

Boris Bajanov told me that he too had visited Blumkin in the mid-1920s. The description he gave pretty much matched Serge's remembrance, but with Bajanov, it took an artificial twist. He made Blumkin look like a character in a wax museum, wearing "a red silk robe with an oriental pipe in his hand." Next to him on a coffee table lay a volume of Lenin's works "always open at the same page," and two or three lines of cocaine on a sheet of silk paper. "Blumkin was a pretentious, vain person," Bajanov told me. "He was convinced he was a historic figure. We used to make fun of his self-conceit."

One day, Bajanov and some friends played a joke on him. They said, "Yakov Grigorevich, we just went to the Museum of the History of the Revolution. There's a whole wall devoted to the Mirbach assassination and to you."

"Really? That's wonderful. What is on the wall?"

"All sorts of newspaper clippings, photos, documents, and citations, and at the top running along the entire wall, a quotation from Lenin: 'What we need is the steady advance of the iron battalions of the proletariat, not hysterical and degenerate petit-bourgeois extravagances.'"

"We made it all up, of course," said Bajanov. "Blumkin was very upset, but he didn't go to the Revolution museum to check on our joke's authenticity."

Blumkin's first cousin told Bajanov that the assassination of Mirbach hadn't happened quite the way Blumkin described it. Said Bajanov:

> When he and his companions were in Mirbach's office, Blumkin threw the bomb and quickly jumped out the window. But he wound up dangling from the fence by the seat of his pants in a very uncomfortable position. The sailor who accompanied him calmly finished Mirbach off, unhooked Blumkin, put him in a truck, and they took off. The sailor died soon afterward on the Civil War fronts and Blumkin was outlawed by the Bolsheviks. But he very quickly went over to their side, betraying the Left Socialist Revolutionaries. He was then admitted to the Party and taken into the Cheka.

Regardless of his exaggerations, I valued Bajanov's accusatory testimony. He claimed that Blumkin had come to Paris in 1929 to assassinate him by throwing him off the Paris–Nice train. But Bajanov said Blumkin grabbed the wrong man and mistakenly sent another passenger to the great beyond. Whether he was lying or twisting the truth, Bajanov had known Blumkin, the "real" Blumkin, a man of flesh and bones—not the figure of ink and paper I was tracking in the archives. In the back room of the café where we met, I can still see the malice in

Bajanov's eyes as he stared at me from behind enormous round horn-rimmed glasses. His memories were distorted by hatred, and at eighty he was struggling to impose his version of history. And that version interested me just as much as the other ones.

It was said that in 1921 Blumkin had been sent to Mongolia when it was occupied by Baron Ungern's troops, to fight at the side of Damdin Sükhbaatar, who was known as the "Mongol Lenin" and led an army of ten thousand horsemen. But had Blumkin really fought "at his side"? Can he be credited with the reported double victory against the two forces that had divided Mongolia between them, Chinese troops and Ungern's White Army? Having reached the gates of the capital, Blumkin supposedly came up with a daring strategy to avoid having to launch a deadly siege. At this point, Blumkin's Mongolian saga slides into myth.

Legend had it that when at war, Baron Ungern always traveled with a pair of eagles from the Mongolian steppes, a gift from the living Buddha and a symbol of his invincibility. Disguised as a lama, Blumkin was supposed to have entered the besieged city and secretly made his way to the baron's headquarters. Getting close to his apartments, Blumkin cut the head off one of the invincible eagles with his saber.

Mission accomplished, he blended into the crowd and spread the rumor that the killing of the eagle showed that the enemy was already within the gates. The city's defenders panicked, and the disoriented Whites beat a retreat in the confusion. Sükhbaatar then made a triumphant entrance into the city. A few days later, during a celebration of the Revolution, the crowd roared when the two friends thundered down the track lying on their horses, and snatched up a silver coin lying on the ground. Blumkin saved that silver coin in memory of the unforgettable Sükhbaatar, who died a few months after his triumph, poisoned by the Chinese or succumbing to tuberculosis, depending on the account.

Back in Moscow, Blumkin published a book about Dzerjinsky and helped edit Trotsky's military writings. One evening, at the studio of the Imaginist painter Georgy Yakulov, he met the celebrated dancer Isadora Duncan, who had come to Moscow at Lunacharsky's invitation, "to teach the proletariat's children to dance." According to the civil registry, that was also the time that Blumkin married Tatiana Feinerman, the daughter of Tolstoy's famous disciple Isaak Feinerman, who wrote under the pseudonym "Teneromo." "I fell in love with a name," Blumkin later confessed to Esenin, who had no reason to envy him, having married Isadora Duncan for the same reasons. Blumkin and his wife had one child, their son, Martin. The name was a double literary reference, to Jack London's Martin and to the hero of Esenin's poem "The Comrade." ("Martin lived, no one knew him. He was the son of an ordinary worker. His comrades were Christ and his cat. His father taught him 'La Marseillaise.'")

I have repeatedly tried to establish an exact chronology of Blumkin's successive missions during the first half of the 1920s, but it was a waste of effort. Not because of a shortage of events, but because whatever connected them had snapped, and the pieces lay strewn across the ground like an airplane crash site. The events I report in this chapter all took place, but it's as if the plane's black box is missing.

Where to begin? And what sources could I trust? I've always liked the colorful English expression to indicate a reliable source: getting something "from the horse's mouth." Assailed at the racetrack by rumors and predictions, professional bettors know to trust only one thing, the condition of the horse. The expression came to mind as I was about to start this chapter and was looking over the blackboard on my office wall, searching for a trail or a hint that would give me a point of departure. An image at the very top of the blackboard caught my eye. It was a reproduction of a 1918 painting of a horse by Georgy Yakulof called *Sulky*. To reconstruct this confused period of Blumkin's life, I would go to the horse's mouth.

I had seen the original painting at the Centre Pompidou in 2013 as part of an exhibition called *Plural Modernities*. I came across it almost by accident. It was hung off to one side and wasn't attracting much attention. I could well have walked past it except that I stopped to read the painting's caption. As usual, it mentioned the name of the painter, the title of the piece and its dimensions, the year it was executed, and the technique used. But I noticed one further piece of information: "Part of the Pegasus's Stall café décor."

I had heard about Pegasus's Stall several times during my research. It was a popular artistic café in the early 1920s frequented by the people who called themselves "Imaginists." This was a group of poets and artists who wanted to revive the noisy and spectacular aspects of prewar literary life in Moscow. They had their bookstore, their review—*Inn for Travelers of the Beautiful*—and their cafés, the Domino and Pegasus's Stall. The job of decorating Pegasus's Stall had been given to the Armenian painter Georgy Yakulov, an Imaginist member known for his theater sets. The horse he painted was a central figure of the café's décor, but also a manifesto.

Pegasus's Stall attracted a colorful coterie of poets, Chekists, prostitutes, and black-market profiteers. The manager, one Anatoly Silin, put his customers into two categories: the "serious," speculators from the Sukharevka, Okhotny, and Smolensk market neighborhoods; and the "not serious," which included the penniless poets and artists that gangsters called "hollow people." The café allowed the first group to launder its money in the name of art, and the second to feed on vodka and vain poetry.

But Pegasus's Stall wasn't merely a gathering place. It was a performance scene that could turn poets into stars whose popularity was measured less by their talent than by their power to transgress. Mayakovsky led the way. His yellow shirt, ringing voice, and provocations had made him famous before the Revolution, before he published a single line. The Imaginists learned from his example: the artist's performance precedes the work of art. In the early 1920s, Sergei Esenin and Anatoly Mariengof dominated the poetry scene and embodied these new poets' status. Mariengof made no apologies. "'Comrades, I am a poet of genius.' That was the line Vadim Shershenevich liked to use when starting his brilliant speeches. We all said pretty much the same thing—Mayakovsky, Esenin, and I, even Ryurik Ivnev, in his girlish voice."

After two years of war, everything was in short supply. The poet Andrei Biely came up with a much-repeated statement that defined an era unable to satisfy even the most elementary needs: "The victory of materialism in Russia has led to the complete disappearance of material in this country." The only thing not lacking were poets. They were in the streets, in the theaters, in the cafés. What were they doing? They were building their legends and short-ening their nights.

Blumkin was one of them, except that he built his legend not only at poetry readings but with a weapon in his hand in Georgia, Siberia, and Mongolia. Since joining the Bolsheviks, he had proven his loyalty more than once. He was spending his nine lives without counting, dodging ambushes and exposing himself to the greatest dangers. Blumkin was a man of action. He wanted to be a real hero, the only way for a poor Jew like himself to gain notoriety. That was his only allegiance and his only loyalty. Poetry would come later, when he was thirty. Then he would have all the time in the world to draw from his experiences what he called "the honey of words."

"In the beginning," wrote Mariengof,

> Blumkin held back a little from our glory, as we pompously called our scandalous renown. We had gotten there by many paths, difficult paths. One dark night in the fall, we even "debaptized" certain Moscow streets. We tore down the "Founders Point" sign and replaced it with "Esenin Street, Imaginist." We pulled down "Petrovka" and put up "Mariengof Street, Imaginist." Ahead of May Day, we spent our last kopecks to have our pictures taken and framed in red calico. We displayed them in store windows on Tver Street from the Chasseurs alley to the Passion Monastery. The store managers had a sense of humor, and gladly gave us permission.

A number of sources describe the relationship between Blumkin and Esenin and the Imaginist movement. But they aren't to be found in the Russian Federation archives at 17 Bolshaya Pirogovskaya, where they are now both available and reliable. Instead, they are in literary chronicles, a generally unreliable source because of writers' natural tendency to make themselves look good, and which become veritable fabulation machines in times of war or revolution.

Mariengof devoted three books to this period, two of which have been published in English: *A Novel Without Lies* and *Cynics*, which Joseph Brodsky called a masterpiece. As for the third, a collection of remembrances translated as "My century, my youth, my friends and lovers," I knew that it mentioned Blumkin several times, but I had searched for it in vain. Not only was it out of print, but I couldn't find it at the French national library, and none of the various online booksellers carried secondhand copies. I finally wrote Mariengof's French translator, Anne-Marie Tatsis-Botton, and got this answer:

> *Dear sir, unfortunately, "My friends" isn't out of print, for the simple reason that it was never published! I translated it seven or eight years ago for Anatolia, the publisher. I corrected the galleys and noted the book's publication date, but a dispute arose between the series editor and the publisher, and everything stopped. The translation is sitting in boxes at Noir sur Blanc, which*

owns the rights and is trying to contact the appropriate
people in Russia to restart everything more "legally." I
haven't given up hope of the book's coming out "within a
few years." A translator's job sometimes involves a lot of
patience.

To this she added:

I am happy to send you the draft of my translation,
which was a great pleasure to do. It's a very good book,
and I would be delighted if at least one person read it.
The part you are interested in starts at page 204. If
you quote my text, you can caption it, "Forthcoming
from Noir sur Blanc, publishers." That might be a good
augury. Sincerely yours . . .

I immediately opened the file to page 204 and
started reading with the excitement of an explorer
setting foot on terra incognita.

Almost every evening, Blumkin, the former terrorist
and Left SR, would sit at a little glass table. He had
a black beard and was past twenty-one, so no longer
a youth, by the criteria of the times. Another of our
friends, who also had once been a Left SR (Yuri Sablin,
a handsome man with a natural beauty mark on his pink
cheek), was younger, yet already commanded the army
that had routed Kolchak in the Urals . . .
Blumkin was a lyrical being who loved poetry and
glory, his and other people's. How could he have not

joined us, since he viewed us as among the elect? He was faithful, friendly, and accommodating. But the Central Committee of the Left SR Party had come to a decision: eliminate the traitor. For Blumkin, this brought a whiff of coffin wood, a smell he didn't like any more than we pitiful mortals do. So Blumkin made us his bodyguards. After all, the Left SR terrorists weren't about to throw their little bombs and kill two young poets just to get one "disgusting traitor," as they then called their delinquent "hero."

When the Poets' Café closed for the night, Blumkin would always beg us, "Tolia, Serioja, my friends, walk me home." He was then living at the Metropol, which we called the "second House of Soviets."

We walked him home almost every night, more or less risking our skins. After all, there might have been an enthusiast among the ardent bomb throwers who didn't give a damn about Apollo's Russian devotees. I usually walked on the left, Esenin on the right, and Blumkin in the middle, holding tight to our arms.

One night when Blumkin was going home with Alexander Kusikov—they were sharing an apartment on Afansevskaya Street near the Arbat—they spotted a suspicious-looking man on a street corner. Blumkin took out his pistol and pushed his friend aside. From the darkness, a shout rang out: "Halt!" Blumkin ran away. Behind him, shots were fired. Kusikov was arrested by a group of Moscow Chekists on night patrol. Blumkin came back and said to them: "It's a good thing I didn't shoot you. I'm a good shot. I could've killed one of you, comrades." But the Chekists weren't having any of this and hauled the two suspects to the Lubyanka. Everything worked out, though. The commissar of the guard knew Blumkin and had him driven home. After that, Blumkin liked to wear the hat with the Chekist bullet holes. Once again, he had dodged a bullet, literally.

Mariengof was busy building his own legend, putting himself and his friend Esenin at center stage. The legend couldn't stand any rivals, especially not a former terrorist and Chekist, much less a secret GPU agent. Can you imagine the Verlaine-Rimbaud duo founding a literary movement with Bakunin or Netchayev? This complicity between poets and Chekists—an alliance of Parnassus and Lubyanka—is hard to imagine today, because it upsets our settled ideas about police and poetry, which are as far from each other as good and evil. But in the first years of the Revolution, it was perfectly natural. Among the poets and artists, the German ambassador's killer basked in the aura of the SR and its Combat Organization.

The poet Vladislav Khodasevich, who was married to the writer Nina Berberova, described a scene he witnessed at an evening party at Alexei Tolstoy's in the spring of 1918. Esenin had come with a bearded, dark-haired man wearing a leather jacket. He listened to the conversations and occasionally said something, always apropos. That was Blumkin, who would kill the German ambassador three months later. He and Esenin were clearly close. Among the guests was a woman poet, K. Esenin found her attractive and started to flirt. To impress her, he baldly declared: "Would you like to see a killing? I'll arrange it with Blumkin right away!"

When Blumkin was in Moscow, he spent his evenings with his Imaginist friends at the Pegasus's Stall. He was one of the founding members of the "freethinkers," a society that Esenin founded and whose goal was to give the Imaginist group a legal existence, support from Lunacharsky, and maybe some subsidies. A freethinkers charter was drafted on the corner of a table and signed by a dozen members, including Blumkin, Mariengof, Shershenevich, and Kusilov, who was called "Sandro." The freethinkers were committed to the spiritual and economic union of thinkers who created in the spirit of world revolution, in speech and writing. At the first meeting of the association on January 20, 1920, Esenin was elected president.

The first page of the first issue of their magazine, *Inn for Travelers of the Beautiful*, carried this manifesto:

"Beauty in the arts and letters used to be summed up by expressions: 'beaux arts,' 'belles lettres.' What does that mean? To speak in the language of images: the mountains are not especially high, the slopes are not especially steep, the cliffs . . . Oh, the cliffs! Best not have any at all, people might fall off them!'"

For the Imaginists, the Revolution shouldn't bring only better living conditions to the people, but also a deliberate beautification of life. In this way, a small elite, divorced from village reality, undertook a process of general aesthetization of existence and romanticization of life: "the era of the image." Re-making a new image of man. Refounding a new idea of beauty. "How the nature of beauty has changed in our times! We seek and find the essence of beauty in the catastrophic upheavals of the contemporary mind, in the dangers of setting sail toward new Americas, toward new ways of being in the world. That is how we understand the Revolution."

"They philosophized at the drop of a hat, and always went to extremes," writes Vladislav Khodase-vich in *Necropolis*. "They worked on a vast scale. The ate little but drank a lot. They blasphemed with fire, unless that was their way of expressing faith. They went with prostitutes to preach revolution, and beat them. They basically fell into two types: the bearded, dark brooder, and the blond adolescent with long hair and seraphic gaze."

The seraphic blond was Esenin, the leader of the Imaginist group who had traded his peasant shirt and boots for a dandy's cape and top hat. The dark brooder was Blumkin, devoted factotum, always ready to do a favor and protect the Imaginists from the authorities and the police. Several times, he freed poor Esenin at dawn when he'd gotten himself locked up in the Lubyanka.

————

We know one thing for sure: Blumkin, Esenin, and Mariengof were all in Moscow at the same time in the spring of 1918. Esenin was already famous. How did they meet? Probably at the Domino, the literary café that Blumkin and Esenin frequented assiduously before Pegasus's Stall opened and became their headquarters. Above the Domino's sign, and stretching across the entire first floor, another sign in big black letters on a white background read, "Psychiatric Clinic." "That sign was the delight of our many enemies, and our despair," says Mariengof. "For us, it was a real catastrophe. But there was nothing we could do. Up on the first floor, they really were trying to cure crazy people."

Below the psychiatric clinic, poets and writers of various persuasions gathered: Futurists, Imaginists, Acmeists, revolutionaries who loved poetry and poets fascinated by political violence. You might run into Blumkin in his leather jacket, or Esenin and Mariengof in patent-leather shoes, black capes with white scarves, and bowler hats. Past a certain hour, arguments became frequent and would erupt over anything: the role of the verb or the image in prosody, or that of the Party in the Revolution. Blumkin actively participated in those debates, and when he ran out of arguments would pull out his gun. "He seemed to have a pistol where other people had a hand."

Within a few days, the two young provincials became inseparable. The poet and the Chekist spent their evenings at the Domino and slept together in the same bed. But it would be wrong to jump to a hasty conclusion about that intimacy: it was due to the housing crisis. When winter approached, it was the cold, not the fire of desire, that brought their chilled bodies together. Mariengof says that Esenin one day got the harebrained idea of offering a woman poet who was looking for work a secretary's salary in exchange for doing a job that would take her less than a quarter hour a day. Her task was to come to their apartment around one in the morning, undress, and get under the covers. When she had warmed the bed for them, she would get out. For their part, they promised to turn their backs during the operation so as not to offend her modesty. Which they scrupulously did while the poetess got undressed. The arrangement took an unexpected turn, however. After a few days, the irritated poetess refused to go on serving as a warming pan. "I didn't hire myself out to warm the sheets of saints!"

That kind of childishness is hard to imagine in the capital of a young Soviet state suffering from famine and epidemics, a city that lacked everything yet overflowed with provocateurs and spies. What we forget was how very young those revolutionaries were. We can list the Revolution's excesses and faults forever, but shouldn't ever forget its authors' ages.

This is a constant misunderstanding. Revolutions are made by young people and described by old ones.

One evening Blumkin went after a certain Igor Ilinsky, a young actor in Meyerhold's company. Given those revolutionary times, the reason seems almost trivial: Ilinsky had used an old curtain to dust off his shoes. "You uncultured boor!" screamed Blumkin, pulling an impressive Browning from his pocket and pointing it at the actor. But he let Esenin immediately disarm him, while muttering an explanation: "This is a socialist revolution, so we have to kill the boors! Otherwise we'll never get anywhere." "A true romantic!" concluded Mariengof, who described the scene in his memoirs. "There were lots of people like that."

The wounds of the Civil War were not yet healed, and the benefits of the New Economic Policy (NEP) were just beginning to be felt. Two eras were overlapping and doubling their psychological effects: the cruelty of war and the cynicism of prosperity. And this amalgam of terror and cynicism produced a particular sensibility that the Imaginists expressed in their own way.

Esenin and Mariengof wrote side by side in an apartment on Theologian Street, Esenin his poems and Mariengof the draft of his novel *Cynics*, which would not be published until 1928. "Scraps of paper covered my desk," he wrote. "Sheets of soft paper covered with my notes wound up spiked on the nail in the meditation room." Blumkin would visit every day, bringing a fresh crop of news items and anecdotes harvested at the Lubyanka. So a direct line connected the Lubyanka with the novelist's writing desk, except that the "bugging" worked in reverse. The novelist listened to police informers, not the other way around. In the information Blumkin brought from the Lubyanka, Mariengof saw the chaos of the era, "its face as if reflected in the swollen belly of a samovar. A face deformed and fierce."

Samples: In the Kama region people were eating a kind of clay. In Tsaritsyn, they ate grass previously reserved for camels. Acorns were now considered luxuries. People were baking cakes of lime-tree leaves. The Caspian was shipping camel meat. In Slovenka (Pugachyov district), a peasant woman named Golodinka cut up her dead daughter's body to feed her surviving children. The Selyanov orphans stole a dead woman's wrists.

Cannibalism and necrophagia were happening on a massive scale, reported *Pravda*. The Bolshevik Factory shipped the first tractor built in its workshops to the Timiryazev Agricultural Academy experimental station. Typhus had affected 1.5 million people in the republic since the start of winter. The Council of People's Commissars decided to erect a monument to Spartacus, the Gracchi, Brutus, and Babeuf. The Icarus National Aeronautical Enterprise organized a solemn festival to celebrate its first delivery of large-displacement motors. And so on.

Mariengof stuffed his narrative with newspaper headlines, clippings, fragments of government decrees. Events accumulated in successive layers, in shards of reality.

Seismographic writing.

Alfred Döblin used the same collage technique to describe postwar Berlin in *Berlin Alexanderplatz*, published in 1929. At the same time Dos Passos was drawing inspiration from newsreels, press clippings, official declarations and excerpts of manifestos; his *Manhattan Transfer* came out in 1925, Mariengof's *Cynics* in 1928. The three novels are contemporary without it being clear which was the earliest. They expressed the sensibility of an era. "You can't take a picture of a world that is blowing itself up," wrote Hermann Broch in 1934.

The Revolution aimed to change the distribution of wealth and the power imbalance between classes, to invent new law, a new economy, and new political forms of participation that would bring the working and peasant masses into politics. It struggled to impose new forms of expression capable of accounting for a shattered world. It sought new angles to penetrate reality, a different idea of movement.

For the first anniversary of the Revolution, the composer Revarsavr (Arseny Avraamov) proposed to the Soviet government that he conduct a heroic symphony of his own composition. It would be played on the sirens of all of Moscow's factories and workshops, and on locomotive whistles. He also wanted to destroy all the pianos currently in use. "The piano is the international balalaika!" he told anyone who would listen, while touting a revolutionary modification of the bourgeois piano. So as not to bother Lenin, who liked violin and piano music, the concert of sirens took place not in Moscow, but in Baku. A year and a half later, Revarsavr played his "Revopus" no. 1, no. 2, no. 3, no. 4, no. 5, no. 6, no. 7, etc., at Pegasus's Stall. They were especially composed for the grand piano he had modified. Ordinary human fingers were obviously unsuited for playing "revmusic," so our Imaginist composer strapped little garden rakes to his hands.

In Moscow, we spent a long time looking for Pegasus's Stall. An old map put it at 37 Tver Street, at the corner of Gnezdnikovsky Street, where the Café Bom and its clowns stood before the Revolution. But the clowns, like the Imaginists, were no longer of this world, and their haunts impossible to find. We had to face facts. After spending days poring over old Moscow maps at the land registry, I finally gave up. The street had been dug up and widened several times since the 1920s, and the mythic Pegasus's Stall lay under the ruins of old Tverskaya Street.

One night at the hotel, Emmanuelle torpedoed my last hopes by showing me a photo of a torn-up Tverskaya Street on her computer screen. The

Russian caption, soberly translated by Google, read, "Pegasus's Stall, here somewhere."

My only link with Pegasus's Stall was *Sulky*, the horse painted by Georgy Yakulov. It was the sole survivor of the Imaginists' nights. I had to make it speak. At the Centre Pompidou, I stood for a long time in front of the painting, as if hesitating on the threshold of an abandoned house. Before me, *Sulky* glowed like a radioactive object, or rather a "memory-active" one, charged with traces of life and memories. It was the only "real" material piece of the puzzle I'd been trying to assemble for years. I had read accounts, consulted archives, assembled maps and photographs, but I had never seen an object from Blumkin's everyday environment up close before.

Blumkin and his Imaginist friends must have passed in front of Yakulov's painting hundreds of times. Had they looked at it carefully? They probably did in the first days, and then got used to its presence, and forgot it. The horse retreated into the silence of objects. But it made me dizzy to think that it had been present at all those Pegasus evenings—the readings, the bravado, the arguments, the glances. By a bizarre effect of translation, I could see, through the horse, the inside of the café decorated by Yakulov: the entrance, hung with a sign he painted with a winged Pegasus bordered with stylized, old-style calligraphy: "Стойл Пегаса." I could see the chandeliers and wall sconces repeated in the mirrors that widened a space so narrow that the tables were practically stuck together. On the stage, a Romanian orchestra was playing. On either side of the mirrors, nude women were painted with an eye instead of a navel, along with Imaginist slogans and Esenin's golden curls haloed by his verse: "Плюйся, ветер, охапками листъв" (Spit, you wind, leaves by the armful). On a wall, *Sulky* galloped though the cigarette smoke.

Blumkin would sit at a glass-top table facing the entrance. He kept his back to the wall, because he didn't trust his former Left SR comrades; they had already tried to kill him three times. Overhead, *Sulky* watched over him like a guardian angel. When Blumkin's thoughts ran away with him, whipped by liquor and cocaine, the faithful horse ran by his side without leaving its plywood backing.

Sulky is a pictorial demonstration of Yakulov's technique for portraying movement, and is opposed to that of the Italian and Russian Futurists. His horse is a collection of separate fragments, a heterogeneous mix of individual pieces and signs: gears, pictograms, fan-shaped ideograms, curls, spirals, arabesques, vague nuances, and splashes of color.

Futurism and chronophotography try to portray the tension of movement using a multiplicity of shapes in motion, as in *Dog on a Leash*. By contrast, Yakulov tried to bring that movement out from within lines and planes, from the very texture of the painting. "The Futurists' attempt to give a walking dog forty paws is naive," he said, "and it doesn't make the dog go any faster."

In a 1926 article on Picasso, Yakulov wrote that earlier artists had worked through a series of perspectives: "conventional flat" perspective in the Middle Ages, "three-dimensional" perspective in the Renaissance, and "pure photographic" perspective in the twentieth century. "Today's artists face a new task, that of determining and expressing the perspectives of objects in oscillation." The painter's eye wasn't a camera; everything was vibration. The whole era was intoxicated with speed, with the energy of movement. "The railroad has changed the whole course, the whole structure, the whole rhythm of our prose," wrote Mandelstam. Yakulov put his galloping horse on a sheet of plywood. Esenin searched for the verbal image to convey the vibration of the real and its life principle.

Esenin, Duncan, and Yakulov. All three would soon find themselves together in the painter's studio in Moscow one night toward the end of 1921.

Isadora Duncan had just arrived. It was her first invitation to Yakulov's. The little Imaginist gang was all there. The scene was legendary. Duncan lay stretched out on the sofa with Esenin at her feet. The dancer ran her hand through his curls and whispered, "*Zolotaya golova!*" (Golden head). Duncan didn't know more than a dozen Russian words, but several witnesses claimed to have distinctly heard her say those two words. She then kissed the poet on the lips and, in a strong accent, said, *"Angel!"* (Angel). She kissed him again, and said, *"Chort!"* (Devil). Standing off to one side, Blumkin observed the scene with one hand on the grip of his Browning—you never know. At three o'clock in the morning, Duncan and Esenin went off together.

A friend of Duncan's named Mary Desti gave another version of the evening, probably inspired by Duncan. "Suddenly the door opened, and on the threshold appeared the most beautiful face she'd ever seen, crowned with golden hair. Piercing blue eyes gazed at her. There was no need for introductions. She opened her arms, and he fell to his knees, hugging her knees and tearfully repeating, 'Isadora! Isadora! *Mia, mia.*'"

A third version of the encounter came from a witness present at the evening. "Isadora spotted the blue-eyed poet and cried, 'Who is that man with the face of a debauchee?' They were introduced, and gossips claimed they slept together that very first night."

Georgy Ivanov, whom we encountered earlier, also had a version of the event, a colorful story no more credible than his account of the Blumkin-Mandelstam quarrel. "At a banquet in her honor, Isadora kissed Esenin on the lips. The poet, who was drunk, pushed her away, and when she kissed him again, he slapped her hard. Isadora began to sob, and he comforted her. She then wrote on a window, 'Esenin is a hooligan!' 'Esenin is an angel!' That was the start of their love story."

Isadora's own account drew from the canons of mythology. According to her, the union of their two souls began while they were asleep, when "his soul soared up to meet mine."

The affair was the talk of the town. A legend was born, and it didn't lack for memorialists. Dance and Poetry. America and Russia. A flood of more or less apocryphal novels, essays, and memoirs followed, including a Franco-British film, *Isadora*, directed by Karel Reisz, which earned Vanessa Redgrave a best actress award at the 1968 Cannes Festival.

The worst enemy of truth isn't a lie, it's pathos. In his memoirs, Mariengof is harsh. He thought that Esenin was attracted not by Isadora Duncan, but by her worldwide fame—a religion he wasn't about to join. His account is merciless. "She only came to Soviet Russia because Lunacharsky, the culture commissar, had promised her the Cathedral of Christ the Savior. Ordinary theaters no longer inspired her. The barefoot dancer's spirit was soaring very high. Instead of the dust in theater wings, she wanted to inhale the sweetest incense."

The government put a town house on the Purest Icon of the Virgin Street at Isadora Duncan's disposal to establish a dancing school. She taught there for a time. Short film clips show children jumping, spreading their arms like wings, their legs moving, and their bodies rising into the air before falling back to the ground, imitating the flight of birds.

Esenin's marriage to Duncan proved a disaster. They left for Europe and the United States to escape the ghosts hovering around them. Esenin was in bad shape when he returned. They'd had many fights, in private and in public. When they came back from the European tour they separated for good. Esenin continued his long descent into hell, sinking into depression and displaying growing signs of paranoia.

"Toward the end of 1925, the idea of 'leaving' became Esenin's idée fixe," wrote Mariengof. "He would lie down on train tracks, try to throw himself out a window, cut his veins with a shard of glass, stab himself with a kitchen knife. Eventually he cut his veins. He left a few lines of a poem written in his own blood." The Imaginist years ended with Esenin's death in late 1915. Blumkin left Moscow for Mongolia. Mariengof got married and wrote his masterpiece, *Cynics*. Yakulov died in 1928. Isadora Duncan abandoned her dancing school and fled to the Riviera to write her memoirs. She died on September 14, 1927, in the most melodramatic possible way. Her scarf got caught in the wheel of a Bugatti convertible she was riding in, and strangled her.

November 13, 2015, our last day in Moscow. We went to the New Tretyakov Gallery, which was showing works by Chagall, Mayakovsky, Kandinsky, and Malevich. I wanted to see *Sulky* again, and Yakulov's self-portrait. The museum, which covers a square block, is set in a large park near the Moskva River that is planted with trees and statues. Children call it "the statue garden" and guidebooks refer to it as the garden of "fallen" or "torn-down" statues. A poor translation calls it "the garden of fallen monuments."

The Muzeon Art Park, to give its proper name, is a fifty-acre square created in 1992 that features some seven hundred bronze, wood, marble, and stone sculptures among trees and playgrounds. At the park entrance, we passed a big granite Stalin with a broken nose surrounded by cages piled high with stone skulls, which were added in 1998. The statue originally stood in Theatre Square. A little farther, the tall bronze statue of Felix Dzerzhinsky that dominated Lubyanka Square from 1958 to 1991 rose high into the stormy sky. It was the work of Evgeny Vuchetich, Party member and hero of socialist labor. A specialist in warlike gigantism, he also created monuments to soldiers of the Soviet Army in Berlin and Volgograd. Turn a corner and you encounter a large Sverdlov, the reputed brains behind the November 1917 insurrection. Also several Lenins, an immense Gorky, and a Kalinin, along with anonymous workers, a vigorous couple brandishing hammer and sickle, and a dairymaid.

Soviet statuary was born soon after the 1917 Revolution, contradicting the Old Bolsheviks' cherished
principle of anonymity. Before the August 1918 attack on Lenin, few people knew what he looked like.
To the revolutionaries, the hero was the people, a
faceless entity as difficult to portray as productive
forces or the means of production. But since there
was no point in decorating streets with tractors and
machine tools, it was decided to revert to statues of
great men. It would be a transitory measure while
waiting for the triumph of the people, faceless and
nameless.

What followed was a tremendous boom in monumental statues that made the USSR a gold mine for
the sculptors who got commissions from the state.
Among these, the famous Sergei Merkurov—he
made Leo Tolstoy's death mask—became the Soviet
regime's official sculptor. His fifty-odd commissions included a Dostoyevsky for Tverskaya Street
and a few Lenins put up here and there. Merkurov
had studied sculpture in Paris, where he was influenced by Rodin. "Carried away by the energy
of the Revolution, he became its spokes-sculptor."
Mayakovsky ridiculed the official sculptor for pro-
ducing "bronzes by the kilo" and "slick marbles."
But Merkurov had the last word: he made the poet's
death mask after his suicide.

Following the collapse of the USSR, the Russian
government relegated the bronze ghosts to this park,

where they are enjoying a second life while awaiting history's final verdict. Whether purgatory or *salon des refusés*, it stars the has-beens of the Revolution, now demoted and harmless, that you can study at your ease. Men once feared in their day are at the mercy of children's jokes. Honeymooning couples kiss at their feet. Those nostalgic for communism can gaze at them and ponder the unfairness of history. In this Disneyland of communism, Western tourists take selfies. We took pictures, too. Standing on tiptoe, Emmanuelle barely reached Gorky's knees, which gives an idea of the monument's scale. A little farther, her gloved hand wiped a dusting of snow from Lenin's smooth pate. In another photo, I have joined a group of revolutionaries with martial profiles, led by a gesturing woman. I am marching with them toward the radiant future of communism.

That was November 13, 2015. Our last day in Moscow, a carefree, happy day. A peaceful day, until the moment our smartphones started to vibrate in the middle of the night. Terrorists were shooting in Paris. Under the muted Euronews screen, the news crawl read, "Paris Under Assault," and a figure: 140 people dead. The Bataclan facade. Ambulances' flashing lights. Café terraces. Terrorists...In our Metropol hotel room, images were splattering the screen. A line from a Heiner Müller play came to mind: "When she walks through your bedrooms carrying butcher knives, you'll know the truth."

CHAPTER

11

From the airport, the taxi sped down the highway along the Bosporus. It was snowing heavily, and the domes of the two great mosques on the hills overlooking the bay were drowned in dense fog and barely visible. It was a freezing late afternoon typical of Istanbul in winter. On the Galata Bridge that links the city's two coasts, a line of fishermen with rods in hand and buckets and baskets at their feet made a human chain linking East and West. The taxi raced across the bridge, heedless of the icy patches that punctuated the pavement. It drove for a while by the docks on the western side, then the driver suddenly braked and pointed to some huts with steamed-up windows. That was where the ferries left for Prinkipo, an island in the Sea of Marmara that I planned to visit the next day.

In Blumkin's day, Istanbul was still called Constantinople, but he was no longer Blumkin; he was Sultanov, and later, Sultan-Zade. You went to Constantinople if you wanted to disappear. You could enter with one identity and leave with another, changed from head to toe. The archaeologist turned out to be a secret agent, the businessman was a diplomat, and the rug seller was negotiating mining concessions for British or American consortiums. It was a dangerous city, with many diplomatic representatives; a nest of spies. You could vanish without a trace, under a false name or six feet under, the victim of a contract or a settling of scores.

The Western powers had their spies, and the Soviets kept an eye on them. They also infiltrated the circles of White Russians who had emigrated en masse at the end of the Civil War, and watched the representatives of ex-empire nationalist movements from Kazakhstan, Armenia, Georgia, and Azerbaijan. Between the Turkish and Soviet secret services, traded information was the coin of the realm. For the Soviets, Turkey was at their doorstep, an intelligence hub. The steamer *Ilyich* shuttled between Odessa and Constantinople with cargos of coded messages, documents written in invisible ink, and undeveloped microfilm.

In the mid-1920s, a new generation of Russian military experts, spies, and diplomats was graduating from the Military Academy of the General Staff, and in particular from its Oriental

Studies department. They were assigned to Istanbul, Shanghai, Ulan Bator, New Delhi, and Cairo. The victorious Revolution was forging its way along the railroad lines to Asia. The mission of "illegal residents," who did not have diplomatic immunity, was to redraw, stabilize, and strengthen the Soviet Union's borders to the south and east. They organized uprisings, supported strikes, and pressed local populations' demands against the British Empire.

Blumkin was probably too individualistic for a military career. His shadowy personality was better suited to espionage, and his knowledge of foreign languages more useful in diplomacy than in the army. But he started his career by killing an ambassador. This left secret diplomacy, so he elected to go into intelligence. As a secret agent, he spent his whole career first in the Cheka foreign affairs department, then the GPU, carrying out secret missions in Inner Mongolia, Tibet, northern China, and Palestine. But after 1925, his footsteps disappear into the fog that surrounds clandestine operations overseas, which are secret by nature, but also into the mists eddying around the legends that were increasingly being told about him. Spies and defectors. Infiltration operations on foreign soil. Unexplained murders. A chart of Blumkin's missions looked less like pieces of territory than a horizon where the clear interests of the new Soviet state and the inclination of a generation of young diplomats to the Orient converged. Blumkin hopped from one city to the next: Ulan Bator, New Delhi, Shanghai, Lhassa, Jaffa, Jerusalem, Cairo. The stories of his exploits hopped also between literary genres, from coming-of-age story to spy thriller, from war memoir to adventure novel by way of travelers' tales. Majestic scenery unfolded behind a series of stage sets: the Gobi Desert, the Manchurian Railway, the slums of Shanghai, the cliff-clinging roads of Tibet.

Istanbul was the final stage of my journey tracking Blumkin in the eighth and ninth stages of his life. In 1928, he was named "clandestine resident" and tasked with creating a counterespionage network in Palestine, Syria, Jordan, and Egypt. When it became operational, the network was to gather information on English and French Middle East policy and infiltrate liberation movements in the British protectorates. The GPU and Komintern's Foreign Departments were concerned about the situation in Palestine. There was a risk of war or clashes between communities. Palestine was a launching pad for revolutionary actions and intelligence gathering in all the Arab countries. But the Secret Intelligence Service, which looked out for British interests, was omnipresent in the region. It had highly trained agents and thousands of informants. It wouldn't be easy to establish a local presence without attracting its attention, and recruiting on the ground was practically impossible. So Constantinople was an ideal rear base for Blumkin's network.

With Constantinople, Blumkin's life reached a kind of acme. He was at the summit of his career as a spy, a clandestine *rezident* of the KGB. Yet in less than a year, he would tumble from those heights into a cell at the Lubyanka and be executed without a trial on Stalin's personal order.

The chronology of events in Blumkin's life, which was so difficult to establish in earlier sequences, now became easy to follow. During the last year of his life you could follow his movements almost week by week. They all lead in and out of Constantinople, to Europe (Paris, Berlin, Frankfurt, and Vienna) or to the Middle East (Palestine, Egypt, Syria, Iraq).

But Constantinople wasn't only the *rezidentura*, the GPU's headquarters. It was a kind of motif, an image in the carpet where all the threads of intrigue in Blumkin's life came together. In the center of the tapestry was the face of his absent father, or rather those of his two substitute fathers: Leon Trotsky and Mendele Mocher Sforim. The creator of the Red Army and the grandfather of Yiddish literature. The instructor and the teacher. The strategist and the poet. In early 1929, Stalin drove Trotsky out of the USSR and exiled him to Constantinople. It was there that Blumkin visited him in the spring and summer of 1929, a visit that should have remained secret and would cost him his life. Mocher Sforim, who died in 1917, would be a ghost that haunted

Blumkin during the last year of his life. And at this point, the affair took a truly novelistic turn.

After the fall of the Soviet Union, a note drafted by Blumkin and addressed to the head of the OGPU Foreign Department was found in the Russian Federation's archives. The note was titled "Proposal for the Creation of a Clandestine Network in Palestine." It specified: 1. The identity of the members of the initial core of agents. 2. The conditions of their recruitment. 3. The modes of communication between them. 4. The rules to follow for physical meetings. 5. Forms of communication with the Foreign Department. Blumkin proposed including Iraq and Persia in the new network and naming a permanent representative in each country. Objective: to oppose the region's omnipresent Secret Intelligence Service in case of war. Blumkin planned to travel to all the countries to supervise and direct the activity of the *rezidents*.

But first, he had to come up with a fake name and profession that could serve as a cover for his espionage work. During a trip to Europe Blumkin had met a dealer in rare books in Vienna. The man told him that since the end of the war demand had been strong for collectible works, incunabula, holy books, old Bibles, Torahs, and Talmuds. Dealers had already ransacked Galicia and Poland and were now scouring Turkey, Syria, and North Africa.

"The sale of antiquarian Jewish books overseas is doing very well," wrote Blumkin to Mikhail Trilisser, the head of the Foreign Department. "The potential buyers are not museums, but mostly collectors who made their fortune during the war and want to invest their money by collecting valuable books. What better cover for our work! It would give us the opportunity to make connections and would explain our presence anywhere in the Middle East."

Increasing postwar demand had driven up the price of rare books in the marketplace, and Russia had a great many of them. Some had passed from private collections to the state libraries during the Revolution, but many works were to be found in Jewish villages of the former Pale of Settlement, in people's attics and cellars. To Trilisser, Blumkin suggested selling these treasures abroad, since Russia had no use for them, and setting up a legal protocol to facilitate the purchase, not to say confiscation, of the books from individuals. To make it impossible to trace commercial operations that amounted to pillaging national treasures, Blumkin suggested using shell companies and smuggling to get the works out of the country.

In November 1928 several paintings from the Hermitage and Imperial Palace collections had been sold for low prices in auctions in Berlin and Vienna. They included European paintings from the sixteenth and seventeenth centuries, porcelain objects, and furniture. The émigré press raised a

hue and cry, accusing the Bolsheviks of plundering
the national patrimony. Blumkin heard about the
scandal and sent Trilisser another note.

> *The sale of holdings held by the state and in muse-*
> *ums has proved inefficient, for two reasons. First, items*
> *are being sold at a loss, which doesn't bring in much*
> *money. Second, the fact that Soviet institutions are*
> *selling these confiscated goods themselves creates legal*
> *and political complications, exposing them to lawsuits by*
> *their former owners. Future operations of this sort should*
> *be carried out by shell companies, not directly by official*
> *Soviet organs. Items must be chosen whose transfer*
> *would do no harm to science, and at the same time bring*
> *in significant amounts of money. Ideally, we would select*
> *items that would not be the subject of lawsuits by their*
> *prior owners.*

Selling Jewish books filled all three conditions.
There was no demand for those kinds of religious
works in the USSR, confiscating the books from libraries "did no harm to science," and selling them
abroad avoided the possibility of legal action against
the state, their sole owner.

Blumkin suggested that the state sell the books
to the Iranian merchant Yakum Sultan-Zade,
meaning Blumkin himself, who would be responsible for having them appraised by experts. The
books would then be put on the European market.
It's not impossible that by getting these books out

of the USSR, Blumkin was trying to save them. He had seen Jewish works stolen and burned in autos-da-fé during the Civil War pogroms. He may have thought that by selling these treasures of Jewish culture to Western collectors, he would be sparing them a possible collapse of the Soviet Union, where anti-Semitism was on the rise in the late 1920s, during Stalin's Great Turn.

Blumkin was now walking in the footsteps of Mendele Mocher Sforim, his old teacher at the Talmud Torah in Odessa. After all, didn't the man's name mean "book peddler"? Hadn't he crisscrossed the Pale of Settlement roads before him? Once Blumkin obtained the legal authorizations, he left for Odessa. Traveling through little Ukrainian towns with the authority of a Chekist, he knocked on bookstore and synagogue doors and inspected peoples' attics. In exchange for a receipt, he confiscated Talmuds, Torahs, prayer books, psalms, *Tanyas* ("which are a guide to life"), Hassidic tales of unexpected depth, stories marrying the mystical to daily life; in short, everything that could be read about a life with a connection to the divine.

Back in Moscow, Blumkin made an inventory of works held by the state libraries. In the Lenin Library he found a collection of Hebrew manuscripts confiscated from Baron Ginsburg, as well as a great number of uncataloged works. His friend and neighbor A. V. Lunacharsky, the education commissar, wrote to the director of the Public State

Library and the director of Leningrad State University as follows: "July 26, 1928, to the Public State Library: The RSFRS People's Commissariat for Education requests that all sixteenth-century Hebrew books held by the State Library be removed and sent by courier to the Leningrad GPU at my personal address. [Signed] People's Commissar for Education Lunacharsky." Blumkin was living at the same address as Lunacharsky at the time, and even on the same landing.

Leningrad Chekists were pressed into service and sent to libraries, where they confiscated rare books. Between the end of August and the middle of October they sent more than a hundred books to the GPU Foreign Department, including incunabula, two Tanakhs published in 1462 and 1491, and a four-volume rabbinical Bible on parchment.

For the last time, the book and the sword were crossing in Blumkin's life, as they had in his youth in Odessa. He tried to reconcile the one with the other. He wielded the sword of the Chekists to confiscate sacred books. Selling the books confiscated from libraries would finance that sword in the Middle East. It was now time to make contact with antiquarians in Constantinople and negotiate the first transactions.

In mid-September 1928, two and a half months after his initial letter to Trilisser, Blumkin returned to Odessa to start the process of getting a visa for Turkey. This took two weeks. The moment he got it, he telegraphed the GPU Foreign Department: "I received the letter. I am in good health. Love to Mom. Liza." On October 8 another telegram reached the GPU: "I am worried about the lack of letters. Nadia." This meant that he had arrived in Constantinople. It would take him a couple of months to rent a space, buy furniture, and order seals, paper, and envelopes with his new import-export company's logo. In late October 1928, the first batch of books reached him in Constantinople. Blumkin stored the rarest ones in the Deutsche Orientbank's vaults, and the others in those of the Ottoman Bank. He made contacts among Constantinople's Jewish merchants and rabbis and brought from Vienna the first Jewish resellers, with whom he undertook what he called "complicated Jewish negotiations." They were all dazzled by his collection. His reputation crossed borders and his name spread among booksellers and antiquarians. In November, Blumkin received an attractive offer from the Kaufmannverlag-antiquariat company in Frankfurt am Main. He promptly traveled from Vienna to Frankfurt to meet Herr Kaufmann, bringing three incunabula: a three-volume Tanakh with commentaries (1486), the Naples Bible in Hebrew (1488–1491), and four volumes of the Bomberg rabbinical Bible (Venice, 1518). Blumkin conducted the negotiations with brio and received $6,000 for the sale of the three works. But that wasn't all. Kaufmann agreed to make "Sultanov" his representative in Turkey and the other countries of the Middle East. The metamorphosis was complete. The secret agent had become a seller of rare books. In a few months, Sultanov's reputation was established.

In Moscow, there was some concern that Blumkin might get carried away by this commercial activity at which he was so successful and forget about his principal mission, the counterespionage network in Palestine. "Don't forget that your main task consists in organizing the network," wrote Trilisser, his boss. "Palestine is important from a strategic point of view, because in case of war with England, the disruption of Red Sea shipping would be very helpful for us." It was time for Blumkin to go back to Constantinople. An unexpected development would precipitate his return.

On February 12, 1929, a steamship from Odessa docked at Constantinople in bitterly cold weather. Aboard were Leon Trotsky, his wife, and their son Lev Sedov, who was twenty-three. An icebreaker had had to clear a path through the frozen Black Sea. "The *Ilyich*, which carried no cargo or passengers, cleared about one o'clock in the morning," wrote Trotsky in his autobiography. When in Turkish territorial waters, he handed the customs officers who came aboard a letter for Mustapha Kemal Atatürk, Turkey's head of state: "Dear Sir: At the gate of Constantinople, I have the honor to inform you that I have arrived at the Turkish frontier not of my own choice, and that I will cross this frontier only by submitting to force. I request you, Mr. President, to accept my appropriate sentiments."

In a single night, the founder of the Red Army had become an exile that Churchill called "a bundle of old rags, stranded on the shores of the Black Sea." The man Churchill couldn't defeat on the battlefield was leaving history by the back door, and Winston could now give his contempt free rein. The news of Trotsky's expulsion from the USSR hit like a thunderbolt. Stalin tried to delay the announcement as long as possible, but the news spread undercover and caught the attention of the worldwide media. The journalists pouring into Constantinople all asked Trotsky the same question: "How could you lose power?" Losing power isn't "the same thing as losing a watch or a notebook," he explained, but is the result of a political and ideological shift. "When the revolutionaries who directed the seizure of power begin at a certain stage to lose it, whether peacefully or through catastrophe, the fact in itself signifies a decline in the influence of certain ideas and moods in the governing revolutionary circles."

After Lenin's death in 1924, Trotsky lost every battle he fought, one after another. First he was excluded from the Central Committee, then from all Party proceedings, and finally he was deported to Alma-Ata, where he was closely guarded while a suitable country was found to send him to. Stalin eventually gave the order to deport him to Constantinople, where Moscow had powerful connections who could keep him under surveillance while his elimination was being prepared. And killing Trotsky might not even be necessary. The city was infested with White Russians and Western spies who might well decide to eliminate the person responsible for their exile and defeat.

Trotsky was initially lodged in a wing of the Russian consulate while his wife and son looked for housing in the city. But there was no way he would stay at the mercy of his enemy in the consulate, where his every move was watched and his correspondence opened. But then, the entire city felt like a prison. He stayed closeted in the consulate just a few days, only going out to walk a few steps in the snowy street. He could be seen along the tramway tracks on the Grande Rue de Péra, in the company of his guards. He was offered several housing options, but none suited him. After a few weeks, the Constantinople GPU representative moved the family to the Hotel Tokatliyan near the consulate, from which Trotsky's wife could continue her search for a place to live. In reality, Trotsky distrusted the consulate and wanted to escape its burdensome protection as soon as possible. The isolation was weighing on him. For more than ten years he had been at the forefront of all the battles of the Revolution, Civil War, and reconstruction. He had no desire to permanently settle in a country whose language he didn't speak. He hoped to soon get a visa from England, Germany, or France, where he had many supporters and friends made during his first exile. That way, he could continue the political struggle on an international scale. During his first months in Constantinople, Trotsky repeatedly requested visas for Europe. But European capitals feared the contagion of Bolshevik ideas, and the aura of the Red Army founder was such that nobody wanted to risk welcoming such a dangerous exile on their soil. The doors closed one after another. First it was Germany, then France. In the spring of 1929, when Labourite Ramsay Mac-Donald won election, Trotsky began to hope for an exile in England, but his hopes were soon dashed. Except for a short visit to Copenhagen, the Trotskys would remain in Turkey for more than four years. As Trotsky biographer Isaac Deutscher put it: "They sat there all the time as in a waiting-room on a pier, looking out for the ship that would take them away."

The new guard was already coming from Prague and Berlin, however. From Paris, Raymond Molinier and his wife, Jeanne Martin des Pallières, sailed to Constantinople, burning with the fervor of the first apostles. They were the first settlers of that "planet without visa" that Trotsky would roam for his eleven years of exile. Molinier was able to find a large house on the island of Prinkipo overlooking the Sea of Marmara, about twenty miles from Constantinople. Irony of history: the "Princes' Islands" were so named because Byzantine monarchs used them as a place to exile royal heirs they wanted to keep away from the throne.

The day following our arrival in Istanbul, we took the ferry for Prinkipo. After an hour-and-a-half crossing, we docked at the little carless island where Trotsky spent the first four years of his exile, from 1929 to 1933. A group of donkey-drawn buggies awaited us near the dock. It was raining, so we climbed into the first one we saw and took off under a dripping canopy, in search of Trotsky's house. The buggy drove along a road lined by shuttered villas, their gardens planted with jasmine and bougainvillea. Then the driver pointed to a little side street that ran down to the sea. "Trotsky! Trotsky!" he repeated, with such a strong accent that it took me a moment to understand what he was saying. A driveway led to a big redbrick building with a shattered roof, surrounded by bushes and weeds. A crumbling six-foot fence protected the garden, which sloped toward a small dock. The vacant house stood motionless, facing the sea. Its roof had collapsed, and vegetation made its way from the garden into the rooms. A few miles to the east of the island, the Asian coast could be seen, once deserted but now covered with buildings and houses. The European coast was just visible much farther to the northwest.

This was the place where Blumkin had visited Trotsky in total secrecy, linking his fate to that of the man Stalin considered his worst enemy. In 1929, Stalin was preparing the second Soviet revolution, the collectivization of the farms, and he needed a free hand. Blumkin knew that if this visit reached his superiors' ears, he would be shot. The leaders of the Soviet Union would consider his loyalty to Trotsky to be an act of high treason, and Stalin wouldn't bother with a trial. "The GPU doesn't need me to execute its agents," he'd warned. Yet Blumkin hadn't hesitated. Trotsky's safety was his first priority.

Blumkin located Trotsky very quickly. He arrived in Constantinople on April 10 and was embracing him on the 16th. How could he have found his mentor in a city as big as Constantinople? What connections did he have within the Soviet *rezidentura* in Constantinople? How often did Blumkin visit? Were these just courtesy visits, or a conspiracy to overthrow the regime? During the meeting, did he raise practical matters connected to establishing an actual clandestine organization? What role did Trotsky's son Sedov play in arranging these secret meetings? Had Trotsky discussed political subjects? What was in the letter that Blumkin agreed to deliver to Trotsky's supporters in Moscow?

In the postwar years, all sorts of legends were going around. For example, the authors of *The Secret War Against Soviet Russia*, a Cold War bestseller, claimed that Blumkin was the head of Trotsky's bodyguard on Prinkipo and served him "with dog-like devotion."

Others claimed that the GPU had sent Blumkin to Constantinople to assassinate Trotsky, but he changed his mind at the last moment and elected to help him instead. In the most crazily romantic version, Blumkin was sent to Constantinople in the company of a GPU Mata Hari who was ordered to overcome her "bourgeois prejudices" and seduce him, so as to discover the exact extent of his collaboration with Trotsky. Gordon Brook-Shepherd, who wrote *The Storm Petrels*, claims that Liza Gorskaya, "one of the most attractive agents at the GPU foreign affairs section," was instructed to make herself available to Blumkin and get him to spill his secrets in pillow talk. Gorskaya was a beautiful woman and an experienced agent, known to American intelligence as "Liza with the big hands and the big feet." Soon after betraying Blumkin, she married Vasily Zarunbin, a GPU *rezident* in Berlin. Under the name Elizabeth Zarubina, she played a key role in spying on the atom bomb project code-named "Manhattan Project" in the 1940s by befriending Robert Oppenheimer's wife, Kitty Harrison, who sympathized with communist ideals.

Until the opening of the Trotsky archives at Harvard's Houghton Library, anyone was free to say almost anything about Blumkin's relationship with Trotsky without fear of contradiction. I remember how excited we became as January 2, 1980, approached, the date the archives would be opened. Would we find Trotsky's letter to the opposition that he entrusted to Blumkin? Did Trotsky mention his meeting with Blumkin to any of his correspondents? What role did he want him to play?

At the end of 1929, Trotsky publicly admitted receiving Blumkin's visit. According to Trotsky, his son Lev Sedov ran into him on the street in Istanbul when Blumkin was returning from the Far East and on his way to the Soviet Union. Sedov then supposedly persuaded Blumkin to "come to the house" to see Trotsky. In reality, a document that Blumkin wrote, dated April 3, 1929, which I found in Sedov's papers at Stanford, suggests that Trotsky's contacts with Blumkin were no accidental meeting, but an organized liaison with the USSR in which the secret agent was clearly a key element. This meeting would cause Stalin to have Blumkin, a Bolshevik, executed on his return to Moscow. It would be a first.

A man with a bloody face regains consciousness to find himself in a wrecked train on the edge of a cliff surrounded by snow-covered mountains. Debris suddenly rains down on him. He trips and falls, and winds up dangling in midair from a train car. Despite his pain, he manages to haul himself up the cars and reaches the tracks just before the train falls into the void. He slumps against a crate, exhausted. When he wakes up, he's in a sunny Tibetan village, his injuries healed. He promptly sets off for Shambhala.

The man is the hero of *Uncharted 2: Among Thieves*, a video game released in the United States in 2009. In the plot, a treasure hunter tries to learn what happened to explorer Marco Polo's fleet, which disappeared when he was returning from China in 1292. Overcoming one obstacle after another, the hero reaches the gates to the kingdom of Shambhala. The game is testimony to our enduring fascination with a Tibetan Buddhist prophecy that appeared between the eighth and tenth centuries.

Shambhala means "the source of happiness" in Sanskrit, "a place of peace and tranquility." It's a mythical land whose inhabitants are said to possess the gift of clairvoyance and enjoy very long, prosperous, and conflict-free lives. Shambhala is one of those sunken Atlantises that have haunted people's imaginations since the Middle Ages.

At the end of the nineteenth century, Helena Blavatsky, a founder of the Theosophical Society, described Shambhala as the hidden home of the Great White Brotherhood, a community of physically perfect and spiritually enlightened humans who guide the evolution of the world. Hitler, Himmler, and Hess saw Shambhala as the mythical birthplace of the Aryan nation, and organized an expedition to Tibet from May 1938 to August 1939 to find it. Less well known but more surprising was the Bolsheviks' passion for Shambhala. An improbable meeting of Soviet secret services and Petrograd occultist milieus, combined with mysticism, geostrategy, sorcery, and espionage.

In the West, the name Shambhala was popularized by the well-known Theosophist painter Nicholas Roerich. He is considered to be the inspiration behind Shangri-la, the hidden Himalayan lamasery that is the romantic setting of James Hilton's 1933 movie *Lost Horizons*. Among the five million hits that Google produces for "Shambhala," you can find some of the seven thousand paintings that Roerich made in Tibet, accompanied by space music by Vangelis.

Roerich hobnobbed with American diplomats and Soviet spies, Japanese politicians and the president of the United States. Aside from the ethnographic and artistic aims of his expedition, Roerich promoted an international agreement to protect works of art in wartime, which earned him a nomination for the Nobel Peace Prize in March 1929. He worked to create an international network of personalities that would support his efforts. On their return from their travels in Asia, Roerich and his wife were triumphantly welcomed to New York City. On June 18, 1929, they were received by the mayor. Three days later, they met Herbert Hoover at the White House. In the spring of 1930, French president Gaston Doumergue welcomed them to the Elysée Palace. In 1935 the Roerich Pact for the protection of works of art in wartime was ratified in Washington, DC, by twenty-one American states.

Thanks to a strange power of persuasion and a consummate gift for publicity, Roerich managed to enlist in his mystical scientific crusade an American millionaire who built a Manhattan skyscraper that houses a museum named for Roerich. He also attracted famous scientists, Intelligence Service spies, Comintern agents, Soviet ambassadors, and even Commissar for Foreign Affairs Chicherin, who received him in Moscow. In exchange for Soviet support for his new project, the painter offered to spy on British activities in Tibet. Chicherin saw the Shambhala prophesies as geopolitical weapons rather than psychological techniques aimed at perfecting the human mind. He thought the mystical considerations enveloping Roerich's expedition project were so much gobbledygook. The Bolsheviks persecuted Orthodox Christians, but they respected Tibetan Buddhism, which they considered to be the religion of an oppressed people.

Like any rationalist, I am distrustful of paranormal phenomena. I've never been drawn to New Age mysteries, and I've preferred to focus on real societies rather than vanished civilizations. After all, I didn't give up the naive faith of my childhood to turn myself over as an adult to some mystical belief, whether draped in saffron saris or stored under shaved pates. Tantric rituals have always repelled me, whether or not enhanced by hashish and aromatic herbs. A Bolshevik I was; a Bolshevik I remain. At a time when many young people of my generation were heading for Kathmandu with guitars, flowered shirts, and water pipes, I spent my afternoons under neon library lights, consulting volumes on history and political economy.

That the highest leaders of the Bolshevik state should follow the teachings of Tibetan Buddhism has always been an enigma for me. Yet the Bolsheviks had put their faith in such eccentricities, invested secret funds, dispatched their best agents, and furnished arms and ammunition to expeditions to Tibet in search of Shambhala. Even Blumkin, who displayed a healthy pragmatism all his life, may have led expeditions to Tibet with the Roerichs. Disguised as a lama (a Tibetan or Mongolian Buddhist monk or priest), Blumkin supposedly participated in the journey into the Himalayas, lending the painter and his family the GPU's moral and logistical support. It was even said that he had met the Dalai Lama in person and suggested an alliance, with Soviet power guaranteeing Tibet's independence.

Shambhala was rumored to be located where India, Tibet, Kashgar, and Afghanistan meet. According to an old manuscript, it was north of the Tarim (Sita) River. Certain ancient Mongolian tales say that its entrance is near Wing-Shan. Helena Blavatsky put the entrance to the forbidden kingdom in the Altyn-Tagh mountain range, at a point never reached by any European. She claimed that the Ellora, Elephanta, and Ajanta caves were linked by underground passages to the White Island of the Gobi Sea. The Ellora and Ajanta caves appear in Roerich's paintings. The Ajanta temples (twenty-nine caves) are carved out of a cliff high above the river. Roerich supposedly hid clues in his paintings that gave access to the underground tunnels leading to Shambhala.

People have long had their own ideas about finding the forbidden kingdom, and that includes those for whom Shambhala isn't a physical territory, but the metaphor for a spiritual quest. In his novel *Against the Day*, Thomas Pynchon describes Shambhala as "an ancient metropolis of the spiritual, some say inhabited by the living, others say empty, in ruins, buried somewhere beneath the desert sands of inner Asia." Addressing rationalists like me, he writes: "You've got your choice—either Shambhala, as close to the Heavenly City as Earth has known, or Baku and Johannesburg all over again, unexplored reserves of gold, oil, Plutonian wealth, and the prospect of creating yet another subhuman class of workers to extract it. One vision, if you like, spiritual, and the other, capitalist. Incommensurable, of course." Toward the end of the novel, Pynchon's hero finds his way to the forbidden kingdom, but it isn't a real country peopled with living beings. "For me, Shambhala, you see, turned out to be not a goal but an absence. Not the discovery of a place but the act of leaving the featureless place where I was."

By studying materials at the Roerich Museum in New York, I was able to retrace the family's expedition in Asia. Accompanied by his wife and his son Yuri (George), Nicholas Roerich left from Sikkim, traveled to Ladakh and Kashmir between March 6 and September 1925, crossed Xinjiang, and wintered at Khotan from October 1925 to January 1926. Then he traveled to Moscow from June 1 to September 9, 1926, before returning to Siberia. From there the group traveled to Ulan Bator in Mongolia, staying from September 1926 to April 1927.

Blumkin was also in Ulan Bator around that time, simultaneously overseeing Soviet intelligence in Tibet, Inner Mongolia, and northern China. So unlike the other rumors surrounding him, his participating in the Roerich expeditions to Tibet is perfectly plausible. Considering how indiscreet the two men were, Blumkin and Roerich were bound to run into each other in a provincial town like Ulan Bator. Blumkin may have been sent to Mongolia to assist Roerich in the preparation of his expedition to Tibet, but also to keep an eye on him. Accounts vary. Some claim that he followed them from a distance, spying on their moves and actions. Others, that Blumkin set off alone from British India to find Shambhala by himself and plant the Red flag in this first republic of the mind. At the Indian border he supposedly disguised himself as a dervish and joined a caravan of Ismaili Muslims traveling on pilgrimage. Or he may have been arrested by English frontier police who had been alerted about an incursion of Soviet agents in India, and interrogated at length on his comings and goings at the frontier.

It was up to me to find proof of all this. The presence of Blumkin in Roerich's company couldn't have escaped the many British agents in the region. The Indian Office archives in London would certainly have some trace of him. While reporting on Bobby Sands's hunger strike in Northern Ireland, I stopped in London to do some research in the Indian Office archives. I had planned to spend a couple of afternoons there; I wound up staying about ten days, buried under a mountain of documents. I came home loaded with hundreds of photocopied pages, which I found miraculously preserved ten years later, at the bottom of the Blumkin Project trunk. Some are now mounted on my office blackboard, their faded color revived by red and blue felt-tip pen.

But I couldn't find any evidence of Blumkin's participation in Roerich's two expeditions. I did find a report by MI6 agent David Petrie, who ran England's counterspy service in British India from 1900 to 1936. It stressed the danger of a fresh Soviet offensive against British interests in Asia, imperiling their presence in India and their influence in Tibet.

In the Roerich Museum archives I ran into a French academic, Dany Savelli, who was working on a book about the Roerich expedition in central Asia. She had cataloged the various accounts of their travels: the Roerichs' son Yuri's travel journal, *Trails to Innermost Asia*, published in 1931 by Yale University Press and two years later in French by the Orientalist publisher Éditions Geuthner; newspaper articles based on press releases from the Roerich Museum in New York; reports from British secret agents concerned by the expedition's detour to the Soviet Union; fantastical instructions from the supposedly higher beings, or mahatmas, diligently recorded by Helena Blavatsky, the Theosophist painter's wife, etc. These different documents reflect a wide range of styles, from the coldness of white papers and classified espionage reports to the incoherent account of a Theosophical quest. Savelli wasn't merely cataloging these very different kinds of documents; she was evaluating their status.

We can get a specific idea about this voyage to Tibet from Yuri Roerich's journal and the trip's extensive press coverage. The little group crossed vast deserts, faced storms, and suffered in freezing temperatures. In the Qaidam Basin, their camp was wrecked and their caravan tents destroyed by a flash flood fed by torrential rains. In the desert, they exchanged gunfire with brigands. They endured weeks of detention at the Mongolia-Tibet border, during which time five members of the expedition died, along with nearly all the caravan's animals. Roerich, who traveled with a gramophone, played Wagner in the Himalayas. "It echoes remarkably in the mountains," he said.

But in his journals, Yuri Roerich says nothing about the days spent in Moscow between June 13 and 26, 1926. He doesn't even reveal that the expedition doctor, a Russian named Riabin, had been authorized to leave Leningrad and traveled to Ulan Bator to join their expedition. So why would he mention Blumkin's presence with them?

Appropriately for such a nebulous intrigue, the answer came to me high in the sky. It was on a Moscow-to-Paris flight, in the form of a remarkably discreet, quiet seatmate—in itself a gift from heaven. The moment we took off, the man buried himself in a book, carefully inserting multicolor Post-it notes while taking notes in a spiral-bound notebook. Feeling relieved, I turned to the window and contemplated the cumulus clouds that the plane's wing cut as the plane climbed.

We might have stayed like that, he with his Post-its and I with my cumulus, if the plane hadn't hit some turbulence and lurched violently a couple of times. The book flew out of his hands and landed at my feet. When I leaned down to pick it up, I noticed a Roerich Tibetan landscape on its cover. Their glowing mountains with chalk-white summits make them easy to recognize. I handed over the book and asked my seatmate if it indeed was a Roerich painting. A broad smile lit up his face. He was delighted to find someone who shared his interest in the subject. The man's name was Andrei Znamenski, and he was reviewing the book about the Roerich expeditions in Tibet for an American university press. The author, Alexander Andreev, had been granted access to the archives on the Bolshevik Tibet project, and drew on them to write a book that revealed the Bolshevik side of the Shambhala myth: *The Shambhala Myth Revisited: The Occultism of Alexander Barchenko and Soviet Power.*

Znamenski was on his way to Paris to give a talk at the École des hautes études en sciences sociales on "The Shamanism Metaphor in Western Culture." He himself had written a book about the relations between Roerich and the Bolsheviks, and published an essay about their search for Shambhala called "Red Shambhala: Magic, Prophecy, and Geopolitics in the Heart of Asia."

A few years earlier, while researching the cultural history of shamanism, Znamenski accidentally discovered the existence of a secret laboratory deep in the Soviet state establishment that was conducting research on Kabbalah, Sufism, Kalachakra, shamanism, and other esoteric traditions in preparation for an expedition to Tibet in search of the legendary city of Shambhala. The laboratory was run by two men who would seem to have nothing in common. The first, Gleb Ivanovich Bokii, was the head of the GPU's "Special Department." The second, Alexander Barchenko, was an occultist writer and science popularizer who had published occultist novels before the Revolution.

I had already heard of Bokii, a former companion of Lenin who had taken part in the October 1917 days. After the Revolution, he ran the Petrograd

Cheka, and in 1921 was named head of the GPU Special Department. Its job was to decode foreign diplomatic cables and develop unbreakable secret codes for Soviet embassies and spies. Bokii recruited the best cryptographers, linguists, and translators in the country. The British, Austrian, German, and Italian cables held no secrets for them, and they were able to partly decode the Japanese, American, and French ones. Bokii also enlisted the expertise of specialists in graphology and even chemists, who were working on explosive compounds that could be detonated remotely.

The Special Department was not housed in the Lubyanka building. It occupied two floors of the Foreign Affairs Commissariat, at the corner of Lubyanka Square and Kuznetsky Most Street, and enjoyed a great deal of autonomy. Bokii was curious about anything that had to do with communication at a distance, an interest that sometimes led him to go beyond the frontiers of experimental physics into the terrain of such paranormal phenomena as telepathy, hypnosis, and table-turning. His researchers didn't hesitate to enlist the help of shamans, mediums, and hypnotists, in hopes of understanding the source of their powers. They were particularly interested in telepathy. Bokii was convinced that the world around him constituted an interconnected system of information.

Barchenko, who was half guru, half science popularizer, had equally wide-ranging interests. He hoped to prove connections between luminous and acoustic phenomena, influences on the sprouting of seeds, gas exchange between plants, the growth of amphibians, and human sensory reception. Barchenko also conducted experiments on telepathic thought transmission. No domain was foreign to him, and you could sum up his thinking with the words "Everything is in everything." By his own admission, his eclectic thirst for knowledge was a synthesis of "Saint-Yves d'Alveydre's Agartha, the Tibetans' Shambhala, and Gurdjieff's knowledge of the ancient science of Kafiristan." Quite a lot! "This all relates to my mystical aspirations related to the search for the remnants of ancient science and its guardians."

As he read vulgarization works on hypnosis and magnetism, Barchenko became convinced that all the new discoveries that scientists were so proud of had already been known by the ancients, but erased by barbarian invasions. He thought that modern science's pursuit of truth through an analytical approach led to the "scattering" of wisdom, whereas everything in the world was subject to a single law. Influenced by the French mystics Éliphas Lévi and Saint-Yves d'Alveydre, Barchenko determined that the remains of this universal knowledge lay in a subterranean country hidden deep in the Himalayas, at the junction of the Indian, Tibetan, and Afghan borders.

After the Revolution, Barchenko excited the minds of Baltic fleet sailors with his talks about Shambhala. He told them about a golden age on Earth and a primitive communist society, "The Great World Peoples Federation." Only those who had reached moral perfection, who were "independent of objects" and egoless, could find the path to Shambhala. The Bolshevik sailors apparently fit that definition perfectly.

Barchenko was recruited in 1921 by the Psychoneurological Institute founded by Vladimir Bekhterev in Petrograd. Bekhterev sent him to Murmansk in the far north to study the phenomenon known as "meryachenie" ("a psychic illness midway between hysterical crisis and shamanistic trance"). Barchenko spent two years studying seaweed at the Murmansk biological studies station, and in his free time looked into the region's past and its inhabitants' mores and beliefs. On his return he claimed to have discovered in the distant Lovozersk tundra the remains of the most ancient human culture, earlier even than Egyptian civilization.

Did Bokii share Barchenko's mystical belief? Znamenski told me that it didn't seem very likely. On the other hand, it was perfectly possible that Bokii liked the idea that Tibetan Buddhist and Sufi mystics possessed superior psychological techniques that could strengthen the communist project. This was a common basis on which the two men could understand each other. One wanted to rationalize the occult; the other wanted to re-enchant the Revolution. Bokii was thinking of "bolshevizing" Buddhism, while Barchenko wanted to convert Bolsheviks to his esoteric knowledge. The two enthusiasts' feverish work seemed designed to reconcile the irreconcilable.

After several informal meetings, Bokii invited Barchenko to give a talk on Kalachakra and Shambhala at GPU headquarters in Moscow. It was the evening of December 31, 1924, and included the head of the Cheka, Felix Dzerzhinsky himself. Imagine this learned gathering of the top leaders of the secret services on New Year's Eve, forced to listen to the ranting of a Buddhist guru about the splendor of Shambhala and its race of zombies. After brief deliberation, Dzerzhinsky decided to turn the matter over to Bokii and give Barchenko the means to carry out his projects. This was probably done to cut short the Chekists' suffering, who were eager to go celebrate the New Year.

And that's how Barchenko became a consultant to the GPU Special Department in early 1925. He was given significant resources to prove his theories about mind reading, telepathy, and remote sensing. He developed a practical experiment to test thought transmission, which was said to produce satisfactory results. Two volunteers with completely shaved heads put on aluminum helmets of his design and were connected by a copper wire. Thoughts immediately began to circulate like electric current between the transmitter and the receiver with remarkable fluidity. Barchenko's research promised revolutionary applications in espionage and intelligence.

On the strength of those encouraging results, Bokii and Barchenko organized a series of talks in private homes. There Barchenko pitched his project for an expedition to Tibet to find the hidden kingdom of Shambhala. Among the people who attended his talks on Oriental wisdom were some of Bokii's university classmates, engineers, important Bolshevik executives, and a few of Chicherin's deputies. Even the famous Yagoda, who became head of the GPU after Dzerzhinsky's death in 1926, was curious enough to come.

On July 31, 1925, Barchenko met Commissar for Foreign Affairs Chicherin, whose accord was essential for an expedition to Tibet. Barchenko described his research and presented his plans for a voyage to search for the traces of a prehistoric culture. A note written in Chicherin's hand exists about the expedition planned by Bokii and Barchenko, whom he describes as "scientifico-propagandists." "For the last nineteen years one Barchenko has been searching for the remains of certain prehistoric cultures. He theorizes that in prehistoric times humanity developed an extremely advanced civilization, far beyond contemporary civilization. He believes that it is possible to gather surviving elements of the knowledge left by this advanced cultural civilization in the holy sites of central Asia, in particular in Lhasa, and among certain secret fraternities in Afghanistan."

Chicherin, who was a reasonable man, didn't believe a single word of Barchenko's stories, needless to say. "I am absolutely convinced that there has never been a very highly developed culture during prehistory." But Bokii's pressure was strong. In the letter he sent to the Politburo the next day, Chicherin wrote that contemplating a voyage to Afghanistan was out of the question. "Not only would the Afghan authorities not allow our Chekists to meet any secret fraternities, but their mere arrival could lead to great complications and even a press campaign in Great Britain." On the other hand, Chicherin was open to an expedition to Lhasa, which might strengthen relations with Tibet. But he set certain conditions. First, more information on Barchenko's background had to be gathered. Second, Barchenko had to promise not to engage in political conversations in Tibet. Finally, he had to be accompanied by "sufficiently experienced inspectors, chosen from among serious Party comrades." Among these was Yakov Blumkin. But Barchenko was immediately hostile to him. So Blumkin pulled a few strings, and at the last minute "someone" refused to deliver passports to the expedition members. The Soviet expedition to Shambhala was canceled, and that is why

Blumkin's name briefly appears in the record of the Soviet Tibet expedition project, and is connected to the legend of Shambhala.

As our plane began its descent to Roissy and our ears buzzed with the change in pressure, I decided to put the question to Andrei Znamenski. Had Blumkin been part of the expedition to Tibet, yes or no? Znamenski laughed. "That's a legend. Blumkin didn't participate in the Soviet expeditions to Tibet, either Barchenko's, which didn't happen, or the very real ones led by Roerich, which did. The story that Blumkin accompanied the Roerichs disguised as a lama comes from one of my colleagues, Oleg Shishkin. He wrote a book that mixes fiction with authentic archive documents called 'Battle for the Himalayas.' There were Soviet agents on the expedition, but they were Cheka agents from Mongolia. Shishkin put Blumkin among them to enhance his story with a nice legend. Having Blumkin alongside Nicholas Roerich allowed him to mix the Roerichs' spiritual quest with a Soviet intelligence operation. But it's an invention."

In 1926, when he was on assignment in Mongolia, Blumkin had probably given Roerich logistical support by providing automobiles, and may have persuaded the local warlords not to attack the members of the expedition. But nothing more. In exchange, Yuri Roerich agreed to serve as his interpreter with the Tibetans, to whom Blumkin was supplying weapons. So Blumkin was involved in the Roerichs' project, but only indirectly. If he ever mentioned the old Mongolian-Tibetan legend that salvation would come from the north, it was for geopolitical ends, telling the nomads that the savior was the Red Army.

Since perestroika, the Russians have gotten very interested in occultism in the USSR, a renaissance accompanied by renewed interest in astrology, magic, and various esoteric practices and teachings. And since 1990, Alexander Barchenko has experienced a kind of rehabilitation in post-Soviet Russia, with followers who consider him a holder of superior "cosmic knowledge." Some claim that Barchenko was a close collaborator of Roerich and his wife, Helena, and had a relationship with the "Masters of Shambhala." In Russia, Roerich is considered an important patriot and spiritual master. In the United States, he is seen as a dangerous guru who ensnared Henry Wallace, Franklin Roosevelt's agriculture secretary, and ruined his political career.

Gleb Bokii hasn't enjoyed a similar return to grace in occultist circles. Like all the Old Bolsheviks, and especially Lenin, he is going through a period in the wilderness under Putin's Russia. The centenary of the October Revolution didn't seem to change that very much. But while Bokii's efforts to find the Buddhist Shambhala weren't crowned with success, he has experienced a kind of literary reincarnation. He survives in the skin of a character in a novel, one of the masterpieces of the twentieth century: *The Master and Margarita*, by Mikhail Bulgakov.

This isn't a theory or an interpretation of the novel, but established fact. Bulgakov's publisher Boris Sokolov revealed in the first edition of his collected works that Woland, the character of the Devil in *The Master and Margarita*, was modeled on Gleb Bokii. It seems that Bokii and his friends weren't getting together just to talk about an ideal society and spiritually and physically perfect human beings. And the head of Bolshevik cryptographers had more than a secret laboratory in which to work his experiments. He also rented a dacha—a kind of country house—in Kuchino, in a Moscow suburb. In this retreat far from prying eyes, Bokii and a few trusted men and women from the Special Department practiced nudism and threw wild parties, following rules that Bokii drew up for their rites and rituals. Members had to contribute 10 percent of their salaries to sustain the commune. On weekends, weather permitting, Bokii and his friends worked naked in the garden, growing fruits and vegetables, which he dubbed "the cult of union with nature." The "summer commune" rule required sunbathing and shared baths for men and women. Communal work was followed by drunken meals and group sex.

These practices weren't seen as especially shocking in the 1920s. Practicing free love and rejecting family values were even thought of as a form of Bolshevik morality. Nude people were often encountered in the streets and on public transit in Moscow and Leningrad. They considered baring their naked bodies to be a revolutionary act.

The Kuchino orgies weren't without conflict, however. Some spouses had trouble accepting the new revolutionary morality, and the collective frolics sometimes turned into pitched battles. Two cuckolded husbands committed suicide; one jumped in front of a train, the other shot himself in the head with his service weapon.

To justify these orgies, Bokii pointed to Kalachakra tantric rituals, a teaching of Tibetan Buddhism. And everyone had to participate, including his own daughters. To increase his sexual power, Bokii turned to esoteric rituals and wound up owning a collection of mummified penises.

Bokii's former colleagues in the Special Department described the dacha as a place of drunkenness and sexual orgies. According to one Klimenko, who participated in these "retreats," the Special Department "natural beings" went beyond gardening and sex to organizing parodies of religious ceremonies, in particular black masses and funerals. Dressed in clerical garb confiscated from the clergy, some community members took the role of priests while others played the dead. During one black mass, a certain Filippov was so drunk that he nearly suffocated while being buried.

Bulgakov was kept informed of what was going on at Bokii's dacha by the poet Andrei Biely, who lived in Kuchino then. Many scenes in the novel, like the Devil's Grand Ball, were directly lifted from the banquets there. Bulgakov saw the Kuchino commune as a prism that revealed the truth of a society "under mass hypnosis." The appearance of the Devil in a Moscow park revealed the deep roots of belief buried under the veneer of positivism and atheism: mysticism, black magic, esotericism, and occultism tearing through de-Christianized Russian society. Pentecost in reverse. When the Devil falls from the sky, he doesn't bring knowledge, but ignorance. He doesn't reveal previously hidden meaning, but obfuscation, eclipse, and the dislocation of all sense and meaning. The effect isn't to enlighten the witnesses of the event, but to disorient them, bringing them not faith, but incredulity.

Like most of Bulgakov's readers, I long saw the book as a fantastical novel, the fruit of its author's unchained imagination, with its series of burlesque scenes and incongruous apparitions: the enormous cat buying a tram ticket, Margarita flying over Moscow on her broomstick, or Natasha astride the severe Nikolai Ivanovich now transformed into a swine. This is partly true, but *The Master and Margarita* is also a realist novel, the kind of realism that describes an enchanted, bewitched world carried off in a whirlwind of burlesque figures. *The Master and Margarita* is justly considered one of the masterpieces of the twentieth century. It is a seminal novel, like James Joyce's *Ulysses*, that has inspired many others, notably *The Satanic Verses* by Salman Rushdie. It took Bulgakov twelve years to write, and the manuscript went through several successive versions, taking its definitive form only when the author died in 1940. It was long forbidden and was published for the first time in the 1960s in a partly censored version. When the complete book was translated in 1973, it was seen as a satire of Stalinist society, with Stalin portrayed as the Devil. But when Bulgakov conceived the novel in 1928, what he had under his eyes were the 1920s, not the Stalin years. His Devil isn't a dictator, but a facetious provocateur that inspired the Rolling Stones' famous song "Sympathy for the Devil."

"Where would your good be if there were no evil and what would the world look like without shadow?" the Devil asks. "Shadows are thrown by people and things. There's the shadow of my sword, for instance. But shadows are also cast by trees and living things. Do you want to strip the whole globe by removing every tree and every creature to satisfy your fantasy of a bare world? You're stupid."

Like Flaubert before him, Bulgakov unmasked the stupidity at the heart of his era's scientific socialism, and it bore the traits of occultism and magical thinking. Bokii and Barchenko were Bolshevism's Bouvard and Pécuchet. Their thirst for knowledge led them to absorb all the knowledge of their day, from life sciences and occult beliefs, Marxism and Theosophy, to physics and esotericism, with a soft spot for paranormal phenomena like clairvoyance and hypnosis. With Flaubert, this was confined to provincial Normandy, but in Russia, it rose to the highest levels of the Soviet state, infecting even its top leaders.

Osip and Lilya Brik's little apartment on Gendrikov Lane was gradually filling up. Friends hurried over when they heard the news. A man in boots and a white lab coat, probably a doctor or a nurse, came out of the bedroom carrying a basin covered with a damp cloth. Holding the basin in both hands, he made his way through the crowd, ducking between the guests. Nobody knew him, except maybe the secret police, who were guarding the dead man as if he were a national treasure. The basin held the brain of Vladimir Mayakovsky.

"Isn't it the strangest thing," wrote Yuri Olesha in his memoir, "that in this very apartment, where we played cards until dawn, we should see Mayakovsky's brain!"

We know the details of the operation thanks to an account by the painter Nikolai D., who watched

the operation from start to finish. He was called in
to join the team from the Brain Institute, which
was shorthanded that day. According to D., the surgeon first slit Mayakovsky's scalp with a scalpel, then
ripped the skin away from the skull, pulling it on
either side. It made an unpleasant sound, said D.,
"like when you tear adhesive tape off a dry surface."
Once the skull was exposed (the flaps of scalp hung
down on either side of the head, like earmuffs you
put on children when it's very cold), he drilled a
hole in the skull and enlarged it with a hammer. He
then cut the skull with a bone saw. The split skull
fell away, exposing the white surface of the brain.
The surgeon severed the connecting nerves and
blood vessels, then gently seized the ovoid mass with
both hands to lift it out of the skull.

"We weren't allowed into the room until much
later, after the Brain Institute men had left," Olesha
wrote.

>Mayakovsky was lying on the bed, his head turned
>to the wall. His features were drawn, his color gray, and
>he had heavy yellow bags under his eyes. His body was
>covered with a blanket up to his waist. Above that he was
>wearing a light blue open shirt with a bloodstain over
>the heart. The Institute men had left their instruments
>on a glass-topped table nearby: a scalpel with hair stuck
>to it, the bone saw, a hammer, and a chisel whose edge
>was studded with small bits of debris like crab fragments,
>probably bits of bone. Mayakovsky's mouth hung open,

*as if in shock from firing the revolver into his heart, or
maybe it was just a reflex connected to the operation.
The skin over the skull had been hastily stitched together,
and was bumpy under his short hair. There was a scrape
on his right cheek; a bit of skin had been torn away by
the sculptor Konstantin Lutski, who had rushed over at
six thirty to make the death mask. Some historians claim
that he hadn't spread enough Vaseline, and that they'd
had to call in a second sculptor, Sergei Merkurov. This
was the same Merkurov that Mayakovsky had mocked in
his "antimemorial" poems, saying he sculpted "bronze by
the kilo" and "slick marbles."*

    *Two convoys were used to transport the poet's
separate parts, one the body, and the other the brain.
The body, relieved of its gray matter, was driven at a
stately pace by truck to the Writers Club, where the
viewing would take place the next day. The poet's brain
was driven at top speed (for obvious reasons of pres-
ervation) in a Packard limousine preceded by a squad
of motorcycle police to the "Brain Pantheon" at 43
Yakimanka Street. The two vehicles left Gendrikov Lane
around midnight, as Mayakovsky's friends and neighbors
watched from the windows, some waving handkerchiefs.
The body's truck and the soul's limousine drove together
for a while on the empty streets before separating at
an intersection; the body turned right while the soul
continued straight ahead. The Chekist Yakov Agranov
removed the cloth covering the brain, and kept an eagle
eye on the precious organ during the entire trip as it was
jostled in the bumps. As the car passed, a student turned*

to look, wondering what important person deserved such a police escort. To his amazement, he saw a brain on the rear seat, illuminated by the yellowish ceiling light. "Even Gogol didn't take things this far," he thought. "His nose went around the streets on foot!" In those fantastical times, nothing surprised people anymore. The brain went on its way without generating further comment. At most, an old woman, intrigued by the glitter of the motorcycles' reflectors in the darkness, leaned out her balcony. "Yet another official host making comrade soldiers work at night," she thought, closing her window.

The Pantheon's facade had been lit up for the occasion, and a double row of militiamen stood in front of the main entrance as a welcoming committee. When Agranov got out of the limousine, carefully holding the basin so as not to spill any formaldehyde, they snapped to attention, forming a line, then marched inside as one man, escorting the brain into the Pantheon. Their boots on the marble made a martial ring, enhanced by the clatter of rifles when they started up the narrower stairs. They climbed the stairs heavily, rifles slung across their chests, to the hall reserved for elite brains. Mayakovsky had been assigned a place of honor to the right of Vladimir Ilyich. The militiamen arrayed themselves in a semicircle, and Agranov walked to a kind of altar covered by an embroidered white tablecloth in the center of the room. He gently set down the basin, which he had carried at arm's length all

the way. The Institute's director, who had held back
up to then, approached and delicately removed the
cloth, revealing the naked brain for all to see. It was
the size of a skinned rabbit and displayed many deep
convolutions. Wearing surgical gloves, he picked up
the brain, let it drip for a moment, then put it in
a glass bowl full of fresh formaldehyde. The militiamen, who briefly thought the professor was per-
forming an elevation of the host, bowed their heads;
a few instinctively bent their knees. But at a sharp
glance from the officiant, who didn't tolerate the
slightest religious manifestation in this temple of
materialism, they immediately thought better of it.
Among the people watching the ceremony, no one
could remember seeing a brain that was so folded,
with so many convolutions and such deep crevices.
The anterior and superior cerebral lobes were especially well developed. The bowl, which was en-
graved with bas-reliefs, was smaller than Lenin's,
even though Mayakovsky's brain was clearly superior
in volume and weight. How should we interpret this
difference in weight, which tended to diminish the
difference in importance between the two recipi-
ents? Can we conclude that one genius is superior
to the other? Does poetic genius outweigh political
genius? But the militiamen, in a hurry to be finished, shouldered their rifles, clicked their heels,
and marched toward the exit. They departed almost
with relief, as always when you leave a funeral. The
Brain Pantheon rang with the sound of their boots

in the staircase for a moment, then fell back into the usual silence of empty halls and the hum of neon lights.

The Institute for Brain Research was located on the second floor of 43 Bolshaya Yakimanka Street, a neo-Gothic palace built at the end of the nineteenth century whose imposing facade aped Old Russian style with tall, pointed gables, turrets, and little arcades.

The Brain Pantheon was supposed to serve as not only a science laboratory, but also an exhibition hall. By putting the brain as an object on public display, the Institute wanted to contribute to the education of the masses. The Institute director had big ideas. He had to make do with this inconvenient building for the time being, but he could imagine a palace built along the lines of the new architecture, with soaring spires, inclined cylinders, and hemispheres rotating around their axes. Good riddance to the necropolises and catacombs, to damp pantheons in obscure basements. The Pantheon would be a house of glass, a crystal palace that would pull the veil away from the functioning of the cerebral cortex. It would be possible to display as many as five hundred brains belonging to society's elite: generals, strategists, neurologists, physicians, composers, poets. Why limit ourselves to the brains of executed criminals, soldiers killed at the front, and disease victims unclaimed by their families, as was done up to then? Research would take a leap forward if we concentrated on the human brain, this "terra incognita of modern times," on the era's intellectual elite, whose central focus would of course be the brain of Lenin, primus inter pares.

As the commissar for health described it, the examination of Lenin's brain six years earlier had started very badly.

> *The autopsy lasted four and a half hours. The defenseless body lying in front of us wasn't just any cadaver. To be honest, it wasn't very easy for me. I had never seen such flaccid convolutions. The two lobes showed unusually large areas of softening. I was also taken aback by the cerebral substance's color. It should have been bright gray or whitish; instead, it appeared orange, like a quince. Looking at such a brain, you could hardly imagine the historic importance of the man it belonged to.*

If the plan was to come up with a benchmark for genius, it was a failure. Even the brain's weight (1,340 grams) was below average. Just imagine, Turgenev's brain weighed 2,012 grams; Byron's, 1,800; and Mayakovsky's weighed in at 1,700. Brains average between 1,395 and 1,400 grams, but the Institute decided to set the average at 1,300, so that Lenin's brain was just above average. One of the doctors confessed his disappointment: "It is surprising that such profound thought could have come from such a small mass."

Nadezhda Krupskaya, Lenin's wife, had agreed to answer the Institute's questionnaire. In spite of her conflict with Stalin (who had threatened to "name another Lenin widow in her place"), she had to overcome her reticence in talking about their conjugal life and her intimacy with the great leader. If she didn't, heaven knows who would do it in her place. At least the questionnaire had the merit of protecting her against attempts to rewrite history. Moreover, it was hard not to answer questions put by doctors trying to pierce the secret of the human psyche.

Krupskaya's answers are found in an eight-page typewritten document simply titled "My Answers to the Brain Institute Questionnaire in 1935." Studying the manuscript, you notice that certain passages have been crossed out, and some words and expressions added, to bring the description of Lenin's character as close as possible to the idealized image of the proletarian leader. So the myopia afflicting the leader of worldwide revolution isn't mentioned, probably so as not to contradict the visionary character of Leninist genius. Krupskaya said Lenin had a tenor voice. This was replaced by "baritone," which sounded more dignified for an orator. Sentences describing Lenin's hallucinations and convulsions were simply crossed out, so as not to feed the rumor of syphilis that had pursued him since emigration.

On the other hand, comments about his insomnia were retained. Krupskaya said that Lenin constantly moved his legs in his sleep. When he woke up in the morning he sometimes told his wife that he felt like he'd "been walking all night long." We know today that this is a relatively benign neurological problem caused by sensations of pins and needles, tingling, or a burning. It was suggested that Lenin had this irresistible desire to move his legs at night because it was symptomatic of the impatience sweeping Russia. In a way, Lenin somatized the forced immobility of a country bursting with the irrepressible thrust of productive forces. The report's bold conclusion: "In those years, all Russia had the feeling of walking at night."

The Institute researchers liked to compare themselves to people of the Renaissance. They navigated by the imprecise maps of lobes and hemispheres. Their eyes were glued to their microscopes, like sailors to their telescopes, looking for waves of the mind. They were exploring nocturnal areas abandoned to beliefs and superstitions where thought and feeling arose. Wasn't the brain said to have one hundred billion neurons, as many as there are stars in our galaxy? Where would we find the star of genius in those constellations?

While waiting for a true cartography of the brain, the Pantheon's statutes dictated that research be guided as much by anatomy and neurology as by observing the subjects' near and dear. Institute researchers were as interested in hereditary factors that might play an important role in the emergence of a genius as they were in "fugitive facial expressions," or an individual's walk, "which sometimes reveals more than his opinions." In this way, Mayakovsky's "character portrait" included a detailed description of the "coordinated, quick, precise movements" that marked his apparently many walks in the streets of Moscow. "He walked quickly, swinging along," noted an observer, "helped in this by comfortable shoes with soles lined with steel plates, and made to last." As a matter of fact when Mayakovsky was cremated, all that remained of the six-foot, two-inch giant was a pile of ashes and his metal soles.

The autopsy report dwelled at length on Mayakovsky's mobile face; a heavy jaw and eyes deeply sunk in their orbits, whose expression alternated between luminous anger and the lugubrious mien of a convict. According to Lilya Brik, Mayakovsky was very proud of his voice. Some described it as a bass; others said it had a metallic timbre. All agreed on its power and expressiveness. Didn't he himself say that "the modern poet must have a good throat?" He had no musical talent, but Mayakovsky's friends all stressed his extraordinary sense of rhythm, which "captured the waves of poetry that were constantly rising in him."

Though it doesn't have any connection with the foregoing, the report mentioned Mayakovsky's great love for animals. In 1924 in Moscow he apparently lived with a squirrel. In 1927–28 he adopted a goat. This inclination was also expressed by "an indulgent tenderness for the weak (children, etc.)" and generally, by a love of nature shown in the obvious pleasure he took in climbing steep cliffs and playing outdoor games (bowling, etc.).

The Brain Pantheon soon gained great notoriety among the Soviet elite. For anyone of any note, the hope of being admitted to the Pantheon was a legitimate ambition. Oldsters intrigued for recognition of their right to be trepanned. Some used their dying energies to secure a spot on an Institute shelf the way others might pursue an academic chair. The Brain Pantheon offered what no church ever could: a guarantee against being forgotten. Some people tried to influence the choice of bowl, the quality of the glass, even the engraving patterns, which were usually drawn from Greek mythology. Some chose Pluto, others Hermes, preferring to settle this while alive, instead of having their descendants hastily point to some vase in a catalog of standard models.

To display the collection's most representative brains, some thirty illuminated niches were built. By the late 1930s, the Pantheon's new tenants, in addition to Lenin's and Mayakovsky's brains, included the precious encephalons of Clara Zetkin, the German revolutionary; Commissar for Culture

Anatoly Lunacharsky; symbolist poet Andrei Biely; and biochemist Vladimir Gulevich. Later, the Institute welcomed the organs of Konstantin Stanislavski, the great dramaturge; Maxim Gorki; Eduard Bagritski; Pavlov; and such eminent leaders as Sergei Kirov, who was killed under mysterious circumstances, and Nadezhda Krupskaya. The brain of Lenin's widow was placed next to his, so they could continue in death the dialogue they had started in life. Eminent foreigners, like the Frenchman Henri Barbusse, also received Pantheon honors. On the day of his admission, "La Marseillaise" was played on the forecourt.

The Brain Institute was divided into three distinct zones, according to a principle common to all theologies: Inferno (Hell), Purgatorio (Purgatory), and Paradiso (Paradise). Over time, some brains fell from Paradise down to Hell (as happened during the thaw), while others rose from Hell to Purgatory or Paradise (by rehabilitation). This tripartite division also allowed the Pantheon to broaden its conditions for admission. In addition to geniuses, whose number is necessarily limited, the Institute could welcome all sorts of lesser notables crowding the streets. Couldn't a brain's inclination lead some individuals to genius and others to crime? Everything depended on circumstance. Some geniuses might undergo an evolution toward crime, just as it isn't rare to see criminals change their ways and become benefactors of humanity. After all, not every genius is an angel, and nothing is closer to genius than a criminal, as history has shown time and again.

Oskar Vogt, a prominent German neurologist who studied Lenin's brain and helped establish the Institute, suggested replacing the concept of "genius" with a broader personality category: "beyond the norm." To illustrate this, the doctor pressed a button in front of him. In a moment, a staffer in a white lab coat entered holding a tray covered with a silver dome that he set before the professor. Almost like a maître d', he solemnly raised the cover with his gloved hand, revealing a brain in a light haze of condensation. Practically licking his lips, he announced, "Yakov Grigorievich Blumkin!"

Vogt nodded the staffer to the door and introduced the candidate.

"Comrade Blumkin is a legendary figure in our Revolution. He was executed a few weeks ago for reasons that have not been made public. His brief appearance on Earth was marked by two gunshots, like a parentheses in the void," he added. "The one inflicted on the German ambassador on July 6, 1918, and the one that ended his life on November 3, 1929. He was not yet thirty years old. Between these two detonations, Blumkin's life unfolded in a sky of conjectures like a luminous phenomenon that burns itself up before our eyes. He was a Chekist and a poet, a mystic and a killer, friends with both the greatest poets and the executioners at the Lubyanka.

He was called 'Zivoi'—He's Alive—and had an epic life that deserves to be told."

Mayakovsky's archive has nothing on Blumkin's. Under the heading Блюмкин Проекта—"The Blumkin Project"—it consists of some fifty numbered boxes organized in nine sections. Not the Blumkin file, but the Blumkin *Project*, as if his destiny had not yet been settled, even though he was dead. Despite all the efforts made to gather everything that could be known about the man in these archives, his biography still looked like an active construction site.

Yakov Agranov, the same person who would oversee Mayakovsky's official funeral three months later, ordered the firing squad to aim at the condemned man's heart, sparing his head. Blumkin had just time to sing the first bars of "The Internationale" when the shots rang out.

His skull was trepanned on a steel table in the Lubyanka canteen. The Party hoped to extract from his brain something about the psychology of its opponents. Truth requires us to say that few precautions were taken. Since he was going to be cremated, the surgeon, a prisoner, didn't bother sewing the scalp back, just wrapped the head in a rag. Blumkin's lifeless body was led to the incinerator. As it slowly rolled into the oven, the alcohol- and blood-soaked cloth was the first to catch fire. In this way, Yakov Blumkin slipped into the flames headfirst.

CHAPTER

14

In the early 1980s in Rome, I met a Russian historian named Aleksei Velidov at a conference on Nikolai Bukharin organized by the Italian Communist Party. I told him about my interest in Blumkin, and he promised to find me some information when he returned to Moscow. Years passed, and I forgot about the encounter.

Almost twenty years later, in 1998, when I had once again abandoned the Blumkin Project, Velidov wrote me a long letter. The GPU archives were being opened and he had gotten access to the Blumkin file. His letter was accompanied by a number of pages titled "Adventures of a Terrorist: Yakov Blumkin's Odyssey." They had allowed Velidov to re-create the events and the chain of circumstances that led to Blumkin's execution almost day by day.

We learned for example, that Blumkin started an affair with Liza Gorskaya, one of the best GPU agents, at the end of summer in 1929. So Liza didn't have to overcome any "bourgeois prejudices" to start a relationship with Blumkin. She had simply fallen in love with him. He was also in love with her, as a scene at Kazan Station revealed.

On Saturday, October 5, 1929, Liza was coming back from vacation. Blumkin was on the train platform waiting for her, holding a bouquet of flowers. Next day they went to the theater and spent the night together. Blumkin was due to leave on an assignment the following week, but he didn't want to leave Liza.

On Wednesday, October 9, Blumkin phoned Liza to announce that he had successfully passed the so-called purification exam, a procedure the Party periodically held to test its members' loyalty.

On Saturday, October 12, Blumkin spent the evening with Liza, who found him depressed. In a report to her supervisor Agranov, she said that Blumkin was saying strange things that evening. "He wanted to prove to me and to all the comrades who didn't trust him that he was honest and brave." When she asked the reasons for this sudden need for recognition, Blumkin enigmatically answered that he "had to settle his accounts."

The next day, still according to Liza, Blumkin again launched into digressions about fault and punishment, the meaning of life, etc. "I then firmly insisted that he tell me what was going on. And he wound up admitting everything: his meetings with Trotsky in Constantinople and the letters he'd agreed to deliver to members of his family."

Blumkin then confided to Liza that he had decided to write a letter to the Central Committee, confessing everything. She advised him to first speak to Mikhail Trilisser, their superior. But Blumkin felt that he was guilty before the entire Party and that it was for the Party to judge him.

Here is part of Liza Gorskaya's account to Agranov:

> *On Sunday, October 13, at ten o'clock in the evening, I was at home. I'd barely had time to think of what Blumkin told me when the telephone rang. It was him. He asked me to join him at the house of some friends. He absolutely wanted to see me, so that I could help him draft his "confession." I promised I would come the next morning. But by the next day, he had changed his mind. He was in a bad mood. His courage and his firmness had disappeared. He repeated that he was going to be arrested, that the punishment would be merciless, probably even a death sentence. I left. I felt strongly that Trilisser should be informed first, before Blumkin admitted everything in front of the Party Central Committee. I was under his orders and my responsibility was involved. I had to tell him everything.*

On Monday at around eleven in the morning, Liza phoned Trilisser. Their meeting took place the next day.

In the meantime Blumkin went to see his doctor and begged him to give him some sort of poison. The doctor refused. Next day, Blumkin decided to run away. He had his suitcase brought to a café near Kazan Station and went to the house of the painter Robert Falk, who lived nearby, at 21 Myasnitskaya Street, in the famous Yushkov House that was home to Vkhutemas, known as "the Soviet Bauhaus." The painter wasn't at home. In the apartment Blumkin found Falk's wife, the poetess Raisa Idelson, and three of her women friends. Blumkin told them that the GPU was looking for him because of his links with the opposition. He wanted to spend the night at her place.

"He looked like a madman," said the poetess when she was interrogated at the Lubyanka. "He was saying contradictory things. He would get ready to flee, and then be overcome with discouragement. He collapsed into an armchair, saying that there was only one thing left for him, to shoot himself in the head. He kept taking his pistol out and putting it back in its holster. Then he would come back to his escape preparations. He had to change some money. He needed Falk's passport, and the train schedules."

On Wednesday, October 16, around eleven o'clock in the evening, Blumkin telephoned Liza.

He had come to a decision. He was going to disappear for a while. "I've decided to hide for two or three years. I'll head south. I have a good plan." The couple headed for Kazan Station. Was Liza thinking of having the transit police arrest Blumkin at the station? Or did she want to give him one last chance? We will never know, because fate made the decision for her: there were no trains until the next morning. Upon learning this, Blumkin's face fell. "Not being able to leave today is the end. The catastrophe is inevitable. I won't escape death."

Georges Agabekov, who succeeded Blumkin as *rezident* in Constantinople, published a memoir in the West called *OGPU: The Russian Secret Terror*. In it, he describes Blumkin's middle-of-the-night arrest near his place in the Arbat neighborhood. It was carried out by the GPU's operational section, and led by one Vanya Klukarev, the treasurer of the Foreign Department. Klukarev went to Blumkin's home on Denezhny Lane at one o'clock in the morning to arrest him.

> *I went upstairs alone, but Blumkin wasn't at home. As I was leaving the building, I saw a taxi arrive: Blumkin and Liza Gorskaya were in it. When he saw us, Blumkin understood what was up. Before we had time to approach the taxi it had already made a U-turn. We drove after it. The taxi raced at top speed through the empty streets, but you know what our cars are like. We caught up with them near Petrovsky Park.*

Seeing that he couldn't get away, Blumkin stopped the car. He got out, raised his hands, and shouted, "Don't shoot, comrades. I give up." To me he said, "Take me to Trilisser, Vanya. I'm so weary!" And Blumkin turned to the taxi, in which Liza Gorskaya was still sitting, and said, "I'm sorry, Liza. I know that you betrayed me." That's all he said. He smoked in silence during the whole trip to the Lubyanka.

"Writers think they choose their stories in the world," the Indian novelist and essayist Arundhati Roy once said, "but I'm starting to think that vanity leads them to believe that. In fact it's the reverse. Stories choose the writers. Stories reveal us to ourselves. They grab us. They invade us. They demand to be told."

I don't know if Roy is right or if it's always that way, but it certainly was the case for this story. It has been following me for more than thirty years. It began when I was the same age as Blumkin when he was executed, twenty-nine. I wanted to write the story of a legendary hero. A Bolshevik Lord Jim. A story of loyalty and betrayal. Crime and punishment. The epic story of a terrorist who also was a poet. In the end, the hero who had faced so many perils and overcome so many dangers was destroyed by his love for a revolutionary as intrepid as he was, in the name of the higher interests of a Revolution that itself had been betrayed.

I now know that I was clinging to Blumkin in an era that was so unheroic, the 1980s, an era of abandonments and betrayals of socialism's ideals. That's why this book is also the story of a failure: that of a generation, my generation, that wanted to change the world.

I am finishing this book where I began it, in this house on the banks of the Marne, where, three years ago, I found the trunk that contained the Blumkin Project archives. The chalky facade of the house stands like an unmarked white page in the evening light. The now-empty trunk sits beneath the blackboard, which has been cleared of the city maps, photos, and the multicolored forest of Post-it notes that covered it. The books it once held are on bookcase shelves, and the archives entered into my computer. Blumkin's nine lives are contained in a USB thumb drive, like ashes in an urn.

Night is falling.

There's a thunderstorm outside. The storm outside. Why do we write books, if not to lead a life that is more real?

Joinville-le-Pont, May 15, 2017

CREDITS

Verse on page 58 from E. G. Bagritski, *Stikhotvoreniia* (Leningrad: Sovetskii pisatel', 1956), 167–71.

Dialog on pages 219–20 from the film *Reds* (1981), written by Warren Beatty and Trevor Griffiths.

CHRISTIAN SALMON is a writer and researcher at France's National Center for Scientific Research (CNRS). He founded and was a member of the International Parliament of Writers from 1993 to 2003. He is the author of several books, including *Verbicide*, *Devenir minoritaire: Pour une nouvelle politique de la littérature* (coauthored with Joseph Hanimann), and *Tombeau de la fiction*.

WILLIAM RODARMOR has translated some forty-five books and screenplays in genres ranging from literary fiction to espionage and fantasy. In 2017 he won the Northern California Book Award for fiction translation for *The Slow Waltz of Turtles* by Katherine Pancol. His recent translations include *And Their Children After Them* by Nicolas Mathieu (2020) and *Article 353* by Tanguy Viel (2019).